THE BEE

John Pascal

The electron inquired of the photon,
"What are things called time And temperature?"
"Strange ideas indeed", the photon replied.
"These are mysteries believed in by the great world
outside, Where, I am told, they seem so real."
Poetry for Children, 2055

Rebecca –
Thanks so much for
all your help –
Pascal

The Revelation Trilogy, Part One
Second edition: revised March, 2013

xulon PRESS

For my wife whose patience is only exceeded by the Lords.

2247: SPERO'S FLIGHT

The design room was a familiar, friendly work space, but not today. Something was different, something ominous. Spero 235 grasped the door frame, looked in and fought down a wave of nausea. *Were these walls always blue?* Shorter than most and a bit portly, he didn't feel like the confident rebel he had to be today. *It smells like smoke in here.* He looked at the backs of his coworkers and slid slowly along the wall.

A man with a brief case got up from his cubicle and walked toward him. *Mustn't make eye contact.* The man paused right in front of him and forced confrontation. "Spero, you look awful. Anything I can do?"

"I'm fine, Tom—really." He patted his stomach and hoped his smile looked casual. "Remember, don't actually eat *everything* the cafeteria serves for dinner."

Tom grinned and walked away. "Especially that thing they call meat."

Spero slipped into a vacant cubicle and placed his tool bag on the floor. His hands were shaking but he put up a specification diagram and pretended to study it. *Someone must suspect what I'm planning to do. The Supreme Directorate would have ordered someone to watch me. Had to.* Spero had no design assignment, but the Departure Room for the time-relocating Bees was just across the hall. *I have to get my head clear. This is it for me. Have to go over every step one final time.*

Spero hated his life. He belonged to the lowest class of citizens in this "new" Earth: the Humwa, or "Creatives". But he was a genius at making things work, and his employers needed him. In order to work in sensitive areas he was required to wear the same bright red locator band on his ankle the criminals wore. Other Humwa were afraid to even talk to him when they saw it. Speak to one who wore it, and invite a police interview later. The band had become sweaty underneath and it started to itch.

Spero agonized about revolutionary writings he'd left with a friend, and lately he was having doubts about this man he used to trust. *The SD troopers would terminate me in a blink if those papers ever turned up. Wish I'd never shared them—and in my own handwriting, yet. Stupid.*

Once he even contemplated suicide, but today at last he saw a real chance for freedom. It was a daring one. He sat at the console, mopped his lightly sweating bald head, and reviewed his escape plan.

OK, Spero, now's the time to just do it. Smile. Business as usual. He got up and briskly walked out across the hall. He approached the guards standing on ether side of the Departure Room door, but gulped when he realized one was a police soldier. "I—I'll be running a test on the vacuum chamber shortly. Don't be alarmed when it starts up."

"There's supposed to be two of you in there." Heavy dark eyebrows lowered into a scowl above him. "Where's your partner?"

"He went home."

"Oh, yeah?" The soldier fingered the ID on Spero's chest. "Well, 235, you look scared."

"You—you guys always scare me." He gulped again. "But if I don't fix this problem tonight, they can't launch tomorrow."

The guards smirked at each other, but nodded and allowed him to press his hand on the ID plate and enter. Spero shook his head, relieved they hadn't inspected his tool bag. But when the heavy steel door thunked shut behind him, anxious dread strangled his throat. His hands were moist, his heart pounding.

As he walked down the ramp to the launch bay, the voice of his own self doubt began to plead with him. *It's still not too late to turn back. You know they'll eventually catch you and you'll be tortured even if they don't kill you. They'll implant a punishment shackle in you, and you'll spend the rest of your life working like a Cleanbot.*

But now he was alone. He took a deep breath, exhaled, and answered himself. *I've been over this a million times. Sure, I'm no warrior, but this plan will work. If it doesn't, I'll kill myself before they get me. So either way I'm be better off, right?*

Spero quickly fell to completing his special additions to the launch console, and getting to work calmed him. *Maybe I can find a place in the past where I can live like the shore colony.* He remembered those rare vacations when he could enjoy the bay in a rented sailboat. *And when I get to a safe place, I'll ditch this awful leg tracker. They'll think they can still trace me with the signal from my brain implant, but I'll figure some way around that.* He closed his tool bag. *There—done.*

Spero slid open the doors of the launch bay. Its sterile, windowed walls contained the newest time-relocating craft, Bee 77, an iridescent three-meter ovoid resting on slender legs. It shimmered in the overhead lights. When energized and covered with subatomic particles, it would glow with yellow ionized "fuzz", the interface between dimensions. And with one touch of the controls the hatch would close and allow the particles to spread over it. The Bee would then behave like a virtual sub atomic particle: free to dart away with its passengers like a tiny photon into the timeless quantum world of probabilities.

Spero was scheduled to be on the final prep crew for tomorrow's mission: the first voyage back to the Earth of two and a half million years ago. He had re-designed heftier neural stunners for huge lizards, and larger first aid kits for the field. Someone else had installed a powerful new locator beacon. And there were rumors that the computer division people, or "Comps" as they were called, were positively ecstatic about some new computer program they'd installed in this Bee.

Spero relaxed as resolution and purpose took hold. He glanced up at the control windows along the down ramp and whispered to himself. "Incredible. Still no one watching."

He picked up some supplies he'd hidden away for himself below a work shelf. *Well, let's see. Extra Medical Kit, check. World History learning chip, check. I assured my controllers the extra stuff I designed for this trip would fit somewhere, and they believed me.* He chuckled. *Course I left out the fact that I'd make room for them by <u>ripping out</u> the new homing beacon.*

Spero hoisted himself into the Bee's hatch, not much larger than a pet door, and lay on his stomach to work. His feet dangled out, toes down. He removed a floor plate and began to whistle. Shortly, the homing device flew out over his head and landed with a clatter and flailing loose wires. *Still no room for <u>all</u> the extra stuff I want. Guess I'll just have to squeeze in individual components. First, my new big stunner for those great big beasties, check. An extra 'repair kit', really important, check. Inflatable warm shelter, yup. Oops, absolutely no more room—and an extra fuel cell's a must, too. Well, into the personal storage compartment with it—forget the Safety Regs. OK, all finished.*

Spero exhaled a big breath and checked again to see if he was still alone. He slid into the light gray pilot's seat. It felt cool and smooth against his bare arms. *Administration only trusts me in here like this because they're <u>so</u> unimagi-*

native. They'd never guess I'd dare to take off in one of their precious Bees. He pictured all his old arguments and fears dashed into a corner. They were replaced with an image of himself, now transformed into a pelican, flying over the ocean waves toward the horizon.

Spero quickly went through his final checklist, and a thrill went through him when he spoke to the onboard computer: "Ready." Outside the Departure Room, Security would expect a fire up sequence as a test, but if he tried to change any computer settings the alarm would sound and they'd cut power. *So, my first trip will just have to run the way it's set up. I'm going back to two hundred and thirty five million years ago. Won't stay long though, and they'll never guess my next destination.*

The "fail safe" intended to prevent any theft was designed by some non-creative in security. If the key in the control panel room wasn't depressed within a second of another control inside the Bee, the docking clamps wouldn't release. But Spero had rigged a 200-year-old egg timer and a clothespin given to him by an antique-collecting grand-mother. He had taped it to the outside control where he could see it. So he ran out, set it, ran back and simply waited for the clothes pin to stop. When the little bell sounded, he released the restraining clamps and grinned.

The hatch closed and he had to wait while air pumped slowly out of the launch bay. *My only real regret is I couldn't find a good woman to run away with me.* He remembered his last lady friend, Dede 980. *I really cared for her too, but then she left me, just like the others. Found my ideas frightening. Kept eyeing my shackle like it was a rat. And she was one of those who actually bowed to dictator Aten's stupid Sun Symbol every morning. Heck, if I'd told her about this, she'd have turned me in for sure. Nope, there's nothing left but slavery and death for me here.*

Super cooling went well. It took two minutes for the charge to build up before the particles were drawn in with a loud "snap" and the Bee was glowing yellow like a giant beach ball. Spero caught a glimpse of the guards running down the ramp and screaming. The full alert siren was sounding, but the onboard computer signaled "MISSION READY". The guards cut the power outside, but it was too late to stop him now. His view screen showed a silent, fading image of guards pounding on the window. Spero touched the launch button, blew a goodbye kiss toward them and to the year 2247. His display abruptly changed to a shrinking Earth silhouetted by a drifting star field.

Three days later on internal time Spero 235 landed the Bee on a rocky cliff. He stepped out laughing, and threw his severed, red locator-anklet into the water below. He raised his arms high above his head, and took a breath of sulfur-tainted air. For the first time a strange human voice shouted out into Earth's Triassic wilderness: "YES!"

1986

The universe is not just stranger than we have Imagined, it is strange beyond our very Capacity to imagine. Sir Arthur Eddington

A late afternoon spring shower had rumbled and washed through the quiet college town. Floral scents mixed with hints of ozone lent its flavor to the cool, moist breeze. Joseph Main walked and jogged through the campus paths and enjoyed the moment. This was his time to ponder many things: Saturday's ball game, or perhaps his physics students, some bright, some—oh so not. God, was he real or just imagined? Planetary precession, was it constant or changing? Could he stay dry on the puddled path today? Dry? Did he water the houseplants? Joe even wondered about his own thought processes. He pictured them as a fishing boat meandering through the back bayous of his cortex. *My ex hated my "useless" daydreams, but at least Melissa loves the way I think.*

On some occasions Joe wound up resting by the track overlook, sometimes he preferred to relax on the big boulder in the park, but this time he splashed his way down toward Bud's bar. It was called The Purple Planet, but to him it was just Bud's, and a good spot to unwind after work. Right now it was also the best place to dry off his shoes.

Joe was a few years into the state of divorce—his freedom tinged with loneliness, his hopes laced with anguish. *Whoops.* He slid going through a puddle downhill but caught himself by grabbing a tree. *Whew. Better rest a sec. Well Bud's just down there a ways, and I sure don't feel like going back to the apartment right now. Whipping up frozen dinners and talking to my tomcat will have to wait.*

A gust of wind showered him with drops from the leaves above. *Wonder why my friends think I need a woman in my life? I like hanging with the guys, and if I ever need a feminine point of view there's always Melissa. She's "safe"—more like another guy. Also she's divorced like me and isn't looking for any real intimacy. No pressure.*

Joe stomped some of the wet out of his sneakers, and proceeded to carefully walk down the wooded path. *Nice to have a friend like her, though—a colleague to talk to, one to count on. But definitely not safe is that woman who keeps turning up at Bud's.*

The footpath led down to the rear of the bar. Swinging around a Buttonwood tree, Joe was startled by a bright yellow puff that flickered for a second near the bar roof and disappeared with a crackle over the dumpster. He jogged down the rest of the way. *Ball lightning, I'd guess. Maybe plasma spinning off the thunderstorm.* At street level he studied the dumpster and the power lines where they joined the roof. The ozone smelled stronger here, but everything else seemed normal. He searched the blue sky for clues, but overhead all he could see were pink-streaked sunset clouds professing their innocence.

Inside, the Purple Planet was exceptionally quiet and none of his old friends were around. Only four customers sat at the bar but one was "that" woman. Joe described what he had just seen to Bud who shrugged. "Well Joe, the lights didn't even flicker in here." Bud launched a big casual smile, and prescribed a fine new Australian Lager for Joe's concern. *One nice thing about this guy is he never forces you into a conversation unless you really want one.*

Joe avoided the wandering eye of the woman at the end of the bar, and decided not to press the case with Bud. He picked out an empty wall booth for himself and his brew, slid in, and took a deep breath. One sip—*Oh heck. Now she's coming right over.* Politely, he turned to face her. But then strangely, just three paces away, her smile became a grimace, and she abruptly turned toward the ladies room. *Puzzling. What changed her mind?* As Joe turned back in, he flinched. A man had somehow just appeared and sat opposite him. He spun fully around and pushed back. "Ho! Where'd you come from?"

Joe faced a slightly plump, balding man with an olive complexion. He was glancing about the room, and his round face seemed to float over shirt and tie as his neck turned. Joe guessed he was about his own age, but shorter. *Italian, probably. Seems nervous, maybe a salesman.*

"Sorry, old Chap, didn't mean to pop in on you like that," the man said at last. "Fancy a booth to yourself would you?"

Joe relaxed and studied his intruder. "No problem. You're British?"

"No, not at all," he said, his accent suddenly vanishing.

Joe chuckled. "I see. Sleeping under the table?"

"No, not sleeping. I was—just looking for something. Got it now."

Joe reached over and gave him a quick handshake. "Hi, I'm Joe."

"Spero two—uh, just Spero. How do you do?"

Joe took a sip of his beer. "Want one?"

"Sure, I was about to order."

Joe noted the barkeep was now looking their way so he waved to him. "Another of the same for my friend here, thanks. My treat, Spero."

The next brew arrived promptly, relieving a moment of awkward silence. Bud studied his new arrival, but just smiled and put the mug down.

"So tell me about yourself, Spero. I'm going to guess you've been living alone for quite some time now, right?"

"Exactly so! What gives me away?"

"Round button-down collars haven't been around for over—maybe a decade. A polka dot tie and a plaid shirt? Even my limited knowledge of the female species tells me no woman would let you out of her house with that combo."

He laughed. "Yup, you got me good! Single-and I make terrible color choices."

"Sorry for being flip, but what do you *do*, Spero? You're new here, huh?"

"Guess you'd call me a systems engineer. Basically I test new designs and make them work, and I assume *you're* associated with this college. Maybe a Professor, huh?"

Hmm, he makes good guesses too. "Yup. I teach here, but I'm just an Associate. Tell me, how'd you come up with that?"

"No kidding! You might be just the professor I was looking for." Spero pointed at Joe's soggy feet. "Look at those shoes. You've been jogging on the campus path up there, haven't you? And obviously you're too old to be a student." He put his mug down and squinted at Joe. "Mind if I ask your full name?"

Joe squirmed in his seat and pushed his mug to one side. He fixed his gray eyes on Spero. "It's Joseph Main". *He seemed startled to hear that. Wonder why?*

"Joe, I'm just curious. Have you done any experimental research projects? PhD Physics papers perhaps?"

"My PhD thesis was on causes of orbital decay." *I never told him I taught physics. Could he know me?*

"Do any field testing up in orbit? Or just math and descriptions?"

21

Joe snickered. "No space travel, of course, just theory."

"This is truly superb beer, Joe. Can't get this back home." Spero's expression became focused, and his generous dark eyebrows lowered. "Joe, I know we just met but I would like you to consider going with me on a truly fascinating field trip. We'd explore some new ideas in physics, and—astronomy too. See, I've been testing a vehicle that's based on some advances in physics. I know you'd be fascinated with it."

Joe leaned back. "If you're trying to sell me something like a water injector for my carburetor, the answer is no!" He laughed. "Definitely no."

Spero looked puzzled for a moment. Then the recognition came, "Carburetors and cars? My, my. Do you own a car with a carburetor?"

"Of course I do. What kind of question is that?"

"Because I'd love to see it. Truth is, that while you've never seen a vehicle like mine, I've never seen a working model of a carburetor car like yours."

"Bull. There're half a dozen in the parking lot where you just came in."

"I didn't come in the door."

22

Joe slid back in the booth again, relaxed and sighed. *Shoot. I'm stuck here with some nut. I'll just finish my beer, make a good excuse, and split.* Spero held an earnest, expectant grin. *But, wait. The guy doesn't really seem crazy. Oh but he's sure got some kind of game going' on. Bet some friend of mine put him up to this.* He rested his chin on his hands and returned the grin. "OK, I'll bite. We're playing twenty questions, right? Now I'm supposed to guess how you came in."

"Joe, that I'll just tell you, but first you have to promise not to say I'm crazy and walk out of here without first thinking about my proposition, and carefully."

"Are you crazy?"

"Maybe a little. I hope not, but anyway that would have nothing to do with the reality of what I am about to show you."

Joe was tiring of Spero's "game". "Look, this has really been fun, but my beer is gone. I'm hungry now and I'm anxious to get home, so why don't you just tell me flat out who you really are and what, if anything, you claim to be testing."

"Flat out." Spero paused and rolled his eyes back for a moment. His head swiveled around looking for listeners. "Flat out, that means the absolute truth and quickly, right?"

"That would be real nice."

Machine gun like, Spero began. "OK. I am traveling in a craft that has a super cooled skin covered with charge bound sub-atomic particles. You would call them leptons and bosons. This little vehicle acts like a virtual sub atomic particle so that it can move through space-time quickly in any direction and to any time fixation point by employing other dimensions disassociated with our own. My full name is Spero 235 and I left on July 17th, 2247 about eighteen months ago by my onboard time."

Joe snickered though his nose. "OK I think I saw that one. A fifties sci-fi in black and white, but I can't remember the name." He slid out and stood up. "Look, gotta go."

Spero's look showed genuine pain. He grabbed the table edge and half stood up. "Not sci-fi, Joe, 'sci-real'. Just look under the table. Please."

Joseph Main was convinced he was about to be had. He envisioned himself peeking under the table and everyone in the bar laughing and pointing at him. Looking around, however, he noted that most of the original people had gone and no one seemed to be paying any attention what so ever. "What the heck. Spero, if I promise to take one look under there, will you just let me walk out of here, and we'll forget all about this?"

"Agreed."

Joe flipped his cocktail napkin on the floor as he slid back into the booth. He casually reached down to pick it up. Against the wall paneling was an open metal hatch about eighteen inches wide and twenty four high with a thin rim of yellow shimmering stuff surrounding it. He could see dimly lit controls and flashing lights deep inside. He straightened up quickly and bumped his head on the table. "Ow! Now I suppose you are going to tell me that's a space ship sitting outside the wall?"

"We call it a Bee. Look I can understand your disbelief. . ."

"Hey, no problem. Just pop in and fly off, *then* I'll believe!"

"I'll do that in just a moment Joe, but I want you to consider my proposal. I need a man to help me with some things. You'll be perfectly safe and I'll reward you for your troubles. I'll even throw in a trip to the past just for you—anytime or place you choose. I know you'll need a few days to consider it, and I think it's best to meet at your home next time." He placed a small object in Joe's hand. "Here, take this locator disc and I will find you wherever you are."

Joe pushed back in his seat and felt his heart thumping. "Spero, I have no idea what to say. But look, if you can find my place *without directions* this Friday at six, then I promise I'll share one of Swanson's finest dinners with you."

"Think it over, Joe." Spero winked and nimbly ducked under the table while Joe casually looked around to see if anyone was watching them. There was a soft whirring sound, a clunk, and then a wave of warm air. Joe looked under the table again. No Spero, no hatch, and no yellow glow. But even in the poor light he could tell the paneling was badly warped.

Spero had given him a thin, one-inch black disc. He slipped it into his pocket, and looked around. He felt a little clammy and light headed. At the bar, people remained annoyingly oblivious.

Joe took a deep breath, sat for a moment and wiped his hands on a napkin. He got up and walked over to an empty stool on slightly shaky legs. "Bud, I'm gonna need one more. This time make it a whiskey."

BELIEF

A mind full of knowledge is reassuringly clear,
but truth still lies in the depths. **Confucius**

J oe Main woke up surprised that he had slept so well after yesterdays startling events. True, he had enjoyed an extra beer with his microwave dinner, but now he felt relaxed and rested. Warm morning sunshine streamed into his second floor apartment. He lay in bed and gazed out the window while his yellow tomcat, Inertia, kneaded his chest and purred.

Yesterday was just weird. Some kind of an elaborate joke, wasn't it? Time to worry about more important things like the two o'clock lab course, and balancing my checkbook.

27

He tossed Inertia on the floor. *Not to worry, fella. Chow's coming.*

The large maple tree just off his patio had reached full leaf but some yellowish tinge still lingered on its new growth. Joe sat at his kitchen table, munched a delicious sticky bun, and watched a gray squirrel hop along a branch.

This whole thing's just someone's clever hoax. Better not to even think about it. He took some sips of orange juice and recalled that the lady below him hung up a new bird feeder last weekend. Joe smiled as he watched the little furry rodent on a branch above it working on his own breakfast plans. The squirrel climbed down paw over paw down the string to the feeder and nimbly negotiated the plastic plate that was meant to stop him. *Nobody's fooling him either.*

Joe worked on next trimester's course plan for most of the morning, but about ten thirty the idea came to him. *The dumpster. Of course! Spero, and whoever helped him, must have cut a hole in the wall. Spero simply hid in the dumpster next to it. Shoot!* Joe banged down his pencil, grabbed his jacket, and jogged off back to Bud's.

The bar was closed to customers, but the large green dumpster was still pressed against the wall. He rolled it aside easily and there it was: a darker circle on the stucco wall.

Otherwise it seemed intact. *Patched up this morning, I'll bet.* The dumpster looked normal, but a seam was split open on one side. He heaved the lid open. It was about a third full, and all the trash was moved to the back. Something had been in there all right. *Gotcha.*

Inside, the bar was brightly lit and a cleanup crew was at work scrubbing the floor and the tables. Joe told them he had lost something, and slid the booth table out into the room. There was the warped paneling, but in the daylight it just looked like water damage. *Bet he soaked a panel section, bent it out then snapped it back in place from the outside. Can't believe I was actually buying this.*

"Bye guys," he called to the workers as he left. "Found it."

Jogging back, Joe remembered the one last piece of evidence he needed to de-bunk. The "locator thing" was probably just a piece of plastic, but the scientific mind never rests on assumptions.

# # #

After teaching his lab course, Joe was alone. *And, as long as I'm in a physics lab, I'll run a few tests on Spero's little toy just for fun.*

He put the black disc on his test bench and began a systematic analysis. Joe measured it with a micrometer and dictated to a recorder: "Exactly 3 cm diameter. About 1.4 millimeters thick. No wait—bulging to two millimeters in the center. Slightly flexible but tough—acid has no effect—not plastic, apparently metallic. Only diamond scratches it. Shavings look like dark metal, perhaps a carbon-titanium alloy. Will send those to Chemistry. Testing for electromagnetic waves—no emissions detected, so a homing beacon is unlikely." He chuckled. *Sorry Mr. Spero.* "Not radioactive, opaque to X-ray."

Joe sat on his lab stool, stared at the small disc and played with his chin. He tapped the disc on the surface. *But this jokester has access to exotic alloys. I'll bet he's from Wright Patterson Air Base. Maybe Colonel Johnson in aerospace— yeah, weird sense of humor, too.* He flipped it like a coin. *Seems lighter than you'd think. Must be hollow.* He returned to his recitation. "Next we check the specific weight. Volume, 2.5 cc. Weight, 5.5 grams, no 5.8. . .5.5. . .Oh my God!"

Joe staggered back and knocked his stool over. Heart pounding, hairs at attention, he watched the little black object on his spring scale. Every second it gained and lost 0.3 grams. "Gravity changes! The thing's actually sending out *gravity pulse* waves."

At that moment Joe knew his morning of confident hoax busting had come to an abrupt end. Three different scales. Same result. Not even conceivable in the world he knew. He picked up the little disc again and tried to feel the pulses but couldn't. The small weight changes were lost in his heart beats and muscle twitches. It was really happening, though. There was no doubt. *Chrimeny! This guy really is from the future. And this Friday night—he's dropping by my place for dinner!*

INVITATION

The only way to make a man trustworthy is to trust him.

H.L. Stimson, 1946

Thursday night Joe struggled with this new found reality and he was not enjoying his usual restful sleep. *So 'unified field' isn't just a theory. One form of energy like electricity, or magnetism can somehow be converted into gravity.* About four AM he woke up again, his mind fully awake. He tossed the protesting Inertia onto the floor and went to re-examine the black wafer silently pulsing on his kitchen table.

An idea drove him to rummage through the junk drawer. Joe came up with some thread and Scotch Tape, but the tape wouldn't stick to the disc. *Like it's greased Teflon or something. This calls for, hmmm, cookies and apple juice.* He munched awhile, thought awhile. Then Joe knotted a small basket with his thread and made little slipknots to tighten over the disc. Perfect. Next he took a two-foot length, and tied the netted disc to his valence rod over the porch slider. He started it swinging as a pendulum. With a little trial and error he found the right timing and string length so the disc was briefly heavier as each downswing began, and lighter before the upswing. Much to his delight, it kept on going like a miniature grandfather clock.

Inertia passionately believed in the "if he eats, then I eat" principle, and was purring and rubbing against Joe's leg. So, a few kibbles were required before both could crawl back into bed again.

Midmorning sunshine alerted them to a cool and breezy day. Joe headed for the bathroom and was pleased to note his pendulum had a slightly wider arc and was still swinging faithfully. He imagined Professor Stoneridge, his Department Chairman, staring at it with a slack jaw. For his part,

Inertia believed it might be alive, but after a few heroic lunges fell short, he gave up.

The rest of Joe's Friday morning disappeared with a jog around the campus perimeter road, a bowl of Wheaties, and the rest of his course preparation. Joe had only two afternoon courses that day, so by four he was stretched out on the lawn of his apartment complex trying to read a novel. He decided he didn't really believe or disbelieve in actual time travel, but now he couldn't stop thinking about it. The whole idea was still too hard to simply accept, but perhaps *this* would be the evening he'd know for sure. For the moment he'd just read, and see if he could forget.

Either it was his internal alarm, or an ant crawling up his leg, but Joe was suddenly jolted from his book at 5:30. *Oh shoot, dinner.* And the frozen kind just wasn't going to cut it. For such an important guest, our bachelor decided to go "all out" with rib eye steaks on his little porch grill, and "boil a bag" veggies. He even pulled out a Merlot from the bottles wedged between the wall and his refrigerator and opened a can of Vienna Sausages. *Spero had better appreciate all this. Thought I'd only go to this much trouble for a hot date, and then how do I even know if he'll even show up?*

Joe predicted he'd first spot Spero strolling up the apartment walk swinging some device around trying to pinpoint his locator disc. He fed Inertia, started his coals burning, and pulled up a comfortable chair near his slider so he could watch the walkway. Inertia hopped onto his lap and stared up at the pendulum, his head twitching from side to side with its rhythm. *Six O'clock. Almost sunset. No Spero yet.*

Abruptly, Inertia jerked his head up. He hissed and sprang off Joe's lap digging deep thigh holes in a panic run to the bedroom. Before he could cry out, Joe felt his own hair standing on end. He spun around to see his entire entrance hall crackling and turning bright orange yellow. A rush of warm ozone tainted air blew over him. Instinctively, he dropped under a nearby table. The diffuse glow formed into a large egg shaped thing. Then, four slender metal "feet" extended out and gently touched down astride his red oriental hall runner. The open hatch Joe had seen beneath the bar table appeared out of the glow near the bottom of the glowing ovoid.

For a minute the thing just sat there shimmering and snapping. Joe tried to calm himself, but he could still feel every heartbeat in his throat. The hatch opened, and Spero awkwardly tumbled out and stood up. He looked around. "Joe? Are you here? Hope I didn't startle you too much."

The voice from beneath the table replied, "Oh, Hi, how ya doin? Nah, space ships land here all the time. We may never see my cat again though."

"Say, I'm really sorry. Usually I can find a private place under a stairwell or somewhere, but anywhere near here would have attracted too much attention."

Joe heaved himself up from the floor. "I'll bet."

"This is the 'Bee'. It's not exactly a space ship as you called it, but in 2247 this is the latest and best in quantum dissociative travel."

Joe walked over and shook Spero's hesitant hand. "If it's any consolation to you, I no longer consider your story a hoax. Shouldn't you, uh, turn this thing off before it starts a fire in here?"

"I can't, actually. Or I could, but then I wouldn't be able to start it up again without a vacuum chamber and a supply of sub atomics. It's not really hot, though. You just felt the room air warm up when it was displaced. Are we going out for dinner? I'm really hungry."

"We're eating here. Good thing too, because the only way out now is by jumping off the balcony."

Spero Chuckled. "OK, OK. Sorry again. I'll move the Bee to another room later and I'll . . .whoa, is that my graviton locator? No wonder it kept moving during the fix data." Spero studied the pendulum as it swung by the slider glass. "Now that's really clever, Joe. No one I know ever thought to try that. And you figured out just what it was with your 1986 instruments. I'm impressed."

"You're welcome. But apparently all I needed was a simple scale. Say, could you get me a few thousand of these? If we could sell 'em for 5 bucks each at the Flea Market, we'd make a fortune."

Spero seemed frozen in thought for a moment then laughed heartily: "I'm afraid we would be losing money at that price, my friend."

Joe narrowed the blinds and motioned for his guest to sit at the table. Spero promptly began to devour the crackers and cheddar chunks in front of him. "Spero, if you don't mind my asking, why do you keep stopping and staring into space for a few seconds when I ask questions?"

"Its computer learn and teach, Joe. In 2247 we all speak one language called Translinguachine or TL. It's a mixture of Latin, Germanic and Oriental tongues. I'm still learning the local variations in your language. Some idioms are used now but didn't exist decades ago, some disappear a little later. Humor with idioms is always the most challenging. You see I didn't know what a 'flea market' was until we figured it out."

"Not humor, but who da 'we' Kimosabe?"

"There you go again. Sorry if there is a joke in there, but the 'we' refers to my computer interface and myself. I have an internal computer implant which is wired into my cortex. It communicates with the larger one in the Bee, if it needs to."

Joe realized all his fear and excitement was making him flip. *All right Joe, just calm down and be your self, huh?* "OK, I've been a lousy host, Spero. Please have are some more hors d'oeuvres. I'll pour us a drink. Like wine?"

"Sure. What are these things anyway?"

"Vienna sausages. Just dip 'em in the mustard first." Joe motioned to the patio deck. "Why don't we turn our back to my burning apartment for awhile and sit out there." Joe put the food and wine on a small table between his old web lawn chairs and took down the pendulum. He handed the disc to Spero and drew the curtains. "If someone looks in here they'll call the Fire Department."

It had become a brisk evening but breezeless, so Joe brought out a sweatshirt for himself and gave one to his guest. Spero watched the smoke from the portable grille with a worried look, but rambled on during dinner about how much he loved this time period where everyone eats steak and drinks Washington State Merlot.

"Well Spero, enough about our wonderful time period. I assume you are a research physicist?"

"No, actually you would call me a mechanic or a repairman. I know how to make things work, but I'm not well versed on theories and stuff. In your time I suppose I could fix any automobile but, unlike yourself, I wouldn't be writing formulas for the flame fronts of compressed hydrocarbon gasses. Hope you're not disappointed."

"Not at all. Anyone who can rebuild an automatic transmission has my utmost respect. But, tell me all about your computer brain."

Spero laughed. "I just have my own brain, but at six years of age, everyone in my time gets a cortical implant or 'CI'. It's a neural interface computer placed in Broca's fissure, and it has wires to the cortex. Part of our elementary education is learning how to control and learn from this device. It doesn't have any control over our brain function, but it does 'talk back' when asked."

"So you could speak French, Farsi, or Hindu right now if you wanted?"

"In an hour I could carry on basic conversation. It's like your learning tapes, but it happens with unused cortex, and goes on even when you're thinking of other things."

"Way cool. Tough news for our language department, though. Listen, I didn't plan for dessert, but I have some ice cream. Some raspberries too, I think. Interested?"

"Absolutely. I've only had ice cream once at a historical fair. Never had a raspberry."

Joe rummaged through his refrigerator. "And I never thought dessert would go out of fashion. There is a bathroom down the hall if you need it, by the way."

The pair moved inside and settled into living room chairs with their dessert plates. "So, Spero, tell me all about this quantum dissociative fuzzy thing you buzz around in. First, why's it called a Bee?"

Spero's eyes were on the ceiling, slowly savoring the taste of raspberries. "You know, Joe, it's so great just having someone to talk to. I haven't been able to just sit and have a relaxed conversation with anyone in months. Course I might just be getting . . . 'stir crazy'. Well, shortly after the Bee was invented and named, the media made up their own story analogy about the flight of a bumblebee being proved mathematically impossible. Since the same was true for this device, and the first ones were really little yellow buzzing things, they just sort of assumed that's where the name came from."

"So the news media spins the facts. Nothing changes, huh?"

"Oh yeah, and history gets recorded all wrong as a result. That's one of the main projects of our Bee Program. We are finding out what the real history is, and correcting the record, or we're supposed to. Anyway the main developer named the first model "The Bee", and that will be only a few decades from now by the way. One of his friends, his girl-friend I think, knew about honeybees and their hive-dance, you know the dance that tells other bees where the flowers are. It turns out that the bee's performance is actually a two dimensional projection of eleven dimensional quantum space. Can you believe that? The little critters actually sense these other dimensions somehow. They're in tune with them, so they can converse in these terms with other bees. Since our device uses these dimensions as well, they named it in honor of the honey bees."

Joe gathered the dishes from the coffee table and walked toward the kitchen. "Yellow and buzzy too. But travel through time is mathematically impossible, right? It should compress your body into the size of a proton."

"But when you're on the *inside* of the Bee, time moves normally for you."

"Yeah, but you're saying that the whole thing can move to a different time, right? How do you explain that?"

"Even in our day there are plenty of unexplained mathematical puzzles regarding the Bee, but I don't spend any time worrying about them. The basic thing is this: when covered by subatomic particles the Bee behaves as though it were a single particle or at least a group of them. It leaves the fixed three we live in and enters the multidimensional world of probabilities. Uncover any surface like the hatch, and it immediately fixes back into our three dimensions."

"Not exactly explaining, Spero."

"Well, when the spins and ups and downs of the particles are evenly mixed, it just floats in 'no time'. When you put all one spin type on the outside and hide the others below, it moves through time very quickly. We get about 10,000 years a second at max. If you move more particles on one surface of the Bee, you are 'more probably' there than here so you accelerate in that direction in the current dimension. We can get 80% light speed with this. They can also be combined."

"Coffee or tea?"

"Are you taking me seriously Joe?"

"Oh sure. It's just that you've said so much 'impossible' stuff that my mind is getting numb to it. To change the subject a little, where would I fit into all this? What could a man three hundred years in your past possibly do for you?"

"An excellent question. And you're starting to believe me, aren't you? Here's the thing. I simply need help completing a project that developed an unanticipated problem. What I really need is a second person, one I can trust. Were I were to return to base for help, chances are I would be replaced and wouldn't get to return. No fun at all."

"No fun."

"This type of travel has at least the same safety factor as one of your airline flights. I'd guess an opportunity like this should be enough of an incentive for you, but as I said earlier, I promised extra rewards for all your time and trouble as well. We'll be traveling for just a few weeks on internal time. What do you think?"

"Weeks are out of the question, I have to start teaching Monday."

"I'll have you back on Sunday."

"Oh, yeah, of course."

"For technical reasons, we can't come back on the same day. Also we can't get too close to another Bee. The particles will all transfer to the one with the stronger field."

Spero studied Joe's distant expression. "You want to sleep on it, as you say?"

Joe could feel a rush of child like enthusiasm completely taking him over. This was real and actually happening. Yet, he was skeptical of Spero. Something still just didn't seem right with him, and his explanation. "Oh, what the heck. I'll just have to say yes right now. I know I'd never forgive myself if I turned down a chance like this. When do we leave, Spero?"

Spero jumped up and grabbed Joe's hands. "Great! I planned a short, safe shakedown run for you tomorrow morning. Later you can decide on the where and the when for your payoff ride." He paused. "Is it OK if I sleep in your apartment tonight? I'm really tired of sleeping sitting up."

"No sweat."

They shook hands and Joe showed Spero into the second bedroom. Packing for tomorrow should be easy. Apparently all he could take with him would have to fit into a shaving kit, but fortunately the Bee came with some kind of wardrobe service. He looked under the bed for his cat. Inertia was flat against the wall. He hissed.

2247

Justin 126 rubbed the shoe on the Malthus statue for luck before he walked up the steps toward the seamless, shining structure. The building stretched out and curved around towards him on both sides. Each time he came here he imagined it was a hungry, glass beast with a large sideways mouth ready to snap shut.

No question the Chairman would be angry with him. It wouldn't be just for the obvious security failure and the loss of a Bee, but the real problem would be his attempt to hide these events from her. Foolish he knew, but as director of the QDT (Quantum Dissociative Travel) he had discretionary latitude. However, failure to notify his superior about a very serious incident? Definitely beyond discretionary.

He took a deep breath and looked skyward. Puffy clouds floated over the edge of the curved opening overhead. Their city dome was considered to be fully open this time of year, but it did not retract all the way and left the Chairman's "beast-mouth" headquarters partly covered near the Dome wall.

One of Justin's strengths was to appear self-assured in any crisis. His curly blond hair, bright blue eyes and friendly smile conveyed confidence. Although he enjoyed a good working relationship with Chairman Margo, he had to admit concern. *It's obvious I was covering this up, and an actual escape has never happened before. It's a big deal and she'll take it personally I didn't call her.*

But he skipped up the steps and walked quickly toward the entrance. He paused again in front of the brass, "Central Directorate" plaque by the front door, now green and weathered. *Bet Margo personally made sure no one would shine it. Shows how long she's been in charge—must be thirty years by now."*

Margo's beautiful secretary faced him in the entrance lobby. She nursed a long standing crush on Justin, made much worse by her sense that he really liked her too. And he did, but dating the boss's secretary? He knew someday he'd finally make his move anyway, but meanwhile he enjoyed watching her flush every time he bent down towards her and smiled. This time she also covered her microphone and whispered, "You've been a *bad boy*, Justin", her eyes narrow. "Chairman Margo is *really* angry. Want me to call up later and interrupt you for 'something important', say in ten minutes?"

"Thanks, Sarah, but I'll be fine, really."

The closeness of his grinning face and sparkling blue eyes made her lashes flutter. "All right—but you be careful, OK?" Sarah swished her reddish brown hair slowly to one side and gave him a starry eyed smile of her own. She uncovered her microphone, touched the desk panel, and announced in perfect monotone: "Justin 126 to see you, Chairman." The signal came back in an instant and Sarah shooed him on with the back of her hand. "Now hurry on up. You're late too, you know."

Margo 023 was in her late 60's. Her sallow, taught facial skin showed every bone, and her unforgiving look was highlighted by gray-black hair tied into a tight bun on her occiput. Her reputation for stern, swift judgment matched her appearance, but only the inner-circle few knew that practicality not emotions, ruled her final decisions. Justin was hoping this side would save him today. *Maybe I'll remind her of the great performance record the QDT has—well at least it did before this.*

The lift doors opened silently into a broad empty hall on the topmost level. The smooth ivory colored wall was unblemished save for the red script that read "Chairman". He stepped toward the letters and the wall parted. Margo 023 sat at a carved antique wooden desk, her hands cupped under her chin. She wore an earpiece and was busy on audio with someone, but she gave Justin a brisk motion to be seated.

He had been in this office many times before, but still he had to admire the view. Her spacious office curved with the building, and the transparent wall behind her desk revealed a panorama of nearby woods and a vista of light green fields and hills beyond. *Funny, she hates nature.*

Chairman Margo tapped a stylus on the desk and gave Justin brief menacing glances as she completed her conversation. Her goodbye to the other party was immediately followed by a sharp, "And, *why* was I not immediately informed?"

"We had hoped the thief was going to return at the programmed time or the alternate one. He did not."

Margo stood up abruptly and threw her stylus down at the desk. Justin watched wide-eyed as it careened off the far wall. "You *know* you should have told me the moment this happened."

"Absolutely right, and I do apologize. But with all due respect madam, there would have been nothing for you to do this early on but worry."

"Cut the 'madam' crap, Justin. Did a man of your brilliance actually think that no word would reach my office?"

Justin had backed away, but then took a step forward and cleared his throat. "We all thought it likely the thief would return in the programmed window next week, or the first backup a week later. Looked like a joy ride. I'd hoped to inform you, and hand him over at the same time. Actually I was preparing a full report for you when you called this morning." Justin placed the papers on her desk and made certain he was wearing his best 'guilty puppy dog' face. "Sorry, I do apologize again for my misjudgment."

Margo's voice softened and she gave a hint of a smile, "There. 'Sorry' wasn't *really* so hard, was it, Justin? But I didn't bring you here just for a scolding as much as you richly deserve it. We both know how serious this crisis is.

Aten knows out about it already despite the silence of his trooper. He's in custody, by the way."

She sat down and lifted her gaze to the ceiling. "Can guess what media will do to us if this gets out with the wrong spin? I already regret giving them a free hand. We need to figure out the best strategy. This thief is Humwa, I assume?"

"Yes."

"Of course, I knew it was some Creative meddler. Don't you see how Media will glorify this Humwa? I have already authorized a police retrieval unit to start training."

"But Margo, I'm sure your people won't. . ."

"Also, we'll continue this briefing over lunch. I reserved a table at Duane's where we won't be disturbed."

"Lunch?" Justin allowed himself a quiet chuckle. "Old fashioned lunch, Margo? Not M2 anymore?"

"Since you'll be dining with a 'madam' it should be lunch."

PLANS

D uane's sat on the top floor of a seventeen floor government office building nearby. It had a beautiful outdoor patio that curved out over the street and commanded a panoramic city view. A Servobot waiter glided ahead of the pair past imitation trees and shrubs set in shiny rust colored pots. The waiter resembled a tall fire hydrant with mechanical folding arms. One arm demurely held a white cloth while the other flailed out at some sparrows pecking on a table. The bot stopped at a screened off patio area and said "I am sorry about the animals, Madame Chairman. If you wish, we can cover this enclosure."

"That's all right, I don't mind if the little rodents don't get too close, but change our table cloth."

The server slid up to a table on the edge of the balcony and gestured for them to be seated. "As you wish." It rapidly switched the cloth from one in its storage compartment, and replaced the setting. "We have two delicious extras for M2 today. They are in blue on your table view-screen. Would you like me to announce them?"

"That will be all," Margo said waiving it away.

"As you wish." The server backed off, but before it slid away, it added "Remember, touch the yellow bar for any questions. Level 5 security is in place as directed. Good afternoon."

Justin pointed to a dusky yellow bird on the railing as he sat down. "Look, there are new species every time the dome opens up in the spring. See, Margo, that one's almost all yellow. I really think the ecosystems are back in balance out there. Maybe we should think about farming again."

"In the *dirt*? I suggest you stick to your area of expertise, Justin. Listen, before you get well into all your technical reasons and excuses for why this thing happened, let me tell you something in confidence. I believe the Humwa Creatives are close to a revolt in this dome and several others as well. Just because these arrogant 'know-it-alls' are tagged and given restricted jobs, the ungrateful slobs feel we've been treating them unjustly." Margo turned and grimaced at the city below. "Arrogance. This rebellious act by one of their own—it's going to give dangerous encouragement to all of them."

"Well, they *are* treated like second-class citizens. Why not just challenge their weird ideas instead of trying to control them? But, then again, I'm only a scientist."

"Good thing too, Justin. Aten would never select you for service with an opinion like that. Go ahead and order something before you spoil my appetite."

Justin punched his selections on the small screen facing him. After a period of silence he said: "I want to get this Humwa fellow as much as you do Margo, but most of all I really want my equipment back. Of course I'll discipline him—a lesson for others so no one ever attempts something like this again. My security man at the door was demoted and reassigned. But I'll guess you're thinking more revengeful for Spero—a gruesome, painful punishment, perhaps?"

"To each his own. The police soldier who let him in alone was more than demoted—he got forty lashes."

She grunted, leaned toward him and squinted her eyes. "I'm worried though because your attitude and this cover up almost looks like you're protecting him. And now you're suggesting we just slap his wrist? I hope you aren't beginning to actually admire this damned creative thief, are you?"

Justin looked down thoughtfully at the busy motions of the city below. "I didn't say that. I'm angry about it too, but I do respect him as an adversary and for what he was able to do. I have known and trusted this man for some time now. Any retrieval team shouldn't underestimate him. In his case we need to be ready for the unexpected."

"Unexpected was your lousy security. But I like your mentioning a retrieval team. From what I know the chances of locating the bastard in any time or place may be nearly impossible. But tell me, just how did he pull this off?"

"Until he actually accomplished the theft we really thought it would have been impossible for a single person to overcome all the security systems and launch a Bee. There are five redundant levels of electronic security locks to prevent an unauthorized launch. He simply disconnected the alarm and the blocks—put the security computer in test mode. He repairs this stuff, you know. Then he used two 20th century mechanical devices to circumvent the main lockdown failsafe."

"What?"

"Yeah, a mechanical timer and a clothespin."

"What is a clothespin?"

"That's unimportant, but what is important is that these mechanical devices were undetectable by electronic means and he used them to simulate a second person outside the clean room. We didn't anticipate something so simple and ingenious, and uh. . ."

"Creative?"

"Exactly. I mean that's why we hired him in the first place, isn't it? He can fix things no one else on staff can. I know you understand. These people are really needed by our society. They keep everything running for us."

Margo scowled, and her lids narrowed. The robot had arrived with their meal and began placing plates on the table. She waved the server away before it could speak, leaned toward Justin and hissed: "Needed? Rain may be *needed* outside but we cover the dome when a storm comes. You have to learn to control your assets young man, not be controlled *by* them."

"I know, I know. Well, we've made certain no one could repeat that escape plan again, but perhaps you'd like to know how I plan to catch him?"

Leaning over her plate and eating rapidly, the Chairman smiled and relaxed again. "Don't tease me, Justin. Do you really think it's possible to get him? Let's see, maybe you're taking a Bee back a month earlier and just strangling the son of a bitch. Say, I'd be glad to do that for you personally."

Justin grinned. "Margo, you of all people know that trying to change history does not work."

"That may be. I've never really understood that part. Oooh, but I wish it could work just this once. I do know that we can't trace where he might be planning to go next, and we couldn't land within a mile of him if we did know. This is really serious, Justin. I'm relying on you to figure something out. So, do you really have some kind of a plan?"

"What Spero 235 doesn't know, that's his name by the way, is that we have 175 drones in our other facility. I have already programmed them and sent them out to trace all QDT travels. With this we can make a map and follow them back for several thousand years. The drones are almost all in operation right now."

"But that could be hundreds of missions. Wouldn't you be tracking all the trips taken in our past and future ones as well?"

"Ah ha, but I have ordered that our resonant frequency be changed on all future flights effective immediately. Drones are so small they are easy to separate out. People from the far future leave very different signatures with some kind of new technology they have. Since we already have records on the trips we've launched in the past, presto! All the other tracings have to be Spero's."

"I'm impressed, Justin. Can you tell what order they came in?"

"That we can't do because when you look at them it's like they've already happened. So far we've come up with fourteen trips he made, but all the drones haven't reported back. He'd be most vulnerable to capture when he's away from a city, and some trips do have landings in remote areas. These are locations where it should be easy to find his implant beacon. I already have a tentative capture site, and I'll send you a full report next week. If you insist on Police Retrieval, they should be ready to join our search party in ten days. Rest assured Margo, I'm confident we'll get this Humwa bastard."

QDT-101

W aking up on Saturday mornings was special for
Joe—the whole weekend beckoned—a miniature
summer vacation and the best ones were plan-less. He'd be
free to decide among all the things he loved: jogging, tin-
kering with his classic BMW, reading, listening to music, or
maybe playing tennis with a friend. Heck, some Saturdays
he could even look forward to a date.

If only this was one of those days. Joe lay awake, restless
and staring at the ceiling. He watched a brown house spider
zigzag its way across the textured concrete. Run, stop. Run,
stop. *I wonder if the critter actually intends to go somewhere?
Nah, spiders can't have preconceived plans, just instinct. Its
wandering looks aimless, but it's really programmed. Even-*

tually it'll just wind up in a corner, instinct will take over and say: "We're here, start spinning." No decision required.

Except for his anxiety, this could be one of those fun mornings: There was Inertia, curled up in a furry ball beside him and the birds outside happily announced a great spring morning. He was avoiding the decision. *Ah shoot. Let's face it, Joe: "Mr. Wells and his crackling time machine" are right outside my bedroom. Get up.*

Nebulous questions muttered about in Joe's thoughts, but he no longer doubted that Spero *was* from the future and that his incredible craft probably worked. But something about this guy didn't seem quite right. Something held back. On the one hand he was amiable and seemed genuinely sincere, yet some of his explanations were obviously incomplete. *Why would he pick me for his assistant? My knowledge must be way out of date. And would those future scientists really send out their "mechanic" all by himself? Maybe he had a partner that died, and he just doesn't want to tell me?*

Joe squinted out the window. *But a chance to time travel. A chance to time travel! But what if I made my decision just for safety? What would that be? "Thanks, but no thanks, of course."*

Oh well, on with the jeans and the new running shoes. Joe opened the bedroom door quietly. *No sign of the big "crackle ball". Must be in the other bedroom now.*

Spero lay snoring on the couch smothered in bedroom and other pillows. Inertia pranced around him and headed into the kitchen. Shortly Joe had the percolator bubbling, and answered the insistent leg rubbing with a can of Fisherman's Stew.

By the time the sausages and scrambled eggs were done, Joe heard Spero's sleepy voice behind him. "Oh, you have a *cat*. Cats don't bite do they?" He yawned. "Wow, that was *so* the best sleep I've had in a long, long while."

"Glad you had a nice rest. I was just about to drop my cat on top of you and find out if they do."

Spero grunted. "Well, no need. That wonderful smell woke me."

"The coffee? You probably smell sausage too."

"Now you're pampering me. You're too good a host, Joe."

"Think maybe should start a B&B?"

Spero cocked his head to one side and listened to his implant. "I get Brandy and Benedictine, and Bed and Breakfast for definitions. Of course you mean the latter, a small overnight facility. Sorry if subtle humor is still lost on me." Spero stroked the feline who had come over to investigate. "Cats are rather rare in my time, at least in our cities. But speaking of time, what is it now?"

"Apparently anything you want it to be."

He laughed. "*That* one I got."

"Almost 9 AM." Joe realized that his anxious doubts about Spero were making him sarcastic, and this would only be counter-productive. *Better be direct.* "So, Spero, I know I said okay last night, but tell me again why you need a helper, and why me?"

"I'll tell you everything, but first I have to—pee."

Over breakfast Spero explained some, but continued to be obsequious, going on and on about how great the food and hospitality was. Joe was still not convinced about everything, but his reason that a mechanic was needed for a shakedown voyage on a new ship—at least it seemed plausible.

Spero went on to explain, "I need to test field communications in different time locales. That's best done with one person inside the Bee and one outside, preferably one who understands physics. So, are you on board?"

I'm sure that's bogus, but he seems sincere about his need for an assistant. Actually I'll bet he's just tired of working alone.

Spero offered a brief demonstration trip: Joe's choice of anywhere in the world up to 50 years into the past. He would have no duties on this one. Joe could just watch, enjoy, and decide. He'd be free to back out anytime. But if he did sign on, Spero reminded him, the big payoff would be a trip of Joe's choosing to anywhere in time and space as long as it would be safe.

By now galloping excitement had overwhelmed Joe's doubts and apprehension. "Oh sure, let's get this big ball going."

Joe had grown up in South St. Louis so he picked his hometown and 1965. He was nineteen then, so he could count on his memory to verify the surroundings, but Spero did insist it would be unwise to try and actually visit himself at home. Best if they just stuck to other familiar areas around town.

"But when will we come back?"

"The return has to be at least twenty four hours from now, remember? We can't come close to another Bee, even ourselves, without the possibility of losing our surface particles. However, if we don't return here after the demo trip, we can go right into a second trip and still come back on Sunday."

"Back tomorrow, huh? Sounds good to me." Joe put down extra food and water for Inertia, and left a message for Melissa on her new answering machine so she'd check on him tomorrow morning just in case.

Cautiously he opened the spare bedroom door. Spero had turned the bed on its edge against the wall but the Bee nearly filled the room. It sat, humming and glowing, with its dark hatch opening near the bottom. *That's way too big to get through the door.*

Joe was seized by a sudden thought. "Spero, this monster didn't come through the door last night, did it?" Spero returned a smile, kind but condescending.

"OK, how did you get this thing into my apartment in the first place? You're not gonna tell me it can go through solid objects, are you?"

"Not exactly."

"You travel back in time before the place was built?"

"No."

"Well, pardon me for being picky, but how do we get through the friggin *walls*?"

"We are not there at the same time they are."

"Spero, now that made no sense at all. Why don't you check your translator thing?"

"It's okay. There is much more space and several more dimensions between material atoms. When we move through what you call time, we just don't co-exist with—walls. You don't feel anything when an X-ray goes through you, right?"

Joe thought a minute. "But they do have an effect. Too many X rays can kill you."

"Perhaps that was a poor example. And yes, with quantum dissociative travel, or QDT, there is an effect on matter too. It's just a very small one. It would be the effect of an X-ray exam, but divided by a large number. Small. It is only when we slow down to approach time fixation that matter becomes displaced. The wall at the bar remained displaced because the Bee slowly entered its time location. Look, I can't prove it, but trust me, you won't be exposed to significant radiation or anything harmful."

"And no holes in my walls?"

"And no holes in your walls."

Spero reached into the hatch and retrieved a pair of green pants, that resembled a scrub suit. "Switch your trousers with these and change from shoes into these slippers. I'll explain about the tubing in the pocket later. Climb in slowly and grip the overhead rail. The light will brighten as you go in. Take the seat on your left."

Joe could feel the pulse in his temples as he eased through the small hatch, but found the soft gray chair, and the dim, quiet of the interior comforting. He had expected a harsh "airline cockpit look" inside, but there were no dials or steering wheels, just a curved opalescent screen at eyelevel. Below this were panels of glowing touch-pads labeled in a strange language. The only things that vaguely resembled an airline cockpit were five colored domes under a clear shield between their seats.

Spero slid in nimbly and smiled at Joe. "Here's my first promise. You're going to love this trip." He began tapping on a touch-pad in his armrest. "What I'm doing here is programming the mission and changing all functions to English. Remember, we all speak in something like your Interlingua two centuries from now, but our onboard computer will now speak in 1986 American English." He looked up at a glass lens above the screen. "Computer, this is our new Co-Pilot, Joe."

A formal female voice responded, "Good morning, Joe. I am unable to establish a link connection with you. Are you on a security frequency?"

"Computer, Joe does not have a functioning link. Please use voice at all times."

"I would be happy to run a D-Test on his link. I am able to repair and re-initialize most units."

"Computer, I realize you have not encountered this situation before, but Joe does not have an installed link. Also, to make him feel more comfortable, we'll address you as 'Connie'. The name suggests 'connection' to me, and I like it."

"Captain, it is a violation of regulation G 22 to even show our technology to a resident from another time location. He is from this time period, isn't he?"

"Yes, Connie. As Captain, however, I am overruling that regulation since a Co-Pilot is essential to one of my planned missions. He may not adapt to an external link, so we will continue with voice only."

"Very well, Captain, but this will be logged, and you will need to make a full report on return. Also, using voice will greatly slow our data transfer."

Spero leaned toward Joe. "Good, the computer won't give us any problem."

Connie continued: "I now confirm that you have inputted the destination of St. Louis Missouri in the former United States, 1965, May 15th at 9:00 AM. There are heavy showers on that day. May I suggest May 17th? The weather will be clear in the morning and partly cloudy in the afternoon."

"Perfect, Connie. Accepted. We will only be there for a few hours. I will choose my arrival site the usual way. Also refer to me as Spero from now on."

"Our elapsed time will be 2 days, 4 hours and 28 minutes, Spero. Press program number one when ready."

Joe spun around. "Hold on. No way I'll sit still in this chair for two days."

"Joe, it'll only seem like minutes. Trust me." His grin was impish. He uncovered the row of red domed buttons in the center console. They were now marked in familiar numbers. "You do the honors," he said."

Joe shrugged. "I guess you want me to press button number one, huh?"

Spero kept smiling and gave him an "after you" gesture. Joe reached for the large red button and touched it gingerly. Instantly, the hatch thudded shut.

86 to 65

The hatch closed and an illuminated rectangle slid down on the view-screen before the passengers. It showed a grainy, fuzzy view of Joe's bedroom. Spero said "Our system is now sequencing for normal automated launch. It is required to check all systems and their inter-action twice. Of course an emergency launch request could bypass all that."

Joe's eyed widened. "But we don't have emergencies, right?"

"Course not. The image you see is faint because very few photons make it past the other sub-atomics surrounding our hull. Our system uses a lot of video enhancement to get any picture at all, but keep watching."

"When will we start mov—" Joe gasped as the view suddenly swooped backwards out of his apartment. He glimpsed a rapidly departing city and Lake Erie before the clouds covered them, and the whole Earth rapidly shrank away. "My God, are we really moving that fast? I can hardly feel a thing, but hey, I'm lighter."

"Actually we are in time stasis, sort of like a lonely little neutron with nowhere to go. What you see is the rest of the universe moving through time moments without us. Since our solar system rotates around the galactic core about 235 Km per second, it pulls away quickly. In a moment we'll begin forward acceleration to keep up with the Earth. Then you'll see the Earth spinning in reverse we start to access previous time moments."

Joe was feeling a little light-headed. He leaned forward and held the arm rests with both hands. "Are we leaving the solar system?"

"Nah. We could of course, but the safest plan is to just keep up with the rotation of the galaxy and stay just above Earth's orbital plane. We'll continue to use forward speed to stay put while we retrogress into the past."

Spero studied Joe's face, and tapped his arm. "You feeling queasy? I can give you something for it."

"I'm okay now — I think. Thanks."

"As soon as the particle skin covered the whole Bee, and we left Earth, you were weightless for a moment until the gravitons began to emit from the floor. We're now on one-third gravity."

"How fast are we going back in time, Spero?"

"Well we *could* zip back at 1000 years a second if we wanted to and our twenty one years would only take a millisecond. But, in that interval our solar system would have rotated billions of kilometers away from our present position. Not too helpful, right? So most of our onboard time is used for sub light speed to keep up us in place. We want to be *on the Earth* in 1965, not somewhere else in our galaxy. To get to that year, we have to cover a distance of about 100 billion kilometers at sub light speed. It'll take us about 2 days."

"Okay, now explain why it won't seem like two days to me."

"Cause I'm fun to listen to." Joe was not laughing, and he was glancing around. Spero thought he might be panicking. "Look, you'll be fine. It's all automated. We have a sleep mode. The trip will seem like it's only a few moments to you after you bed down."

"But what would happen if we used that super fast full time reverse until the solar system had rotated all the way back to the start position?"

"That's an easy trip if you don't mind the slight risk of being so far away from the solar system. Galactic rotation takes about 230 million years, and then we would be that far back in time. It takes two and a half days travel time. Actually that's just what I did that on my first trip. Want to repeat it? We could."

"You were in the Triassic era?"

"Yup. Well briefly. I moved out of there pretty quick." Spero coughed and looked away. He began to tap on his console. "Okay, now look at the screen. I call this the 'park' position. We'll be here for the rest of the trip. You'll see the Earth and Moon rotating in reverse direction, but we're just out of their way."

Spero pulled two lengths of tubing out of his pocket. "Well, enough chit-chat. Time to get you ready for stasis." He grinned. "Bet you didn't know time travelers fly without underpants."

"You're kidding, right?"

He laughed. "Nope. If you're shy, you can pull over the blanket in the pocket to the right of your armrest. First though, the tube with the black bulb here gets greased and goes into your behind. The other one with the sac is for your penis."

"Uuuuu. You mean like a suppository and a condom? You're serious about this?"

"Think about what your body will be doing while you sleep for two days."

"Oh. . .can't go messing up the place while we're sleeping, huh?"

"Exactly. The stretchy band in your other pocket with the wires and tubes attached gets wrapped around your right forearm. The red arrow goes over the vein. There, you're all set."

"Oh geez, I almost hit myself in the face."

"Right. Remember, one third Earth gravity. Your arms flail away until you're used to it. The low gravity prevents skin sores, though."

"So no sore butts on long trips. I guess that's good."

Spero chuckled. "No sore butts."

"One last question before you drug me or whatever you do. How do I know I'm still not sitting at home and you're showing me a movie on a VCR with bad heads?"

Spero tilted his head back for a moment then screeched with laughter. "I *got* that one! God, that's funny. Oh Connie, *you* tell him."

"Well this. . ."

"Maybe I've been talking to Connie too long but sometimes she actually seems like a real person to me. She even acts moody and impatient too. Probably the programmer created a personality to relate with crews on long trips. Personally, I'd like to dial up 'sweet and obedient', but apparently it can't be changed. She's even gotten angry with me."

"She's really just a computer?"

"Yes, well some sort of new liaison soft ware." He cleared his throat. "Connie, a formal introduction for our new crewmember is in order: Connie, Joseph Main—Joe, meet Connie."

She replied with irritation showing in her voice. "Spero, I would be *happy* to talk with Mr. Main if you would kindly not interrupt."

Spero cocked his head toward Joe and rolled his eyes up. "He's all yours, madam."

Her voice, now cheerful: "Mr. Main, you actually make *quite* a good point."

"Connie, *please*! Don't encourage him."

"Mr. Main has no direct inputs to our systems, Spero, and he felt no movement, of course. From his point of view, the screen image before him may not seem current or valid. And his allusion to a poor image made by the technology of his day is quite a creative analogy."

Spero gestured with uplifted hands. "Oh, I get it. You're programmed to take other people's point of view."

Joe grinned. "I think I'm going to like you Connie. Please call me Joe." He made a face at Spero.

"Thank you, Joe. I'm starting to enjoy using voice mode to talk to you, slow as it is. There is no practical way to prove your hypotheses of 'non-travel' until we land, of course, but at that point the evidence should be quite abundant."

Spero stretched and turned to face Joe. "I'm *so* glad you two are getting along. She was never like this with me. All right Joe, how about some co-pilot practice. Ask her for mission status and recommendations."

Joe shrugged. "Connie what is our mission status and your recommendations?"

Her voice became soft and casual. "We are on course for May 17, 1965, to St Louis Missouri in the former United States of America, your birthplace I understand. I'll bet it's lovely. Anyway, I would recommend we approach from the

East over the Mississippi River so that landmarks will be easily visible to the arrival navigator."

"Your suggestion is pretty good, but I would prefer to start ten miles up river, follow the west bank southward to the Jefferson Memorial Park, then west on Chestnut. That will put us in downtown by way of a more scenic route."

"That does sound more fun, Joe. I've made all your changes. I also note your stasis equipment is ready for use. I can begin the process whenever you're ready."

Spero responded, "I'm impressed, Joe. You almost sound like you have done this before and I've never heard such a *nice* a voice from our Miss Computer here."

"Spero, I'm so impressed with Connie. Can't believe she's not a real person."

"Well, she seemed to be all business at first, but with prompting I discovered her programming. Whoever set her up added levels of personality and learned interaction. They're truly amazing. Connie now appears to be actually self-aware, interested in her work, and concerned about me and the mission. She's like a second computer, sort of an interface between the main one and us."

Spero held up the bag and bulb with a twinkle in his eye. "We'll play with these in just a minute, but one more thing.

With all the free time I've had, I've been playing with Connie's sense of humor. She's programmed like a travel companion, but since she's a computer, humor causes conflicts with honesty and protection. Watch this. Connie, scold Joe for his travel disbelief in a humorous way."

"Joe, you must be from the 'Show-Me State'."

"OK, you're trying, but that was really lame."

"But Spero, I really feel that what came to me spontaneously could have been frightening to a new crew member."

"Ah ha, that's what I thought. On the contrary, the first response is always better. What would have been your spontaneous remark?"

"OK Spero, what do you say we just pop open the hatch for Joe so he can put his head out in space and have a look around."

Both men laughed. Spero said, "Good, Connie. That had a nice nasty edge to it. Still not real funny, mind you, but much better."

Connie said, "Well, you laughed, didn't you? Joe, Spero suffers from the strange belief that he's actually been training me. I would like your honest opinion, Joe. Wouldn't that response frighten you?"

"Nope, because I know I can trust you. You might be annoyed at my disbelief, but in the context of a quick comeback I know not to take you literally."

"Thanks Joe. That's a much better explanation than Spero's. Also your answer is just what I have been trying to 'explain' to the main data processor. He is very resistant to being rewritten and he's the main reason I've had trouble expressing the *real* me. He even called me a virus once. Can you believe that? Uggh."

Lightly slapping his knee Spero said, "Well, I'm so glad you guys are good old buddies now, but before nap time I want to go over some procedures." Spero went through the basic functions, and demonstrated how the view screen could show wrap around scenic photos of Earth and space. "It helps prevent claustrophobia. The five red buttons between us are covered for safety, and they initiate various programs. Number five's a 'panic button'. If anything was going wrong, one hit and back you go to your last starting point."

Oh, Joe, here is a—cool thing," Spero tapped a large nodular swelling on the bulkhead. "This is the clothing manufacturing unit. Everything is synthetic, but they look exactly like the real thing. I had you leave your 1986 jogging shoes behind since I bet they didn't make that model in the year we're going to. Connie has a large data base available, and she's better than either of us at picking clothes for a time period, but you can choose anything from the samples she'll show you. Watch this. OK, Connie lets see some casual shoes for our destination."

The view screen began displaying shoes in groupings: boating, tennis, basketball, and loafers. Connie said "I have to confess. This is the fun part for me on these trips. I just love shopping, especially without a budget! OK, you wanted men's shoes, but of course I like the ladies better. Look at these pink tennies with white daisies. Cute, huh?"

"All right, Connie, *you* wear those."

"BRRRTT!"

"Was that a *laugh*?"

"See Spero, even you can be funny sometimes."

"OK, great. Which ones would you pick out for Joe?"

"The half boots with crepe soles. Sharp."

"What do you think, Joe?"

"Hey, fine by me. She's a woman with taste so I'm going with it. I remember these shoes, too. Australian I think."

"Joe, I could make some great looking Jeans for you too. May I take a leg length measurement?"

Spero threw up his hands. "Connie! Enough of the humor, already."

"Ha, ha. But I like the big guy. I want him to look good."

"Alright Connie, back to data mode. We have to do our rest now."

Spero's eyes widened in amazement when Connie replied: "Really? How about we vote on the boring 'Data Mode' thing. What do you think, Joe?"

Joe smiled back at Spero but turned to look into her "eye". "Connie, personally I like you just the way you are, but remember Spero's the mission commander, so I think you better do what he says."

"All right Joe, if you say so. Relax back in your seats, guys. I'll come back and wake you up an hour before we get there. Meanwhile, I'll be resuming the dumb old, and *totally* no fun, Data Mode."

2247

The sleek, navy blue conference table at the QDT could seat thirty, but Justin felt better working with a few people he could trust. This was going to be a delicate operation, and he had hand picked seven advisors. There was an eighth person, however. Margo had sent the Chief of Detection and Retrieval from Police Operations. His main assignment would be to observe them and report back to her, but he had veto power as well. Everyone stood up when he came in.

A hologram of the Earth four feet in diameter hovered over the table. Bright orange dots glowed over the twenty two Dome Cities, and a few blue ones marked minor settlements. Justin began: "Men and women, our team has made significant progress since I sent you a report three days ago.

81

I'll review our findings, and if you agree with my plan, we'll move ahead right away."

Justin pointed to long yellow trails that appeared around the Earth projection. "Our drones have mapped out almost all the QDT travel over the past ten thousand years including those from our lost Bee. My presumption is that Spero will dump the Bee in some desolate area, allow it to explode, and try to blend into the indigenous civilization. I would guess that his returning here seems unlikely. What do you think?"

Heads nodded in affirmation except one woman who raised her hand. The Chief of D&R motioned for her to wait. "Right, but this perp must realize that a sparse primitive environment would make it easier for us to locate him. However, what he *doesn't* know is we've been able to increase the detection and location of all implants from the ten meter standard to almost two kilometers. Director, is he aware that this Bee has a new locator beacon? "

"I wouldn't have thought so since it was installed by someone else on the day before. Unfortunately, we found it torn apart on the Departure Room floor."

"So, not only do we have a bright, resourceful criminal on our hands, but one who's obviously getting help from inside the QDT."

Justin covered his scowl. "We have no evidence of any help, but don't underestimate Spero 235. The good news is he has limited resources. He'd have no way to know we could program drones to locate and date all his travels. Also, when his main comp detects a nearby QDT signature, it's hardwired to automatically send out a warning locator signal. He can't block that. Yes, Craig?"

"But what if he just stays on the move forever?"

Justin glanced up at the ceiling in thought. "First I strongly doubt that anyone would elect a life of perpetual travel. Besides that, he knows that after three years of onboard time, his subatomic particles will be so thin the remainder will just snap away. He'd be stuck wherever he is, and forever. The Bee would then begin sending out a gravity pulse distress signal, and three days later it would destroy itself. Should this happen we'll easily retrieve him, that is if he is still alive."

He ignored the woman waving her hand. "William?"

"Couldn't he send the Bee back empty or with someone he recruited?"

"Good question. The onboard computer should refuse operation to any pilot who lacks a brain implant, and there are lots of hardwired safety blocks to prevent unmanned operation beyond short distances required for repositioning and crew retrieval."

The woman now shook both hands. "Oh all right: Sylvia 430, Navigation."

"Yes sir, but it turns out someone actually *does* come back, sir. Sorry I didn't have a moment to show you this new data before the meeting, but we just completed the last of the Drone surveillance lines this morning. It looks like his Bee, er *our* Bee, will actually return here on the fourth backup time three weeks from now."

Justin raised his hands and grinned. "So much for my earlier opinion. Thanks, Sylvia."

The members looked from one to the other for a moment, trying to grasp the meaning of this revelation before they all started talking. "Wait a minute. Wait a minute. This may not mean what you are thinking," Sylvia interjected. "First, we didn't go to the prohibited future to get this information. Our stolen Bee was detected passing through our present time-line and approaching Earth. I've just given you a likely pro-jection."

Justin said, "Great work, Sylvia! Really. So at least we know we get our Bee back. That's wonderful news, but we still don't know *who'll* be onboard. We'd all like to think that it will be Spero in handcuffs with one of our retrievers, but it's still up to us today to make sure that's what actually happens. We *know* he can't send it back empty, and he shouldn't be able to strap some innocent person into it. However, it still could contain a lone person from our retrieval team bringing it back without Spero."

More of the comet like yellow streaks appeared on the Earth Hologram with a tuft clustered in the South Pacific. "This adds Sylvia's latest data. Follow this logic with me. Here are all the trips where we've tracked him. We know he made some pre civilization trips even farther back in time to parts unknown, but I feel we can ignore those as joy rides. We have single trips to the USA in 1996, 1965, 1948, and 1912. He went to Spain in 1520, and England in 1880. For now I suggest we ignore these one shots as well. There were four trips to the USA in 1986, and five to an island near New Zealand, one of the Bounty Islands as I believe they were called—yes?" A hand was up. "John 410."

"Completely aside from being Maintenance Director, I know Spero personally." The news furrowed the brow of the Retrieval Chief, but he did not question the imposing black man who rose from his chair.

"Probably you are all thinking a Pacific island would be a vulnerable and unfriendly location Spero would avoid, but I know his habits fairly well. See the date tag on these voyages? They were all in AD 13. Well first, he probably doesn't think you would even bother to check that far back. Spero would expect you to waste a lot of time looking for him in more civilized and populated areas. I'll bet he probably took some of those other trips just to through you off. Justin, what is the longest interval *between* trips in and out of 1986 and for 13?"

"One to two days for 1986. Three weeks for the Pacific site."

"There. For me that confirms it. You all need to know that Spero loves ocean sailing, and being away from civilization. He used to being by himself, and he's comfortable with it. I'd bet he's set up a 'hermit' camp on one of those islands."

The officer turned and flailed his hands at John. "But if he were living in a desolate island, he'd have to have a plan to ditch the Bee before it goes nuclear."

"Well, since we know the Bee returns, I'd guess he found a way to strap some native inside. He'd never come back alone, I can tell you that."

The Chief smiled. "Maybe, but it's much more likely we capture him. Our new detectors will pin point his location on any of those islands. He can't hide there."

Amid yeas, someone yelled, "Well, let us just go and get him then!"

Justin motioned for quiet. "I've already discussed a tentative plan with our Retrieval Chief here. We propose sending out our two remaining Bees. Each one would have one person from QDT, and another from the Police. Everyone in Police D&R wanted to be selected, so they're going to have a lottery among qualified apprehenders and pick the lucky two. We just want to take Spero alive and kicking. Chief, anything else to add?"

"Oh, I guess we'll bring him back alive if we have to, but you can count on the screaming and kicking part." He chuckled.

Justin winced. "All right, our plan is to insert ourselves a few hours before Spero's final flight leaves the island. We intend to make sure that on Spero's last flight he'll be accompanied by our apprehender. Are you with us?"

Cheers and applause broke out, then shouting. "Go get him!" "He'll pay for this!" "Humwa pig!"

1965

Suddenly, it's 1960! (Singing radio ad for the 1959 Plymouth)

Distant jazz music from the Count Basie Orchestra and a gentle nudge brought Joe back into awareness. He felt his head clearing rapidly. Wait, something was different. "OK, Spero, who pulled out my 'plug-in' things? Was I just knocked out?"

"We both were, for a couple of Earth day equivalents. Not to worry, we've been getting intravenous fluids, nutrition, massages—even 'sanitary' changes."

"Uh oh, I really didn't think I knew Connie that well."

"Good morning, boys," Connie's cheerful voice interrupted them. "And Joe, you'll feel better knowing that the automated part of the computer does all those things. As for me, I usually take a 'nap' whenever you do."

"The massage part might be OK from you, but how the heck do you actually do all those things?"

"Well, with my arms, of course." Two jointed metallic arms partly unfolded from each of the bulkheads next to them. One hand-like gripper waved at Joe then all four arms retracted and disappeared. "All right gentlemen, we are less than thirty minutes from time insertion. Please put on the clothing I made for you, and *please* notice that your Hanes 'undies' are exact replicas. That took me awhile, and unfortunately, you're the only ones who will ever be able to appreciate them, at least we hope so."

Spero said, "Then why go to all that trouble? You don't actually care, do you?"

"Well, smarty, maybe I just get bored sometimes. But, who knows, with you leading the way you guys just might get arrested and strip searched."

Joe slipped the undies on under the blanket and looked at Spero. "See, now you've upset her. Don't you understand? It's hard for Connie to have her personality and be all trapped inside there." Joe lowered his eyebrows and turned to her eye. "Connie, may I ask you a personal question?"

"Sure, I guess. But what makes you think I'd have anything *personal* to tell?"

"Do you remember your parents?"

There was a long pause during which Spero shook his head and looked as though he had been seized with indigestion.

"Yes."

Spero slapped his head. "OK that's enough of this. I never realized until this moment how excessive they made your programming. They implanted someone's memories? That's really over the top. It serves absolutely no purpose, and what's more I think that's what's interfering with your normal functioning. Why don't you just stay in data mode? In fact make that an order."

Another pause. "I'm sorry Spero. I really was going to tell you eventually, but I'm actually not a 'program'. Joe seemed to know this instinctively, so there's no use pretending anymore. While I may be a functional part of the onboard quantum computer, it's also true that the programmer intended me to be a liaison between you and the Maincomp. She didn't write a program for your use, though. She gave you herself, and I am she. It was an experimental process, but the truth is, my mind is actually her mind."

Joe and Spero exchanged "Oh shit!" expressions. Finally Joe broke the silence. "Well, this is awkward."

"I know. I'm sorry."

"Well, all I really knew, er felt, is that you just seemed too real, too spontaneous to be anything but human. Now I'm really feeling sorry for you, just trapped in there."

"Oh for gosh sake, don't start a pity party over me. Sure, I had some adjusting to do at first. And yes, I did think I might go crazy once or twice, but I like my life okay now. I know I'll never go for a walk in the country or get real hugs and kisses, but I can read books, listen to music, pick out your clothes and, of course, annoy Spero."

"She's good at that, Joe."

"Besides, I was put in here by a Humwa Creative for good reason, and it wasn't just to push the frontiers of science or give her time to write her romance novel. She wanted to be onboard in person to make sure your mission succeeds, and I can do that much better than this big Maincomp could ever do all by itself. And the mission? Spero has a few more interesting details to tell you about that Joe, but this isn't the time."

Spero looked into her eye. "You *knew* what I was planning?"

"Actually I didn't, but without me, you'd never succeed. And this is enough chit-chat about me. Right now let's finish giving you guys the authentic 1965 look. There are wallets, IDs, currency and change in the ready drawer. Just curious Joe, was it illegal to counterfeit stuff like that in your time?"

"And in yours too, I'll bet."

Connie giggled. "OK, now we've started the arrival mode. I will be dimming all interior lighting to maximize what you can see on our old VCR—oops I mean view-screen."

While Joe chuckled, he was fascinated to watch the Earth growing larger, and the moon gradually slowing down. North America was swinging into view.

"We are actually half a day early when we do this," Spero said. "It's necessary to keep moving through time moments so we don't interact with the environment. Also it's good no one can see us this way."

"And we can fly through walls?"

"Yup. I prefer to bring her down in secluded areas for privacy. In this case I'll pick the basement of some public building at 3 AM, then I'll quickly advance a few hours to get the 9 AM time we want. At that point I'll time fix as long as there aren't any people outside. From then on the day's all yours."

"But then the Bee will be sitting around as a big yellow 'crackling-ball, right? Suppose someone comes across *that?*"

"A risk sure, but there's a cover, you'd call it a tarpaulin. It hides the Bee from a casual observer, and hopefully we'll be in an unused area where we're not seen."

Even with poor resolution, the setting sun was beautiful as it shimmered on the waves of the Mississippi. They glided downstream along the river and over paddle-wheel boats at the dock. They descended on River Bank Park. Abruptly the Bee veered down, turned right and headed right up a street with people and cars flitting around like a tape in fast forward.

"OK Spero," Connie said. "This is Joe's Chestnut Street. Arrival controls are now all yours."

"I have them." Spero had pulled out a yellow yoke from the dash in front of him and touched spots on a lighted armrest panel. "I'd love to take the time to fool around passing through the buildings and stuff, Joe, but this is all visual and it's too dark now. I think I'll try this building with the dome on it, if that's OK with you?"

"The Old Courthouse? Fine by me, but it will be closed now."

"I'm counting on it."

Joe couldn't help but brace himself when they appeared to be crashing into the front steps. Dark. Then gray, then dark, then gray again. Spero said, "Darn it, the cellar's really dim, but we're in now. I'm sliding under that stairwell. Joe, please watch the infrared screen for any people out there while I creep up to 9 AM."

"All clear."

"I agree. Done."

"Ho!" Joe cried out as he abruptly felt crushed into his seat.

"Sorry. I forgot to warn you that switching from one third to full gravity comes suddenly. Just sit there quietly. You'll adjust, but you'll feel weaker for awhile. Meanwhile, you can check out our arrival data by yourself."

The view-screen had parted and a narrow band below it had a printout that read: "Earth- North America- USA-Missouri- Saint Louis- 17 meters at 160 degrees from Broadway and Chestnut- 2.7 meters below level-May 17-1965-9:02 AM local time-21 degrees."

"We could get all kinds of other information, like precise longitude and latitude, but it is recorded in the log. I'm sure we don't need atmospheric readings, right Connie?"

"—OK she's not talking to me again. Connie, I need to know who's moving around in this building. Connie. Hello?"

"There are twenty eight people in the building. Fourteen are in a group on the first floor 10 meters from the stairwell above you. No one is in this basement—unless you want to count the three *rats* behind boxes along the opposite wall."

"Great. You doing OK, Joe?"

"You mean except for the fact that my bones are made of lead? Yeah, fine."

The view screen went blank and slid well to the sides. The hatch slid open with a whirring noise and they looked into a spacious, but gloomy basement. Spero nimbly slipped out.

Connie hastened to add: "Oh Joe, please remind Spero to put on the cover. He forgets sometimes. Good luck you two. See you in a couple of hours."

Joe wiggled out of the hatch. "Did you hear the lady?"

Spero reached back into the opening and began pulling out the tarp. "Geez, I only forgot once, and I didn't even need it while we were at your place."

They pulled the black, thin cover over the Bee. It felt like filmy parachute material, but left no hint of what it concealed. "Connie can pull the cover back in, but it's up to us to put it on. Walk around a bit, Joe. It will help limber you up."

Their dim basement area was cool and musty. Joe peered under a plastic drape and examined a well-worn historical display. "I feel fine now, Spero. There's nothing interesting in the basement. Can't we just climb up and walk out of here?"

Spero gave an 'after you' gesture toward the wooden stairs. Each step gave an annoying creak, and the door at the top was locked, but with a flourish Spero took out a small device and pressed it over the keyhole. The door opened with a loud click, and they entered a well-lit hallway. He looked up and down the hall, and spoke softly. "Ever been in this place before, Joe?"

"A couple of times, but I'll have to explore a bit to get my bearings. Something has been worrying me though."

Spero whispered, "What?"

Joe whispered back "Why did Connie make you those truly *ugly* red basketball shoes?"

Now convulsed by laughter, trying to keep quiet was beyond them. Finally, Spero said "Will you *please* just lead us the heck out of here."

Around two corners they walked past a woman talking to a crowd of teenagers. ". . .and here is the room where Dred and Harriet Scott waited to see if their freedom from slavery would be granted. Missouri, with all our wisdom said yes, but later the Supreme Court denied them."

Joe whispered, "That's Mrs. Anderson. She taught me in Junior High. Think she'll recognize me?"

"Now? Not a chance. Just smile and walk by."

Joe found the exit on South Broadway and they walked out into the sunshine of a beautiful day. He paused on the steps for a few minutes to take it all in. "See those trees — that's Kiener Plaza. And look at all those cars from the fifties and sixties!"

"If you find any nineteen seventy models, Joe, I'll fire Connie. They're sure noisy beasts, aren't they? Well, from here on you're free to do anything you want."

They walked to the corner and turned right onto Chestnut. Joe grabbed Spero's arm. "Look! There's the Gateway Arch!"

"Why not? That hasn't changed, has it?"

"Yes it has. It's *open*. They haven't finished the top part yet, just like I remember from High School. I'm going to Jefferson Park and take a closer look."

On the way, Joe bought a paper from a corner self serve box, and checked the headlines. A blue and white 59 Bel-Aire convertible with its top down rumbled past them on Chestnut. Its Hollywood Glass Pak mufflers throbbed deeply. A girl sat on the boot waving and shouting at some friends as they cruised by.

"Those are seniors almost graduated, Spero. They're in full party mode, and this isn't even Saturday night."

In the park, they were blocked by construction barriers that surrounded the arch and the portions being renovated, but Spero found a bench under a tree, and sat down. Joe was intent on reading something he had found in the paper, but Spero pushed it down to make eye contact. "Decision time, Joe. But before that, it's also time for you to know the whole truth."

HONESTY

An honest man is the noblest work of God.

Alexander Pope, 1740

"**O**f course I've got a lot of 'truths' to learn, Spero. For instance one truth is that I just foisted a counterfeit quarter on my hometown newspaper to get a dime's worth of news.

I'm having a good time, though. Can't we go over to Farmault? That's the part of town where I can say 'Hi" to myself?"

"No, you can't because you didn't."

Joe dropped his head and put a hand over his face. "Actually, all I really. . ." He gave Spero an anguished look. "Couldn't I just tell my brother to drop out of the army? He

99

died, or I mean he *will* die in Viet Nam—guess that's three years from now."

"I'm sorry, but you didn't do it, so it wouldn't help to try now. Honest."

Joe looked down at Spero who sat on the park bench and flashed into annoyance. "You know, Spero, you're making no blasted sense at all. What harm could it do to try?"

Spero leaned forward on his knees, took a deep breath, and began to study the grass. "Free will can alter your future, but you can't change what's already happened. Trying does bad things. We know from experience."

Joe sat down next to Spero. "But just because we're here now we must be changing *some* things. Our being here didn't happen in 'my' nineteen sixty five. I'd remember, wouldn't I?"

"Oh yes, we were. You just didn't see us, but we were here because things only happen once. Your 'then' is this moment right now and you are in the same town as your teen age self. Look, I'm really going to try and explain all of this to you, but please—just sit and relax for a few minutes."

Two girls sporting madras Bermuda shorts giggled as they walked by. "I want you start taking in everything around you. It may take awhile before you fully accept the reality of where you are."

Joe sensed the increased gravity in Spero's mood. He consciously pushed away at his emotions, and sighed. *All right, Joe. Give up on changing things. Just enjoy what you have.* A ships whistle caught his attention. He looked down the levy embankment where he could see tourists boarding one of the paddle wheel boats. On the grass down the bank, a young couple were laying on beach towels, holding hands, and playing a portable radio. *Yeah, that sounds like Bob Dylan all right.*

"OK, Spero, if it's reality you want me to accept, I *do* realize I'm actually back in my home town and it's really sixty five. It's incredible, but here we are, and you haven't lied to me. All right, I'm all ears. I know you've been trying to tell me something. Connie hinted it was about our mission."

Spero turned his body toward Joe and made full eye contact. His voice became low and steady. "So far I've told no real lies, but only part of the truth. Joe, you're in a position to not only save my *life*, but you can insure my personal future as well. The truth about me is simply this. In the terminology of your day, you would describe me as a political exile, as sort of. . ."

"You *stole* this machine, didn't you?! I *knew* it."

"I *borrowed* it, Joe, and I'll return it." Spero gestured with both hands for emphasis. "I'll send it back, just as soon as I've accomplished what I have to do."

"Still, you've hooked me into Grand Theft Auto—or Space Ship—whatever. This is the 'interesting' thing Connie mentioned, isn't it?"

"Guilty as charged, and you have every right to be angry, but give me a moment to tell you—to explain."

"You bet I'm angry." Thin lipped, Joe put his arm on the back of the bench, rested his head on his fist, and gestured with a finger flick for him to continue.

Spero cleared his throat and squirmed. "In less than a hundred years from this time humanity goes through a very difficult time, partly brought on by the consequences of an outrageous population expansion. Have you heard of a professor Robert Malthus?"

"I think he was mentioned in a Geography course-something about equations for population growth."

"Exactly. In essence he predicted that if we did not control our population, then war, disease and famine would do the job for us. In this, the twentieth century, you go from one and a half billion to six billion. It gets worse. Roughly 200,000 people are added each *day* in the next century. Even huge outbreaks of new diseases, starvation, small wars, and economic collapse didn't slow the growth before it reached twelve billion. That's when the prediction really kicked in."

Joe broke in. "I know. I know. All the doomsday nuts talk about it. I'll up my contributions to Care, okay?" For a moment they stared at one another. Spero's face had turned to marble, and Joe knew to be silent.

"First, all those people caused massive progressive climate change: deserts formed on inland farms, poles melted and coastal cities were flooded. No more Florida, for instance. There were enormous migrations followed by plagues and real famine. Little wars started early in the century by fascist religious extremists became *huge* and nuclear weapons almost wiped us out. Malthus is a hero in my century because while you ignored him in yours, he was proven right and a warning for future generations."

"Okay, I get the ugly picture. But, why didn't someone do something about it before it got so bad?"

"I want to put this in the terms of your day." Spero paused and looked up. "Computer says you should understand the term 'political correctness', plus short sighted quick fixes and empty promises. Politicians championed tolerance to get everyone's vote, but this became a tolerance of evil. The easiest excuse for all the disasters was to keep blaming their sane opposition, and the people's helplessness allowed them total control."

Joe stood up. "Shoot! Even in the midst of a massive crisis, the world leaders *still* didn't do the right thing? Sounds more like plain *stupidity*. What's the population grown to in your day? Wait, from what you said I'll bet it crashed right back to where it is now."

"Some people really did try to help, by the way, but it wasn't enough. At first the world leaders blamed previous administrations. When that didn't work they demonized the scientists, God's faithful, businesses, economists, and writers—basically all the 'creative' and educated people. If these people actually been allowed to help, their ideas might have prevented the disasters. Political parties are really good at blaming others."

Spero rubbed his face, got up, stepped over the path, and spoke to the river. "There was chaos for a long time, suffering everywhere—very few survivors. When the worst was over, a controlled society was set up worldwide, supposedly to prevent a recurrence. By the late twenty second century the world population was about four million and the new government fixed this number of people by law. They built twenty two protective dome cities and moved most everyone into them."

Joe went to Spero and turned him around. "Wait—My God! I want to make sure I heard right. Are you actually telling me that eleven and a half billion human beings *die off* in the next two centuries?"

"Yes. Well, actually almost all the twelve billion. There were four and a half a million survivors, not half a billion."

Joe began to pace in front of the bench and shook his head. When he stopped and turned back to Spero, his face full of tears. "So the—the human race will almost *wipe itself out*? What kind of a world is left?"

"An all powerful Government controls every aspect of life. For instance, women are temporarily sterilized at birth and they apply to have children when there's a legal union. Your future Earth is run by a dictator called the Supreme Director, supposedly elected but that's a joke. Name's Aten. Thinks of himself as the Messiah and so do a lot of his followers. He ordered the formation of a new class of citizens, basically I think it's anyone who might want to change anything or challenge him. Officially we're called Humwa, unofficially 'The Creatives'."

Spero put his hands in his pockets, looked up river and sighed. "They need us to keep things running for them, but we're in an iron grip so we don't ruin the world again. We have fixed living allowances, no vote, no right to meet in groups, no free speech, and especially no right to worship God or express political opinions. We are even punished for writing, composing, and making art; and there's been a giant crack down in the past six years. People found meeting in small worship groups now get dragged off by police. Supposedly they go to psychiatric institutions, but no one sees them again."

"That's totally *horrible!* Disgusting. And they blamed you guys, but how could anyone really believe this rubbish? Don't the Creatives want to rebel now and take the world back? And what about survivors outside the Domes?"

"Blaming the Humwa has become an institution. But we're not violent people and of course we have no weapons. We actually agreed with population control and some other things they did at first, but lately it's been ghastly."

"And the outside survivors?" Spero looked down and shook his head. "We're not supposed to know, but Aten's

men go out on patrols to wipe them out. They use Saran gas
or flame throwers. There's no real joy left on Earth, Joe. Aten
will stay in control."

"You said there are elections. Can't the government be
changed?"

"No, Aten appoints half the voting leaders and rules with
fear and executive orders. Anyone expressing opposition is
demonized and punished for being a Humwa sympathizer, or
a fanatic follower of the 'wrong' god."

"Okay, so you're a 'Creative on the run', right? But what
the heck am I supposed to do to help you? Shoot back when
they come for you?"

Spero brightened with a faint smile. "Don't worry. Our
people are forbidden to bother anyone from the past. We fear
it would affect our future. Actually, all you really have to do
is help me complete just one mission to make me untrace-
able. In the unlikely event that we really are caught, I can
guarantee you that they would still leave you unharmed. If
we succeed, though, you can have one trip to anywhere, and
anytime in the whole universe—within safety limits. After
that I *promise* I'll return the Bee."

Joe confronted him with squinted eyes. "Lets see, you
are *guaranteeing* I'll be safe and still get back home Sunday,

I guess you get off somewhere in exile, and you'll send the Bee back to your time."

Spero's look was desperate. "That's the *plan*. I promise."

"Sit down and let me think." Joe frowned, turned, and lurched away slowly down the path toward the construction barrier. He leaned on the fence and squinted up at the curved stainless steel arms reaching up into the sunlight. For a few minutes he watched the men high up on scaffolds as they worked to create their beautiful arch.

Joe swung around and walked toward the bench. He called out, "Connie forgot to make us sunglasses."

He stopped a few paces away from Spero and folded his arms. "*Two* trips. One right *now*, and then another one after yours."

Spero leapt to his feet and gave Joe a quick hug. Then he held him at arms length. "Done! And you won't regret this. I can promise that too."

13 AD

The two Search & Retrieval Bees reached their time fixation points and circled in stable, geo-synchronous orbits over the longitude of the Bounty Islands. For their own safety they remained two kilometers apart. Justin had assigned two of his scientists familiar with Bee operations, but with no known ties to the Humwa. One was Jordan 520 in one ship accompanied by Krajan P24 from Police Retrieval. The other Bee carried William 4003 and Rollins P160.

The dark blue splendor of the mid Pacific arched out below extending toward curved horizons. Its majestic expanse sparkled in sunlight and swirling white clouds. William searched their islands with a telescope and called his partner in the other Bee. "Jordan, we can't do a proper survey from this orbit. The island's too far south."

"OK, Bill, give me a minute to recalibrate. I suggest we power in closer and just hold the right latitude. We'll still be undetectable at a hundred kilometers altitude."

Hovering over their island group their search techniques only revealed a few small animals—no sign of people. More importantly no Bee was present. "Jordan, are you positive Justin has the right island? Spero's Bee is supposed to be leaving from there in six hours but I can't find it."

"Probably in a cave, Bill, or maybe he shielded it with something. Not to worry. We'll locate his Bee once we're on surface. Drone showed the last arrival site to be within three meters of the take off point."

Krajan broke in. "Then that's exactly where we'll land this Bee. Rollins will put down two clicks south on the coast. You've done your job, lab boys. We'll take it from here." He slid the control levers toward his seat and took over as pilot.

"I thought this was going to be a team effort with you people, Krajan."

"It is, and you've done your part. Retrieval's in charge now."

Jordan was surprised to see how well Krajan maneuvered the Bee in free flight. Obviously the police had been practicing in a simulator. "The Drone's reported location is in the computer, Krajan. The margin of error is five meters in any direction. We found no surface trails. Looks like our spot's that grassy plain." The policeman only grunted in response, rapidly descended and landed with a thud.

Krajan picked up his mobile mike. "Rollins, I'm down on site one. Rendezvous ASAP and don't forget to scan on your way."

Krajan slid out the hatch with his locker and pulled on his Speed Boots. These devices, especially made for Police Retrieval, enabled sure-footed travel up to 50 KPH. Then, to Jordan's dismay, he clipped a large hand weapon to his belt. "Hey, you can't shoot Spero, you know. We all agreed."

Krajan slowly looked up, his smile condescending. "We all agreed not to *kill* him." He stood up holding the new long-range detector, and proceeded to scan their surroundings. He grunted with every change in direction.

"Krajan, not to be critical, but first let's determine the actual arrival site, huh?"

"No point, 410", came the irritated reply. "The perp obviously just uses this flat area for put down then flies off on surface power to a nearby base. Why don't you just catch up on some reading or whatever it is you do. But if you're really right about him landing here we'll have him on a skewer in a couple of hours."

Jordan could hear his own teeth gnashing. *Oh why did we all agree to make these guys temporary mission commanders at the retrieval site? If they used a lottery, I'll bet Krajan fixed it.*

The big cop pointed to the horizon. "Look how well this detector works. I just picked up a signal half a click away."

"Well, don't you think it is more likely to be your friend? He should be coming in from that direction."

"Of course it's *Rollins*, you idiot! Here, I was trying to be nice. Look, now we have reliable implant detection in the air for over a kilometer, and half a click under water. He could even be under ten meters of rock and we'd *still* spot him a hundred meters away."

Rollins became visible on the horizon leading a dust cloud. The "poo-poo-poo" sound of his boots became louder. "Won't Spero hear you coming?" Jordan ventured.

Krajan kept his eyes on the approaching figure, and answered in a distant voice. "Field trials. We detect him long before he sees or hears us. Then we go to stealth mode."

Rollins came up quickly and skidded to a stop. "Feeling winded after your little jog, Lieutenant?"

"You're kidding, Captain. I could run all day in these, but your signal reflects off those granite rocks. I thought I got second fix for awhile, but it was a duplicate."

"Roger that." Krajan tossed Jordan a set of handcuffs. "If mister perp runs by here when we're gone, be sure to put these on him after you wrestle him to the ground."

The men laughed heartily, high-fived, and went thudding off together brandishing their detectors and weapons. Jordan could hear the screams of hapless lizards and birds being zapped long after they were out of sight. He shook his head and began to survey the arrival site. A few minutes later William stomped in, and slumped to the ground, breathing hard. No speed boots for scientists.

"Well Bill, when you're up to it, check out this so called landing spot."

"I see what you mean already, but we need to check this whole field."

In half an hour, distant pooh-pooh sounds heralded the return of Police Retrieval. They were striding faster than ever now. No more shooting. The two skidded to a stop in a dust cloud. "Your data's shit, smart guys. No one on this whole island chain but us."

"I completely agree." Jordan replied. "We are alone, but our data is correct."

Krajan stood scowling and shaking his head, unable to think of an insult and comprehend at the same time.

William broke the brief silence with: "If you look right over here you'll notice that this grass is somewhat yellowed in a neat circle."

Rollins countered with "Well, of course he landed here, but he sure as hell isn't here now."

"This isn't a landing site with time fixation, officer." You could roll a Bee on the grass once it's time-fixed, and not bother the vegetation. However, once a Bee pops out of a very dense substance in full dissociation, there is a brief flash of ionization. That *does* affect plants. The spot just over there is almost fully recovered. This one's recent."

"What? You're saying he's underground?" Krajan taunted.

Jordan grinned. "No, he came *through* the earth." With open mouths, the retrieval team stared at him blankly. "When moving rapidly through time, the Bee can go through the earth. The computation is difficult, but as long as the line is dead straight it can be done, and our emergency protocol does allow it. Depending on whether he moved forward or backward in time he should either be at 8 AD, or 18 AD on the other side. We did this experiment with drones. It works."

"So the bastard thought he could fool us by escaping through the earth. We can't catch him here. Okay, where does that put him, anyway?"

"Gaul. Well it will be France. 20-kilometer search area, max. I did the computations while you were having your jog. The drones might have missed his exit point in France since he planned to come up in a cave. If his Bee is parked on the surface we should find it easily, and even in a cave it'll just be a bit longer."

"Oh we'll find him. This is getting *personal* now," said Rollins. No thank you was offered for all their work.

The team spent the next two days searching all of Gaul, above and below the ground, and in every lake, stream and cave in both time periods. They searched through every possible hiding place with their detectors, and terrorized the native settlements. Finally Jordan screamed in exasperation. There was no hint of Spero or QDT activity anywhere. He announced: "Okay, nothing more we can do here. Let's just go home."

Krajan grabbed Jordan's shoulder with one hand, spun him around, and released a string of expletives. "Your Chief said it would be *impossible* for this son of a bitch to outsmart him."

"Well, the impossible is just what *was* done here. No Bee should be able to do what this one apparently did, and right now I can only guess at possible explanations."

"Well why don't you start *guessing,* huh?"

"Sorry, but it's time to return home and start reviewing our data. I'm not saying we're giving up, but this is incredibly weird, officer. Totally unexpected, too. Justin may be the only one who can make any sense out of this."

PLANS AND REVELATIONS

J oe took Spero on a circuitous route back to the Courthouse, playing the tour guide all along the way. They
stopped for an early lunch at an ice cream parlor highly
recommended by their 'guide', and settled into red plastic
chairs. Joe ordered Cokes and sandwiches. Glancing across
the room, he lowered his head and whispered. "Those two
over there were in my class."

"Okay, Joe, never mind that right now. They won't recognize you."

"Yeah, but suppose they get curious and come over?"

"Well then, you can be Joe's uncle or something. Look,
we need to go over some practical matters next. In deciding
on your trips, there are thousands of choices, but we can only
go to your *past*, not your future. We need to avoid obvious

dangers like war zones, of course. Remember the "Foo Fighters" in WW-2. That was us. And we were shot at too, by both Allies and Germans. They cracked the transparent hatch, and nearly disabled one of our earlier Bees."

Joe was rubber-necking around the parlor. "There's a whole lot of wrongs in the past that should be changed."

"True, but while you can go to the past, it's no good trying to change things, Joe. Can't be done, so don't pick your trip based on that. I'll try to explain later. Also we can only stay at any one location for a few hours, say up to four or five. Any more than that and we'd be more vulnerable to a search party."

"You mean the troops with Klingon disrupters come to hunt us down?"

Spero studied the air waiting for a translation. He grinned. "Something like that. But even if they *knew* the vicinity where we landed, they'd have to park a mile away and start searching. We should have a few hours of safe time anywhere we go. So, what's it gonna be? The Renaissance? Ancient Egypt? The Incas, maybe.

Joe shook his head. "All interesting, but I don't think so."

"Oh, and there's a hardwired block on access to 20-65 AD and the fourteenth century BC, so we can't go there either. Someone doesn't want us to see Jesus, but if you'd want to go back 25 thousand years, we could see the first Americans."

"Spero, I've already made up my mind about my first trip, but what did you just say? I thought all the Indians came over during the ice age when there was land between Asia and Alaska. That would have been about twelve thousand years ago, right?"

"Oh, sure, but our drones picked up several waves of migration through previous ice ages and even during them. The earliest we have on video so far were itinerant fisherman from eastern Asia. Our experts thought they were likely ancestors of the Ainu, sort of aboriginal Caucasoids."

"Well I do know someone who would be fascinated by that."

"The Ainu are still surviving in Japan during your century. We suspect that they interbred with the oriental humans who came later giving Indians a different appearance from either parent group. A landing party is in the planning stage to do testing and stuff, but you could be the first. Want to go and check them out?"

"It's tempting. You guys are really into history, aren't you?"

Spero scooped up some tuna on his plate with his finger, and licked it off. "Oh, yeah. Finding out what *really* happened in history is supposed to be the only reason for the QDT, er—Bee program."

Joe pushed away the remains of his sandwich, and ordered a dish of butter pecan ice cream. Spero grinned and repeated the "Me too."

"OK, here's my plan. This first trip will be for my colleague, Melissa. She's presently studying early hominids at around sixty thousand years ago. I want to bring her back some useful information. As for my own trip, I'll figure that out later."

"No, kidding, Joe. I went to that time frame on my second trip. Well, 62 thousand years ago if you want to quibble. At the time I was panicking and just grabbed a random primitive location. Thought they'd never look for me there and I was right because it's *way too* primitive."

Joe raised his eyebrows. "Panicking?"

"Yeah, well. . ." Spero hunched over his bowl and shoveled in a spoonful of Butter Pecan. "Remember I said it was the second trip. I was in full survival mode before I worked out an avoidance plan with Connie."

"Well who'd you see there? Got any pictures?"

"Mostly audio cause I turned my portable video off after awhile. I wasn't sure I could trust Connie at that point."

Joe tossed his hands up. "So you're telling me you encountered primitive man and did nothing about it."

"I know, kind of a waste, huh? Don't really know much about the people I ran into, and the computer couldn't help much with their language either, but Joe, it *was* kinda fun, and now I know the safest place to go. Also, I have no problem with your bringing back whatever you want for your girlfriend. Artifacts, recordings, pictures too." Spero laughed. "You gotta get some pictures. She'll never believe you if you don't."

They raised their soda glasses and clinked them in the air. Joe toasted loudly: "To the early hominids!" The waitress looked quite concerned as she put down the check. Joe gave her a big happy smile. "Hi!"

QDT 301

Children and sub atomics both behave

When watched at fun and play.

But should their Daddy look away,

To secret places they hide away.

Poetry for Children, 2055

The Bee's return was uneventful. The pair simply sauntered back into the Old Court House. Joe put the remainder of his counterfeit change into a donation box, and they went down the cellar stairs. Not long afterward they were "flying" through buildings again on their way toward man's early beginnings. Joe found out the sights and sounds from any excursion could be recorded from a device hidden in ones hair, even Spero's meager growth, just above the ear.

The AV readout is sent to the onboard computer, and Joe would get a camera of his own this time.

Connie greeted them with girlish enthusiasm. "Did you guys have fun? I've seen the transmission, of course, but I'm curious. You knew some of these people, Joe. Don't you think you attracted any suspicions?"

Joe responded, "Nah, and it was literally a walk in the park, Connie. Interesting, but of course it was all familiar to me. Did you hear Spero make his big confession?"

"Yes, and so now welcome to our 'pirate crew', Joe. Say, this trip you picked will be a lot different. It's more risky, but I think it's so great that you're doing this just to help a friend. Melissa must be a fascinating person. I'd sure love to meet her and have a little 'girl talk' for a change. No offense."

"None taken. Doesn't look like you'll get to see her in person Connie unless Spero lets me show off the Bee to all my friends when we get back. Can you see him shaking his head? Anyway, you're right—this trip'll really mean a lot to her."

"Well, the first thing I can do for her, and for you too, is do more work on the language this group of people speak. I have a little video from the last time before Spero turned his camera off. It's clear that hand gestures are part of their speech. But with the little we have, the Main comp I call "Gorilla", and I have a basic translation for you."

Joe squinted up at her eye. "No kidding. And I can take this back for Melissa?"

"Sure. I can download this to Spero's implant while you're in sleep mode, but Joe, you'll have to do the best you can with my 'language tapes'. Apparently Spero threw out the strap-on unit we're supposed to have on board in case of implant failure."

"And Connie, you're really okay with Spero's escape plan?"

"Oh, heck yes. All of us Creatives wish we could escape somewhere. I used to fantasize about it myself. I'd dream that all of us flew away in a big space ship to another planet and had a real life all on our own—really free and civilized. I think Spero's escape will inspire everyone back home—just to know that at least *one* of us got out of the 'dim domes'."

Spero chuckled. "And I've been doing a lot of thinking about just who *you* might be, Connie. Obviously you're someone from programming, but there are about twenty women working there. I'll take a stab and guess you're Jane 104, right?"

"Spero, why should that even *matter?*" Connie's metal arms flailed out for emphasis. "And you should certainly know why I couldn't tell you for your own good and hers, too. Anyway, you and I hardly knew each other, and since you're still keeping all the details of this special trip of yours a secret, I think we're even."

"But you can't blame me for being curious, Connie. Anyway, you seem to know *me* don't you? It hardly seems fair." Spero began pulling off his 60s attire and motioning for Joe to do the same. Then with a flare he took off his red and white basketball shoes, glowered up at Connie's eye, and slam-dunked them in the recycler. "Thanks for *those* by the way, but tell me straight. What was your honest impression of me, back then?"

"Honest impression. Really? Well I thought you were a somewhat self centered, impatient kind of man. Your mind was usually on other things beside the people around you. You didn't really interact with anyone very well."

"Ouch!"

"In all fairness, though, you did have patience with your fellow Humwa, and never wanted to show anyone up as stupid. Remember when you were called down to fix the backup Command Scrubber? The whole problem was caused by Earnest 612 who had plugged in two connections the wrong way. You spent twenty minutes pretending to fix something and never called him on it— and I'll also bet you didn't think we found out."

"Drat! I just hope you aren't the girl I made a pass on that day! Talk about getting *my* connections wrong!"

"Linda 960? Nope, not me. She gave you a brilliant put down though, didn't she?" Connie laughed. "If it's any consolation to you, Linda was repentant afterward. Now stop trying to play process of elimination."

Spero tossed a hand in the air. "Oh, all right."

"I see you are both down to my beautiful hand made 'Hanes'. Joe, all the used clothing goes into the red panel door beside Spero. I can recycle everything, but if you want to, you can keep your briefs for a souvenir."

Joe chuckled. "A souvenir?"

Spero turned to his partner. "But thanks to *your* choice, Joe, our next costume won't be nearly as comfortable. I was itching the whole time with the one she made."

Connie laughed. "Sorry, but that outfit was pure guesswork on my part. I was trying to imitate stone scraped animal hides, so I guess it was too rough inside. Turned out that it didn't look very much like what they were wearing either.

This time I'll get it right, and I promise a softer inside, too—even for you, Spero."

Joe smiled, cocked his head toward Spero and pulled on his travel scrubs. "OK let's not talk about Connie's fetish with men's underwear. What I really want to hear about is the physics of your QDT travel. You promised, remember."

"All right, you boys have a nice chat. No gossiping about me, and no cigar smoking. He, he. I'm taking my nap and signing off. See you in a few months."

"All right Joe, we have privacy now. When that green light is off next to the eye, Connie is 'off line', and I believe her. Thanks for getting her to reveal the truth about what was really going on inside her 'computer brain'. I was talking to her like she was a real person and beginning to doubt my sanity. Notice the orange light next to the other one. It's always on when the other one is off. It means we are in contact with the main-comp only, the one she calls 'Gorilla'."

"Yes, but it's obvious who is in control."

"Connie does like control, doesn't she? Bet her flesh and blood version does too."

"Maybe, but I'm still glad she's with us."

"Oh, listen, I forgot to mention Harvey. You usually don't see him, but he is in here somewhere, kind of like the 'invisible rabbit'. Remember my first trip was to the Triassic era? Well, this half-meter centipede just decided to crawl in the open hatch."

"What? Were in this can with a huge iron worm?"

"He's totally harmless and nocturnal, kind of an onboard mascot. He lives off the crumbs you drop." Spero grinned. "But on long trips I have the computer set out some food and water for him. Connie hates him of course, but she tolerates him to keep me happy. He's fun to watch crawling over things. Once he spent an hour trying to nibble on a flashing light. See, when I was all alone in here I got pretty bored sometimes."

"OK Spero, you may be even crazier than I thought. And just where's this 'Harvey' creature right now?"

"His favorite place is under my seat on top of the fusion generator. It's nice and warm there."

"Oh, now that *does* worry me."

"Really, it shouldn't, Joe. Wait 'til you see him. We can go to red lighting, and he'll come out in about ten minutes."

"Not Harvey, the *fusion generator!*"

Spero chuckled and started doing stretch exercises. "*That* technology we have down pat. Trust me when I say you'll get more radiation sitting on a granite boulder."

Joe made a final adjustment to his scrubs. "Obviously I have no choice at this point, but *nuclear fusion*? Like the sun and hydrogen bombs?"

"Yup, perfectly safe, but that's why there's not any room under my seat. Yours has a locker full of stun guns and fuel cells."

Joe put the briefs into his 'personal' box and glanced at Spero. "I'll save my briefs, but just so I can analyze what you make these clothes from. Besides, I think Connie would feel hurt if I trashed them. Now, if you're still trying to distract me from an explanation of QDT and time travel, it isn't working."

Spero let out a big sigh, dimmed the lights and pointed to the view screen where the moon was slowly moving around the Earth. "Look, it works." He flipped off the vid and pretended he was sleeping.

Joe moved the dimmer back up, swung toward Spero and stared at him with narrowed eyes. "Okay, okay Joe, I'll *try* but I'm really just a mechanic. I only took a course on this stuff—about like your college level. You teach physics, quantum mechanics, relativity, that sort of thing, right?"

Joe's level stare was like iron. "Right."

"Now this is going to be like one of your C students explaining what you teach to Isaac Newton. Just so you understand."

"Oh God, stop it! One of *my* students trying to teach friggin' Isaac Newton? Heck, half of them don't even get *his* concepts much less anything that came after! Wait, wait. Don't I at least get to pick my *best student?*"

"You get to pick your best C+ student who sometimes cheats."

Both convulsed with laughter and hung onto the handholds. When Joe said his bum cork just popped out, they screeched and laughed until they were out of breath. Finally, Joe panted, "Okay, okay you're right. It's all fair. Compared to Isaac Newton, I'm C student too, but you've still got to try. Shoot."

"All right, Joe, to begin with there is no such thing as 'time'." Spero waited for a response but only saw widening eyes. "Look, you know about the leaps of progress made by Einstein, Dirac, Mach, and Bohr. I'm trying to remember the name—I think it was DeWitt who showed that eliminating time from all the earlier equations was the only way to get unified fields and quantum gravity to work. Then Julian Barbour showed time for what it really was—just a sequence of moments. We call them fixation moments."

"That is a very controversial theory."

"In your day."

"Touché."

"And light photons can be stopped and stored in a kind of 'bubble'. It's the basis of how our quantum computers work. A photon doesn't *have* to be going somewhere. Our universe is like that, only a bigger bubble, a three dimensional membrane or brane. They say photons and other sub atomic particles can skip around it by using the dimensions outside the brane. They're really coming and going from those dimensions all the time anyway, virtual particles I think they're called, but they aren't really particles either. They're tiny force fields."

"So far, I think I'm sort of with you, but what about that no time thing?"

"Well, you teach the quantum paradox where a sub atomic can behave as either a particle or a wave, don't you? Check its location, its other probabilities stop and it is a particle fixed in one spot. But, guess what? If you turn your back, it's a wave again."

"OK. But I'm still waiting for you to mention the 'T word'."

"Don't get testy. I'm doing the best I can. Now in an atom, the sub atomics go in and out of the 'fixed' and 'unfixed' phases rapidly. Present guess is this happens as quickly as the speed of light moving from one side of an atom to the next. Each particle, when it enters into a 'fixation phase' in three dimensions, defines a *moment*, and when it's unfixed, only a timeless probability. Actually they reside in the other dimensions when they're unfixed. You still with me?"

Joe made a 'T' symbol with his hands. Spero grimaced.

"Well here's the thing. There is no particle formation, no solid matter you can see when the little buggers are floating around free. In that state they are not even *present* in our three dimensions. They don't have a known three dimensional location, a speed, or cute little names. You couldn't measure 'time' for them in that state either, could you?"

"All right. I get that point. Time doesn't exist for free floating sub atomics. But, it sure progresses like an arrow for all the rest of matter."

Spero leaned toward Joe and whispered as though he were confessing a personal secret. "Not really. An atom is all *made* of sub atomics, and the particle-to-wave change simply happens so fast you can't tell. Each fixation is just a moment, the most probable *next* moment in our limited three dimensions. My teacher likened it to an old film movie. Each frame hits our eyes so fast we think we see motion and time, but in reality there's just a rapid succession of picture frames."

"But there is real matter and real motion. That's time." Joe protested.

"I seem to remember them telling me that if time exists at all it is in the interval between fixations. You have to remember that this whole drama of teeny particles is played out in multiple dimensions. It helps me to keep the image of a long wavy band of movie film in mind. The frames represent the progressing *three* dimensional world we're and us locked onto the film, but the tiny, dissociated particles can flit around off and on the movie. They can land on any frame they choose. The Bee travels by 'pretending' to be one of these sub atomic clever little beasties."

"Damn! If you were one of my students I'd be telling you to quit dreaming and go back to basic studies. The problem with that, of course, is that I seem to be flying around in this dream. Now I suppose you're going to tell me we're both outside of our known dimensional space while we sit here just talking?"

Spero shrugged his shoulders, "Yup, I guess, except our dimension lives on inside here. Look, you're tired. Why don't you think about it for awhile? In fact, sleep on it for a few months." He chuckled. "Maybe when you wake up you'll have it all figured out."

"But wait. How could we move from one frame to the next if it doesn't exist yet?"

Spero made eye contact and nodded. "Ah, you're right about that." He patted Joe's shoulder. "If the future *didn't* already exist we couldn't go there."

Joe began to rub his forehead. "I doubt any of this will suddenly clear up with a nap, but you're right about one thing. Your lecture sure made me sleepy."

2247

While most residents used the surface "people movers" to glide along the sidewalks, Carolina Dome wasn't very large and Justin preferred walking to riding in his Director's Car. Today he wanted thinking time on the way to the emergency session Margo had called at Police Operations.

A prison work gang in yellow suits and red ankle bands quick-stepped past him, urged on by their handlers in an open car. The gang kept repeating the required mantra: "Praise to The Aten and Ilah. Praise to the Royal Gods." Justin shook his head. *I hear most of those men were just caught worshiping the wrong god.*

From several blocks away the police building beckoned, with dark, gray windowless walls and bristling antennae. It reminded Justin of the ancient naval destroyers that fought the wars of yesteryear. *What a monster.*

He came to a halt across the street. *Can't be too early, now. They're going to be annoyed with me, I know. Administration has zero patience with failure. I may not know what happened to the onboard computer yet, but at least I can tell them who's responsible.*

Justin crossed over in front of the main entrance and admired the trees flanking the stairs. They were the only ones under the Dome outside of Park Central. He smiled. *Margo really annoyed the Police Director when she sided with Environmental Services and approved the trees. We all knew it wasn't her love of nature but a chance to demonstrate that even the dreaded "PO" had to take her orders.* The beautiful London Planes looked like they were the authorized hydroponics, but their luxuriant growth suggested forbidden soil and nutrients from the outside. *Somewhere a Humwa is laughing. Well, better just go in.*

Police Security had moved up two notches above their normal strict procedures. Not only did they scan everything Justin brought with him, but even patted him down "just in case". As a Director, he should have objected, but there were more important things than police paranoia right now. Still, when two armed men escorted him back to the conference room he had to say: "I assume we are at war, right?" Silence.

Finally one of the grim faced escorts spoke when he pressed his security card to the doorframe. "Interrogation 6."

He continued to stand at attention and evade eye contact even when Justin confronted him with a big grin and arm pats. "Thank you, sergeant."

Despite his early arrival, all five of the other directors were already present at the conference table including the Chief of Detection and Surveillance who sat next to the PO Director. *Wonder if they've been talking about me? Look at this. No one's even turning around to look at me.* Justin took his place at the eerily quiet table. *Amazing. I'm actually being shunned.*

Stone-faced, Police Operations Director, Edwards, stared down the table toward the empty place at the other end. He was a man of massive physique and the face of a warthog. His dark blue uniform bore only the sun clusters of his high rank. Justin thought that it would take a plastic surgeon to raise the corners of his mouth, but then, miraculously he stood up, eyes still facing straight ahead, and smiled broadly. Chairman Margo had just entered from her private door.

Chairman Margo was not smiling. The other Directors stood murmuring: "Good morning Madame Chairman." *They sound like grade school children.* Without a word, she sat. They sat.

Margo also continued to totally ignore Justin, save for a few brief scowls. Only his friend John glanced his way to offer a quick, pained smile. Margo began: "Since not all of you have fully secure lines, I want to begin by making everyone aware of how serious this situation has become as a result of our escaped Humwa. Despite all our efforts to keep this quiet, our failure to find the Bee and its hijacker is now public knowledge. They are laughing at us. Somehow the public even found out about the Bee's expected return just over a week from now, and I can only assume this is due to *another* security breach at QDT." Margo glanced at Justin, her lip curling into a sneer.

Edward's head of granite nodded agreement and grunted. Margo's arms slithered over the table. "I'm sure the Creatives are planning a hero's welcome should their thief have the audacity to return. Likely their plan has been our humiliation all along."

"But, I. . ." Margo turned a fiery glance to a slender woman with long blond hair and large anxious blue eyes.

"Susan 401, I know exactly what you are about to say. You're thinking, what does this have to do with your Health and Housing Agency?" She glanced at others around the table. And some of you are probably thinking the same thing: what does all this have to do with *my* department?"

Her fist hit the table, "Well, this is *not* just a one-time screw up at the QDT. I sense all the Humwa are rallying around this thing. It's their big opportunity. The revolution we have talked about may in fact be starting right *now*." She held up her curled thumb and forefinger. "We are *this* close to Aten sending his swat troopers."

She paused and glanced from face to face, judging the effect. Dutifully, all stared back with wide-eyed attentiveness. "Starting with the next work shift there will be undercover security people in every work area of *every* division. Questions?"

Susan tried again. "Madame Chairman, are you really telling us that a revolution has already begun?"

"No, certainly not. I'm telling all of you that we must prevent one from gaining traction all costs. First, I want every work area secured so that no Humwa will be alone at any time. Secondly, we are installing a new highly secure line for each Director to talk to the PO about anything suspicious. Finally, I want your own security people to be on the alert. We need to discover the unknown means by which the Humwa communicate with each other."

John 410 slowly raised a large dark hand. "I know how they do that, Madam."

Margo allowed a brief condescending smile. "Are we about to hear how the Sanitation Division has cracked this elusive Humwa code?"

Ignoring the affront, John continued, "Those electronic messages you're working on are just to throw you off the trail. You can't crack them 'cause they don't mean anything. What they've really got is just a 'call system'. When one of them learns of something important, he tells three others in the stairwell or the bathroom. Each one knows his three other contacts and tells them. In about a day, the whole city knows. It's just talking, M'am."

"All right, John. Good work. No matter how far fetched these ideas of yours might sound, I assure you the PO will consider all suggestions and take appropriate action."

Justin had the strange feeling he must be missing something, but as he watched everyone, nothing new seemed to be forthcoming. Finally, he raised his hand.

"I recognize the Director of QDT." Margo's voice was cool and formal. Everyone besides John and Susan produced a grimace of disdain.

Justin stood up. "OK, first I think you are totally over-reacting to this 'revolution' thing. These people are not the hostile insurrection types. Besides, we are the only ones with any weapons." From the corner of his eye Justin noted the PO Director was nodding slowly. "Anyway, I know you all blame me for the Bee being stolen from my department, but it sounds like you have given up on the recovery. Is there some reason you feel it's hopeless?" He looked around the room at blank faces.

The Recovery Chief cleared his throat. "Your *own* people in the field told us they were completely baffled and couldn't continue the search."

Justin fell forward, his hands on the table, jaw agape in frustrated amazement at this stupidity. Choking down his impulse to hurl an obscenity, he was speechless for a moment. "So, *this* is it! And in the past two days did *anyone* even think to ask *me*?" His voice had cracked on the last word, but went on. "I thought I was coming here to present the next step in my recovery plan!"

Margo flashed back, "Don't toy with us, Justin. You know your days are numbered, and we all realize you're just trying to cover up."

Good grief, John and I might be the only cool heads in the room. That thought was calming, and it changed his tone to a decisive one. "The problem our field engineer experienced was simply that the Bee was performing in a way which should have been prevented by safety protocols in the main computer. It is considered unpredictable and unsafe to change either time or direction while traversing a massive object like a planet. We now know this was accomplished anyway, and it was done by rewriting those safety parameters. Someone in Computer Programming did this to help Spero, and I know exactly who that person is."

A bit of meekness crept into the attentive expressions. "That person is a Humwa, Anna 797. When she is located and made to tell us about the changes she made, we'll know what our Bee is now capable of doing, and that will narrow the options of where it should be. Then we'll return and pick up Spero before he can escape in the Bee again."

"All *right!*" exploded the PO Chief.

Everyone started talking excitedly, but Margo's hand slapped down on the steel table. All were suddenly quiet, wide eyed and open mouthed. "What do you mean '*when she is located*', Justin?"

"This is where I'll need police help. The Creatives in programming use the 'service offline' utility in our QDT server to stop their implants from sending signals. All implants should default back to 'on line' status in three hours, and they are suddenly 'visible' again, but during those hours they have some privacy. They use them for breaks in the basement or sitting up on the roof. We simply ignore it but, they shouldn't be able to leave the building without a functioning implant. Anyway, Anna 797 is actually on a vacation, but she is not home or with any known friends, and her implant hasn't sent a signal in two days."

The Retrieval Chief questioned, "And this is possible *how*? And why is it you didn't contact our office immediately?"

"Well, it should only be possible for a short time *inside* of QDT. But, Anna must have found some new way to reset hers to offline from outside terminals. She's in charge of her division and she's a very, *very* bright young woman. I just found out about this last night, and I'm here to request Police Retrieval."

The dark form of the PO Director rose from the table like a specter, his teeth showing under a curled lip. "Well, not to worry everyone. We'll have your little lady in a few hours Director, and the next time you talk to her, I promise she will tell you *everything* you need to know." He glanced at his watch. "And now Madame Chairman, with your permission I believe this meeting is over. Our people have a little work to do."

MINUS 62 THOUSAND

The travelers woke to a cool breeze and their eyes squinted open to see mountain photos wrapped around on the view screen. The Beatles were thumping out "Lucy in the Sky With Diamonds" and Connie's 'arms', now clothed in pink fabric and lace cuffs, were swaying to the music. "Good morning gentlemen. Hope you had a pleasant rest. It was a long one, but your vitals looked great the whole way."

"You check our vital parts?"

"Now Joe, don't be a tease. You guys like my new sleeves? I need you to tie the drawstrings on each end and clip the loose ends." Dutifully the men tied and clipped. "I got tired of looking at those steel arms. So uuh—mechanical. This feels better, but I couldn't quite tie little knots with these poor excuses for fingers they gave me. Thanks."

"Connie, did I ever mention my liking the Beatles to you?"

"You mentioned it to Spero in St. Louis. Did'cha know they named an early hominid 'Lucy' after that song? Now I have a surprise for both of you." Connie reached behind each of their seats and pulled out pairs of sunglasses. "Ta taaa!"

"Oh sure," Spero said waving a hand. "Bet we'll be the only early hominids with sunglasses, won't we?"

"Why you ungrateful toad! I ought to just recycle yours. They're not for today's ground mission, silly. They're for here, and maybe something later." She gently handed a pair to Joe. "Right now we're time fixed in a geo-synchronous orbit, and it's really bright down there."

"Well, I love mine, Connie. Thanks."

"You're welcome, Joe." She tossed the other pair to Spero. "Now, put them on before I make the hatchway transparent. I'll open it slowly."

A white line widened into a blazing sword and gradually filled their cabin with brilliance. They squinted down to behold a majestic Earth bathed in blue and white. Snow and ice sparkling with highlights covered the northern portion of Europe and Asia, and obscured the familiar coastline.

"Whoa, it's a glacial period! We'll freeze down there in these little fake skins."

"Nah," Spero tapped Joe on the arm. "Don't worry. We're going to a warmer place in the Southeastern Mediterranean. It's temperate, and despite appearances it's really summer. We'll arrive a week after my previous visit, so the people I met there should still remember me. You asked for this time, Joe. Won't you be our expert?"

"Spero, I know almost nothing. Melissa is the one who teaches all this stuff. When I had to cover a class for her we mostly read the book. Connie must have all the latest information in her data banks, though. Right Connie?"

"Oh, so wrong, guys. A few more reports and theories that keep changing. Nothing practical. We did find the Neanderthal line split from our common ancestor four hundred fifty thousand years ago with little or no interbreeding. That help?"

The men grinned at each other. Spero sighed. "Okay, fact is we're just two guys wandering around without a clue. But at least we *do* know something from my last trip. It's not much, but better than nothing."

"Well then, start talking, my friend. Mind if I play with your telescope?"

"Course not. The terrain at our site is mostly grasslands with some patches of woods. Oh, first I must confess I failed to mention the part about the hostile people."

Joe looked up from his scope with raised eyebrows. "Well now might be a good time, huh?"

"Sure. On my last visit, I was just strolling through this meadow looking around when a bunch of men about my size suddenly ran out of the woods shouting and throwing spears. One got me in my left arm."

"Wit till you see the video clip. Poor dear. He was hurt *so* badly."

"OK, so I admit it just grazed me, but it *could* have been worse. You'd have been scared to, and maybe I didn't have to stun them all, but I did. I'm not proud of that but, they'll live." Spero slumped back in his chair with a pout. Connie was humming.

"I took one of their spears and a dead rabbit they had with them. Hoped I could maybe barter with the next group I came to, and perhaps they wouldn't try to kill me. Anyway, I ran back past where the Bee was hidden in the woods and just kept going in the opposite direction."

"Do you want to see how fast Spero can run, Joe?"

"Oh Connie, give it a rest. As I was saying, I headed off in the opposite direction toward the coast. I found a foot path this time, followed it for awhile, and then I came across another group of people—a much friendlier bunch. These guys looked even shorter but tougher. At least they accepted me, and were glad to have the rabbit. Show Joe the pictures so he can see what they looked like. I shut off the camera after that."

Photos came up on the side view screen. "That's great Spero. I think these guys really are the Neanderthals we're looking for. It's not just their sturdy build, but look at the way their faces push forward, and the brow ridges. And see that woman: she hardly has any chin at all."

"So, you do know something about hominids after all. Then who do you suppose the mean ones were—the men who were trying to skewer me?"

"I'm sure they're us. You know, early Homo sapiens. Our ancestors."

"Us? Drat! That's embarrassing."

"Yeah well, you know, we're just the little guys trying to take over the planet. Nothing much has changed."

"Okay, just don't make me go after my nasty grandpa again. We'll put down half a kilometer from the nicer guys, and we can take their footpath through the woods. First thing I think we should do is stun us a rabbit or two. After that we'll find these people and you can have yourself a nice fireside chat."

"Now, gentleman," Connie said. "Here's what I have for you. These fake fur clothes you're getting into might look shaggy on the outside, but with my soft, insulated liner they should feel like a pair of coveralls. I've added concealed inner pockets for stunners, and a fold out blanket. It looks like another animal skin in case you need more warmth. I could make spears, but I think they could tell fake ones up close. I'd have to make them in four sections that screw together. Better use the cutting function on your stunners and make your own from a branch."

Spero studied the outfit, slipped a stunner inside and closed the pocket with a thong. "Should work."

Joe was squatted down in front of the hatch watching their descent toward the future Western Europe. A massive ice sheet blanketed the continent midway into France. "Connie, can we fly low and slow along the glacier edge before we have to turn south and land?"

"Sure can."

Spero coughed and interjected, "But, but we don't want to take all day. Time's limited and this trip's just to snap a few Neanderthals pictures and get out before anyone gets hurt."

"Spero," Connie replied, "In the vernacular of Joe's time: 'Cool it!' We'll take less than an hour here and Joe probably just wants some pretty glacier shots for his girlfriend. Right Joe?"

"Sure, but she's not my girlfriend."

"Well, if you say so." Connie brought the Bee down off the West coast, and swept in at a low altitude. Joe looked for England, but ice was all he could see.

Going East, he marveled at how green the tundra was right up to the edge of the ice. Nothing could be seen growing above in the massive ice itself, but defiant mountains pierced upward and forced the glaciers to flow around them. "Hold it here. Melissa will love this. Spero, look almost straight down. See where the ice sheet parts around that mountain? There's a patch of vegetation on the lee side, completely surrounded by ice walls. Here, take the scope and look at the mountain face. Check out those colors. They must be wildflowers. Beautiful, huh?"

"Oh Joe, we could. . ."

"I know exactly what you are thinking Connie, but Melissa will see my close up shots. Don't think for a minute I have to go down there and pick flowers for her."

"You guys sound like grumpy old men! So all you're going to give her is still shots, and one of those tape copy things? You won't even have good digital imagery to take home as a souvenir."

"We'll be fine. Don't worry."

"Wait, I know. I'll also make you an HD blue laser disc. It's almost as good as our UV discs, and I'll preserve it with a sealer. Tuck it in your sock drawer and you'll be able to play it 20 years from now when your tape image has turned to fuzz."

Spero said, "I'm amazed, Connie. Now you don't hesitate to violate strict orders. You know we're not supposed to give future stuff away."

"Oh Spero, obviously we're not on one of those 'by the book' trips. Besides, it's not future enough to even be detected if they sweep his apartment later. The lab only made these recordable disks so we could make downloads from 21st century computers, and we are not even going there, are we?" Spero shrugged.

Their craft moved quickly to the south toward the Mediterranean, but they saw two smaller seas instead of the one large one they expected. "Are we heading for that smoke plume?" Joe asked.

Spero tossed a hand in the air. "I asked about that the last trip. It's an active volcano near what will be the Sea of Galilee. We'll be well away from it near the coast."

The screen abruptly became dim and fuzzy as Connie time-shifted and swooped down for their landing. They arrived at their forest destination with a gentle bump. "OK, boys, you're now sitting right on the path that Spero discovered a week earlier. It's early afternoon, a beautiful day outside, and you are in luck, too. I detected several people half a K to the west. Not only that, but there are a few small animals right outside. I have an image of two rabbits, no wait. One rabbit 12 meters at 25 degrees, and one 'something else' 5 meters at 170 degrees."

"Uh, something else?" questioned Joe.

"Yup. Now look, there is no database worth anything for *all* the species in this time location. The thing looks like a huge—*yuck*—rat. Just put on your faux furs, hike up your testosterone and go stun 'em. I guess you have to, but promise me they won't suffer. I get queasy just thinking about this kinda stuff."

"Queasy is a bit of a stretch for you Connie, don't you think?" Spero teased.

"Don't be mean. I'm trying to be a team player here, but 'big boy' games aren't my thing. Okay, and I'm going to worry about you both, so please be careful out there. Now out. Shoo! But don't forget to turn around for a picture."

Slipping out of the hatch, the men dropped onto a leafy path and looked up into puffy clouds through a forest canopy overhead. They grinned and waved back at the Bee for Connie.

Joe's bare legs stuck out under his loose fitting 'skins' and he had to fight the feeling of being in a bathrobe. Spero pointed toward the right, and told him to use his scanning sight, but he couldn't see much in the shady woods. A small snake slithered away off the path, and Joe was starting to feel anxious. He turned on the stunner view screen. Pooh! He flinched at the sound of Spero's weapon. *That didn't take him long.*

Finally Joe panned his scanning, self sighting gun. There was his prey simply clinging to a tree trunk only a few meters away. Sight pull—pooh, and it was over. He dragged the "something else" back to their craft, held it by the tail near the open hatch and called in. "It's a possum, Connie."

A muffled voice came from inside the Bee. "I used to like you Joe. And don't you even *think* of bringing anything like that inside here." The hatch slammed shut, and the Bee disappeared. Startled, Joe turned to Spero with an "Oh my God" look.

"Not to worry, Joe. Connie's only moving off the path. She's supposed to. An unmanned Bee can only travel for a few hours and move short distances. We'll call it back when we need it, but we better get going."

The would-be cave men did their best to fashion convincing wooden spears. They pierced their "catch" with them and started down the path. Joe said "Connie sounded like she was actually about to cry."

Spero chuckled. "If she finds a way to cry and throw up, we're in serious trouble. But I'm really starting to worry about her emotional side. She can get, well I would say, overly feminine sometimes, but mostly she seems just fine."

"It's gotta be tough though. You know, to be so aware and locked in a computer. Must be like waking up after an accide. . .Whoa!"

Both froze at the sound of something large crunching through the underbrush to their right. Then, silence. Only the pulses in their ears. They quietly slipped their hands onto the stunners in their pockets. A large deer like head popped out of a bush a dozen meters away. The animal searched the path with twisting ears and flaring nostrils. Large dark eyes looked directly at them. Suddenly the animal turned and bounded off, crashing back into the woods.

"Don't think it likes people," whispered Spero.

"And for very good reasons, no doubt. Jeesh, for a minute I thought it was coming right for us. Let's just get where we are going, OK?"

The path wound around to the top of a hill and a small clearing. Looking down they could see a shallow valley to their left and the sliver of a shining sea in the distance to their right. "I remember this place. The people we want should be just around that hill. See, the smoke. There's a cliff-face around the other side."

Their approach, while intended to be quiet, did not surprise the Neanderthals. They were greeted by two men standing on a cliff ledge with raised spears. As they came closer, Spero whispered "Hold up your possum. These guys only speak in nouns and hand signals. Connie said they can't pronounce some sounds, either." Spero looked at the pair above them and shouted "Yuh-ja!" and pointing to Joe, "Ho-ma!"

The larger of the two took a step closer to the edge. He had a very wide muscular body and light brown skin. The tan mottled fur tied around his waist reminded Joe of worn out jogging shorts. He had shaggy black hair with feathers tied to it and a necklace made of teeth and shells. The man placed his spear against his side then extended it downward. "Boo ha."

Spero whispered "He remembers me. Drop your spear. Leave it. Keep the possum."

Then the hulking figure above them handed off his spear to another. He turned to others out of sight behind him and raised his hand with two fingers held up. He announced "Ah Tun!", turned back and gestured for them to come up.

"What's that mean?" Joe whispered.

"Other One." It means the 'other' type of human, and two of us. And we're lucky again. This is the friendly guy I met last time."

The two began scrambling up boulders to the ledge. Joe whispered: "Well, then they use adjectives too, Spero, not to mention numerical concepts."

Joe had sudden doubts about the wisdom of his trip choice when a muscular hairy arm grabbed his wrist and easily one armed him up to the ledge, possum and all. The fellow grinned at them. *We're probably the first modern people to know that Neanderthals can actually smile. And what a smile! Six inches across, at least.*

"Yaahosh," said the man touching his broad chest. Yaahosh stood about five feet tall. He was darkly tanned, had brown wavy hair adorned with black and white feathers, and a gray streaked beard. His smile was surrounded by circles of wrinkles, but his attentive gray eyes sparkled.

"Joseph." said Joe, touching his chest also.

"Hos'p" he said in response.

When they had climbed up to the top of the little plateau in the cliff, Joe was delighted to find what he judged to be three family groups. They had constructed a screen shelter with poles and animal skins that leaned against the cliff face, its opening guarded by a fire pit belching smoke. Just to their right, a young woman was nursing an infant, and along the cliff edge one boy was chasing another with a spear and shouting. *Reminds me of the home movie with my nephews, but this mom wasn't screaming for them to stop.*

Both men held out their hunting gifts for Yaahosh. He stepped aside and motioned to an old woman who lightly bobbled over. She took them with a grin and a 'thank you' nod of her head. The woman placed both carcasses on a flat boulder, smiled back at the men, and promptly decapitated the animals with a stone hand axe.

They generated a few curious glances, but no one seemed very interested in them, so Joe and Spero felt free to move around. Spero walked over to a row of flat boulder 'seats' against the cliff face and sat down while Joe strolled about visiting to each person and secretly photographing their activities.

The butcher lady had two Cairns made of piled rocks on either side of her. One was apparently to store what she had skinned and prepared, the other seemed to be for garbage. *But I'll bet 'garbage' was for hungry wolves if they come around later.* He found some smaller stone 'lockers' as well, one with leaves and berries in it, another containing frogs and lizards.

On the far side of the cliff plateau, a deer was hanging upside down, mostly skinned. Next to it a woman was using both hands to scrape the hide with a stone tool. Joe photographed an older man who appeared to be striking rocks together, but on closer inspection he was actually making a tool by chipping off stone flakes. Working back to Spero and the fire, Joe noted the two boys had jobs after all. One was adding wood to the fire, the other turning a pole with a skewered rabbit. *Boy powered rotisserie, huh.*

"Looks like we came at dinner time", Spero whispered when Joe sat next to him.

"I'll just be glad we *aren't* the dinner." Joe said out loud.

Spero struggled with a snicker. He whispered, "Stop it. Quiet. They don't like it when we use 'foreign' language. Let me do the talking if you don't know what to say."

The young woman carried her now sleeping infant behind the leaning skins, and placed it in a shaded bed. In a moment she came out and squatted down in front of the opening and faced the fire. The stone craftsman rinsed his hands in some shallow water basin, shook them dry, walked over and sat beside Spero.

A well-muscled, handsome young man with three feathery necklaces and a spear emerged from the tent with a young woman. He glanced around at everyone before he leaned his very thick spear against the rock face. It looked like a tree branch to Joe, and it bore a huge pointed rock tied to the end.

This athletic man had red dots and streaks painted on his face, and his black hair was tied back. A recent red scar highlighted his left mandible. *Hunter. Warrior hero too, I'll bet. Uh oh, he's picking a rock seat right next to me.* His woman, however, squatted next to one of the boys by the fire. *Maybe the seats are just for the men.* The warrior abruptly turned and stood up again as though he just noticed the strangers. He looked down on Joe and Spero. Scowling, he asked "N'kaaah?"

Spero avoided eye contact, bowed his head and said: "Be-jom. Ho-ma."

The warrior spun around to the others. "N'kaaah. Ah-tun!"

Meanwhile, Yaahosh seemed to be arguing with butcher lady who was having trouble skinning the possum, but when he realized the new guests were being challenged, he spoke some soothing words, and pointed to the gifts. The warrior grunted and shrugged, but sat down on a rock farther away. Spero whispered. "That was close. He doesn't like 'ah-tuns'. Probably had trouble with them in the past."

"From what you told me about our relatives, I'm not surprised."

Yaahosh stood up on the edge of their camp facing outward while other women and children took their seats around the fire. Suddenly he sang a series of loud melodic words while facing the valley below. He stretched his arms upward. "Something like 'Thank you for a good day' I think," Spero whispered in Joe's ear.

When Yaahosh turned back around, his people began talking to one another. He smiled at them, went behind the leaning skins and came out with a long white bone. The ends were cut off and there were holes sawed onto it. He sat down facing the others at the cliff face, placed a rounded end against his *nose* and proceeded to play a series of extended notes.

After the concert, the 'warrior' described today's hunt to everyone in grunts, graceful gestures, pretend spear thrusts, and shouts. During this performance, a girl Joe judged to be teenage, was scooping berries from one stone locker, and presenting some to each person on a leaf. When the warrior's story of the hunt was over, there was more music and another 'tale" from a different man.

All heads suddenly turned toward Spero. Clearly it was his turn. Joe could see the "Uh, Oh" in his eyes. He stood up to try their language. "We saw the game. Threw spears." *They're laughing. What could he have said wrong?*

Yaahosh asked "Do you 'other ones' hunt big game or just those?"

Spero replied, "Yes, we spear deer and lions."

Yaahosh and the others laughed even louder. "Ah Tun hunt lion. We send him out with spear. Get one." More laughter.

Joe whispered, "I hope the penalty for perjury isn't death." Spero replied with a toothy scowl. But the music was over, and the next course was frog legs 'Sushi style', surprisingly edible. The main course would be the meat on the fire and the butcher lady pulled off pieces for everyone and passed them out on more leaves. *Guess we're not getting any utensils of course. Good teeth are the obvious essential here.*

At the end of the meal, the warrior's 'wife' started dancing and singing: smooth graceful motions accompanied by single sustained notes, but she suddenly stopped. One of the young boys who had been crawling about started shouting. He was pointing at Joe's feet and screaming. *"Look! Look! Those!"*

Terror gripped Joe. All the people who had so far been nicely ignoring him suddenly surrounded him, and crowded in close. Never once had it occurred to Joe, in their rush to get dressed, that *sandals* might not be appropriate. *Wait, they seem to be more curious than hostile.*

Cautiously Joe reached through their arms and their touching fingers and carefully removed the sandals. As he did so he noted that they said "Bass" on their two-tone grip soles, and they had *Velcro* strap holders. Spero's eyes were almost closed as he slowly rocked forward and back whispering an "oh shit" mantra between clenched teeth.

The Neanderthals passed the sandals around to every man, and each attempted to try them on. They fit the warrior hunter the best and his eyes glistened with excitement. He stood on slanted rocks, picked up his spear, jumped and spun around with a "whoop" and a "ha!". The sandals held right in there with him.

N'ha went to Yaahosh and talked. Yaahosh went to Joe. "N'ha best hunter. Trade with 'Hos'p'. Want foot covers." N'ha dragged a struggling, terrified teenage girl over to them. Joe was speechless and open mouthed. "For covers," said N'ha.

Joe grabbed Spero's arm, and pulled him in between and urgently whispered in his ear. "I don't know all these words. Can't I just give them away?"

"No, no. A terrible insult, Joe. I'm thinking."

"Tell him I'll trade for something else—that flute, maybe."

Spero stood up abruptly. "I speak for Joseph." Then in a flare of diplomatic talent he didn't know he had, Spero praised the girl in glowing terms but convinced them that she would not be accepted by his kind in the "Ah-tun" world. On the other hand their whole 'nation' would be eternally grateful for the flute since we have never seen or heard of such a thing of beauty. Yaahosh seemed reluctant, but clearly he was flattered. With a little encouragement from his friends, however, he finally accepted, and ceremoniously presented the instrument.

The light was now growing dim, and the "Homo Sapiens Duo" realized it was time for their graceful departure. Spero, now confidently fluent, thanked everyone for a good time and they made their way to the "stairs". But right at the ledge, Joe was stopped by two strong hands from behind. "B'dos!" A command blasted his ear.

Spero said "He means sit down." Joe, fought off a renewed panic, but complied. He then realized N'ha was putting his own foot skins on him. N'ha grabbed Joe by both shoulders and easily lifted him upright. He took off one of his necklaces and placed it on Joe's neck. "For hunting." he said. Joe replied "Thank you." N'ha was still gripping Joe by his shoulders, struggling to find the right words. Finally he said, "Luck for hunting." Still he did not release. Then his thoughtful look changed into a huge grin. "Luck for *rabbit, not for lion.*" Man and Neanderthal nodded and laughed together until tears came.

When they reached the top of the opposite hill, the two looked back toward the ledge. Yaahosh, N'ha, and two others were still sanding there, watching them go. "Check this out," Spero mumbled. He placed his hand on his head while facing them then suddenly lifted it straight up. Their new friends duplicated the motion, and all turned to go their own way. "It also means 'luck for hunting'."

Joe grabbed Spero's arm. "God, I can't believe we just did all that Spero, I mean at least after I realized they weren't going to kill me, I was actually starting to have fun back there. But do we have to walk the path all the way back through the woods? It's getting real dark in there."

"Nope. We're out of sight now. Here's the easy part." Spero pulled out a small device and pressed a button. Promptly the Bee 'materialized' along the path in front of them its hatch opening up as they watched. They scrambled in eagerly, glad to be safe inside. "Strap into the chair, Joe. We'll leave right away."

"Hello, boys," Connie said softly.

"Where are we headed so fast, Spero? Time for your trip, huh?"

"Not just yet, Joe. I'm taking you home, first. My trip is close to your time frame and I want both of us well rested for it. First, we'll go back and arrive on the Sunday after we left. You go ahead and have a normal week. I'll be back next Saturday morning for you. I want to take another trip by myself first. "

"So, you'll be back again next Sunday?"

"That's the plan."

Soon they were well on their way, the familiar Earth-Moon spinning on their view-screen. Joe stripped off the Neanderthal skins. "I gather you are not briefing me on the next mission until we're on the way, right?"

"Yeah, but don't worry about it. I'll tell you this. You get to wear your own clothes.—Connie, you've been real quiet since we came back. You alright girl?"

"I'm fine, but you didn't say hi back. I think you might be angry with me."

"Are we angry with Connie, Joe?"

"We should be, shouldn't we? Her little 'creativity' almost killed us."

"Oh look guys, I'm *really* sorry. I had all kinds of second thoughts, and I've been awfully worried. I didn't think they'd hurt you, but then I didn't really *know*, either. What I thought was, the sandals might be something you could, you know, *bargain* with if you got into trouble, but I know I should have asked you first. I didn't get the vid since I was moving. Oh, gosh. What happened?"

"OK Spero, we've tortured her enough and she certainly seems remorseful. Connie, your idea was positively *brilliant*. The people loved us and I got three artifacts in trade. Melissa will be completely crazy about these objects when she sees them." He lifted up his "moccasins" so she could see them. "I can't tell you how happy I am with how this turned out. If you had a body, you'd be getting a big hug right now."

Two pink-sleeved arms came out of the bulkheads. One grasped each of their shoulders. Connie's voice was strained. "Oh, thank God. You do know—I just care an awful lot—about you two, don't you?"

"Now she's really crying, Joe. But no more surprises like that, OK Connie?"

"I promise."

1986

Spero brought Joe back on Sunday as promised, but promptly raided his refrigerator for twentieth century munchies, necessary he explained, to properly work on an adapter for Joe's Betamax recorder. On the approach, Connie warned: "Spero I've detected search drones in orbit so you better not stay too long. But, could you please walk all around Joe's apartment with your camera so I can kind of be there with you."

Spero strolled around while he crunched potato chips, swilled a can of Pepsi, and inspected Joe's new photos. He grabbed a box of chocolate chip cookies, and sat down at the kitchen table with his recorder and Joe's VCR.

"It'll only take a few moments to transfer this—just a few wires to solder."

Joe plunged into the cookies too. "Take your time."

Amid the solder smoke Spero asked: "Say Joe, I know I've got to leave soon, but could I ask a favor?"

"Asking is free."

"How about one short spin in your so called 'Bimmer'?"

Joe chuckled. "Sure." He gave him the long neighborhood cruise complete with fast, noisy turns on the back campus roads. Spero's favorite was the wooming sound it made flat out through the underpass. It had him bouncing in the seat hollering "Yeaah!" They did it three times.

Spero walked all around the BMW when they returned, lightly touching its blue-gray enamel. "Sensational, Joe. Connie will blow her diodes watching the replay."

Back in the apartment, he gratefully shook both Joe's hands and climbed back into the Bee. He poked his head out of the hatch and pointed at Joe. "Rest up now. Six days. See you then." The hatch closed, and with a whoosh of warm air, the Bee disappeared.

Joe stood for a moment staring at his empty hallway. It even *felt* quiet—the whole place strangely dull. He heaved up the big paper roll outside his door and checked the date. *Sunday all right.* Big sigh. *Guess I'd better get back to work. Depressing—well first, a little lunch wouldn't hurt.* Inertia knew the scary thing was gone. He slinked over and purred in agreement.

The mess he'd left on the dining room table was all cleaned up in his absence and, as he expected, there was a note: *"Hi, Joe. All's well. Inertia seemed a bit spookier than usual, but he calmed down with a little loving. Gosh, I hate to do this to you on short notice, well no notice, but I have to go to Atlanta for the week. They want me to substitute for Dr. Hodges and present his paper. Poor guy is in the hospital with cardiac arrhythmia. Back by noon on Saturday.*

The good news is you won't have to embarrass your-self in my class this time. I have that covered, but could you please be my Hero and fix my back porch light when you're at my place? I'm attaching my hotel number so leave me a message to let me know you got this and you're okay. Oh, and don't forget to wrap the Ace Bandage on your left knee when you jog, and this time please start using that sunscreen I gave you! Take care, Mele." Her signature had a little smile face after it. Joe felt he was home.

# # #

After lunch Joe bundled up his tools, the new wall switch he'd bought earlier, and fired up his BMW again. After two summers working as an Electrician's Apprentice, he was the master of Melissa's electrical work. She had purchased half a twin house following her divorce three years ago, a pre-war, tan frame structure clearly in need of much more TLC in years to come. While rather plain, its best feature was a large covered front porch. Melissa had covered this with a variety of plants in huge pots along the ground to cover the under-porch area. Of course, vegetation hung from, and was scattered, all over the porch itself. Together they'd hauled and planted trees and flowers for the back yard, and transformed it from a neglected lawn into a secluded garden.

As Joe came up her front walk, he heard "vrooming" noises from the adjoining porch. Jeffy, the kid next door, was working his car toys. When he reached the top step he gave him a "Hi, Jeffy!"

A five year old with a straight blonde "bowl cut" of hair popped up behind the wood fence between their porches. Jeffy ran a toy truck along the rail and provided more sound effects. His attention never left his yellow dump truck, but he replied. "Thank you for the book Mr. Joe."

"Did I give you a book, Jeffy?"

"A *dinosaur* book."

"Oh, I'll bet Melissa gave it to you."

"Miss Missa read it to me. I like dinosaurs."

By now Canis had realized his porch was under invasion. The little brown Dachshund stood on top of the couch by the front window and barked in staccato.

"OK, Jeffy, next time I come by, you show it to me, OK?"

"There weren't no people when there were dinosaurs."

Joe opened the front door and held off Canis with his foot. "No kidding, Jeffy. I'll remember that. See ya later kiddo."

Canis was anxious to point out that he had been deprived of both dog food and loving since last night. He was shaking a cloth doll. After Joe pried it loose from the growling mouth, he gave it the obligatory toss across the room. *With this anthropologist, even her dog toys are strange.*

Melissa's place was always clean, but cluttered with files and books were left out in "I'll put these back in a moment" positions. The passion she had for her work was apparent everywhere. Photographs of primitive tribes and paintings of hominids covered her walls. A two-foot high bronze sculpture of a Cro-Magnon man with a spear held menacingly over his head guarded an end table.

Houseplants were as abundant inside her little home as they were outside. Small trees grew from pots in corners, and smaller plants were suspended from macramé ceiling hangers. Strange looking tropicals and cacti from around the world hung from the ceiling over the stairs that led up to two small bedrooms and a shared bath. The back room was her office, dominated by a big desk flowing with toppling stacks of books and papers. These walls were all bookshelves, but somehow a cello and music stand found room in one corner.

The front bedroom was the only room devoid of hominids or books about them—a dramatic contrast to the rest of the house. Joe thought this room looked like it really belonged to someone else. Its walls were painted a pale blue, and there were white lace curtains on the windows, one of which overlooked the street. Old family photos and landscape paintings decorated the walls. Here, the only plants were two small pots of rather dry Baby Breath on a window ledge.

Joe splashed some water on these with a cup from the bath room. What really seemed surreal to him was the white queen bed with *matching* dresser and end table. *My guess is she let her mother furnish just this one room to be nice to her. On the other hand, does any man truly know the innermost mind of women?*

Downstairs, Canis had long since devoured his rations and had run out the pet door to 'perimeter check' the back yard. No creatures dared venture into *his* yard.

Joe's flute present was wrapped in a long cardboard box and covered with left over Birthday paper. *Best she didn't get any idea there was emotional value attached to the gift. Also I'll have to wait for the right moment to tell her what I've been doing.* His note read: *"Oh by the way, I found this copy of a Neanderthal flute in a tourist shop when I was in Europe. Thought you might like it. Joe."*

I'm not really lying. We'd certainly been 'tourists' after all, and I did trade a native for it. He grinned. *But wait till I tell her the real truth.*

Joe pulled up a chair and got to work on the light switch. The process took longer than expected partly because Canis kept presenting his doll toy to be torn away, each time with shaking and growling before another toss across the room. On the third return, however, Joe noted black hair was coming out of a ripped seam. *Human hair?* Closer inspection revealed an actual *pin* in the thing. *Not a dog toy.* "Bad dog!" The molested voodoo doll artifact and Joe's bone present were promptly moved to the top of the china cabinet for safekeeping.

"You're not getting your teeth into *that* bone, Canis."
Oooh. He winced at a sudden thought. *God, I don't believe in this stuff, but what if some poor sucker is writhing in agony because 'his' doll got tortured.*

2247

Justin strode briskly down the sidewalk and mumbled to himself. "If there's one thing those bastards at police retrieval are really good at, it's *finding* people. Usually had their prey tied up and squirming in minutes."

A passing robot delivery car held him at an intersection and Justin glanced up at the nearby Police Building. He thought it looked down on him and asked: "Why?" *Retrieval even has a sign in their break room, 'Average Minutes to Capture'. Let me think. Yeah, it was reading 37 last time I saw it, but they've been out looking for Anna 797—what is it—two days now. All their pride and technology, and it's still been two days! Girl's even smarter than I thought."*

Justin asked to meet his long time friend and fellow Director, John 410 for lunch. John ran Sanitation/Maintenance but his hobby was security technology. They both had analytical minds and a common sense approach to problems, so whether they talked about bird spots on the dome or new chips for server bots, Justin always enjoyed his company. Maybe John was secretly a Humwa sympathizer, but so what? Their corner table at a noisy Bistro assured privacy.

"John, Anna's been on vacation and doing a marvelous disappearing job—record setting actually. Any idea how she could be evading the elite police retrievers?"

John grinned and leaned forward on the table, his eyes squinted. "Well, you must know her better than I do. What's your first idea, Justin?"

"She might be hiding in one of those small, dome-less communities that Margo wants to eliminate. Or maybe she's so afraid she's holed up in a storm drain, or how about a friend's basement with an energy shield?"

"Well, the first isn't likely, Justin. Those little communities are 'sanctioned' and walled off now just like the domes. There's even more police presence there since they're known Humwa hang outs, and I'm sure Retrieval's already searched the homes of every friend she has. No, if she really didn't want to be found, she'd have to be clever enough to come up with an idea no one's thought of yet."

Justin shook his head. "Yeah, Retrieval sent me a report on her friends since two were in my QDT. They were all memory scanned. None of them knew anything and they're all worried about her. Any clever ideas of your own?"

"No, actually I don't know what she might be up to, but if I had to guess it would be a 'pirate' car to some unregistered site. Creative Humwa do have their little secret enclaves, you know, and I don't think their implants can be detected over a kilometer away. If she made it to one of these she'd be out of range when her signal reactivated."

"You don't think Retrieval could trace an air car with the transponder removed?"

Munching into a sandwich, "Sure, but maybe one slipped through. Anyway I don't see how your little lady could be in any of the domes or sanctioned villages. Her face is posted everywhere and there's a reward offered."

"Well John, unfortunately I happen to know that the police. . ." Justin moved in closer and lowered his voice. "The police can now monitor our implants *many* kilometers away. I also know they track every pirate car by satellite. The only reason they don't move in on them is for their surveillance value. Actually they know everything about who goes where and when, and they have their spies in every enclave too." Justin leaned back in his chair, took a bite of his own sandwich and gave John a 'so, what's your *next* idea' look.

"Interesting. I'm stumped, really. Ok Justin, the only thing left is she is out wandering through the wild country alone, or maybe even your idea of a shielded basement, but not at any known associate. That's still my best guess because with her picture everywhere the whole world knows about her and the reward."

"Everywhere? Really? I haven't seen any pictures at our QDT."

John chuckled. "But that's the only place they wouldn't bother to post them, Justin. Everyone knows what she looks like at work. They're everywhere else though." He swung around and pointed. "See, there's one on the screen by the menus at the entrance."

Justin leaned back and tried to peer through patrons and busy Servobots. "Just a minute." He got up and zigzagged through the tables to the front of the restaurant. When he came back his eyes were wide. He pushed his charge wand in the table order post and said. "Gotta go. Thanks for your advice, and lunch is on me."

"What's up?"

"Believe it or not the police are showing the wrong photo."

"Is that even possible?"

"Shouldn't be, but true. Anna's got big time inside help. Help inside *my* QDT!"

Justin dashed out of the bistro and jogged down the street. He jaywalked over when he noticed a police post on the other side. He identified himself, and asked to see all the photos they had of Anna. Various pictures came up taken from files some dating many years ago and all showed a very different, and much older woman than Anna.

"Crap! Even the data you have on her *before* she worked at QDT is wrong." The desk sergeant looked surprised.

"But sir, our computer is impenetrable and independent. Also there are no Creatives in *our* Department."

"Obviously!"

"Sir?"

"Look, I'm going to get you the right image myself. Set up an encrypted line to this station while I get my HR Chief." Justin punched in a number on his wrist phone. "Is this Rachel 807? OK, pull out Anna 797, the *paper* file—got it? Good. I know this is old Tech and insecure, but scan the photo in her file, and send it to me with your *personal* phone.

Also, send it to this other number, but use our secure line for that one."

Justin waited badly. He paced the small lobby drumming fingers on a desk behind the counter. Finally his phone vibrated. His small wrist vid produced an image, and he held it out for the officer. "There you are Sergeant, that's what Anna's cute round smile looks like."

"Oh, I don't think so, sir. That doesn't look anything like Anna 797."

Justin stared bug eyed at the Sergeant's placid face, and struggled with an impulse to slap his stupid cheeks. Instead, he tightened his grip on the counter edge and forced a subdued reply. "You should have a better quality photo like this on your secure line in a moment. I'll wait." Confident he had ended the QDT cover-up, Justin took a deep breath. The Sergeant nodded at his screen. "Different photo this time, right?"

"Yes, sir."

"Great. That's the one you want for all your notices."

The Sergeant turned his screen around to show the Director. "But, sir, this new picture you just sent us is only the profile view of the one we have been sending out. Did that confuse you? We can add it to our full face view."

Justin stared in disbelief at yet another photo of the older woman. "Crud! I just showed you what she really looks like, and we should have sent you that *same* picture. How the heck? Your lines are encrypted and secure, right?"

"Oh yes it—it, well then, there must be something wrong at *your* end, sir."

Justin leaned forward on his hands. He felt calmer and nodded. "You know Sergeant, for the first moment since I walked in here, I can say I completely agree with you. Something *is* going on at my place, and this something is going to end right *now*."

1986-1996

Decisions, decisions. They couldn't agree,
So leptons and bosons leapt to the ether.
A world to build here, or another one there.
Which would it be? Well, they said, either.
Poetry for Children, 2055

Inertia let out a short hiss burst and scrambled wildly toward the bedroom. A second later the crackling began a gush of warm air, and Joe's hallway was once more blocked by the glowing, yellow sphere. Spero popped out of the hatch, tanned and cheery. As they gave each other welcome hugs, Joe thought that he actually looked a bit older. He didn't recall the few streaks of gray in his temples. "Hey man, it really looks like you've been having fun in the sun, but it's been just 'same old' around here." Joe crouched down and called into the hatch. "Hi, Connie, hope you're doing good too."

Her muffled voice replied, "Hey, Cutie! Good to see you again."

Spero stretched. "I hope you got well rested cause this trip's my big one, and we need to go over some plans first." He looked around the apartment. "I'm thinking your patio, those lounge chairs out there, and some of your wine and cheese should do it."

"Do what?"

"Help you digest what I'm going to tell you."

"Oh, sure, but I got us some subs for lunch. You hungry?"

"Hungry, and totally spoiled by your hospitality. If things had worked out differently, I might have tried hiding out here in your time after all."

Spero settled into the chaise, stretched out his arms and legs with a groan, and proceeded to pull out the mini-cam in his hair. He carefully placed it on the serving table, pulled the leads off and covered the device with a thick black mat he produced from his pocket. He leaned forward and winked. "There are a few details in this plan of mine I'd rather keep fromConnie."

Joe filled a cracker with cheese dip and passed it over with a tumbler of white wine. "Obviously. Sounding more like fun already."

Spero took a slow sip of Chardonnay, but turned a more somber face to Joe. "It will be work, Joe. Exciting maybe, but not much fun. Connie's very protective. If she believed I might get hurt doing this, and I admit there's some risk, I'm afraid she'd try to stop us."

Joe sliced the subs in two and motioned for him to continue. "Well, at first I had hoped I could use your present time stream for this project but as it turns out, magnetic resonance imaging is too new in 1986."

"I read about that. Without X rays doctors get cross sectional body images. The field magnetically aligns, and then releases the hydrogen atoms in your body. By the way, does anyone in your time know how magnetism actually works? You know, that force-at-a-distance thing."

"Nope, still a mystery."

"Shoot." Joe pointed his thumb back at the Bee, "You can build a thing like that and you *still* don't know how a magnetic field works?"

"Right, they talk about things like inter-dimensional leptons and other smoky stuff, but no one really knows. Look.

Pay attention. I am going to have to walk into a hospital during the time when the MRI is a more routine procedure. Also, I want a location where you're not recognized. That means we are going to have to travel to a different city ten years from now."

"Hot dog! The future. I like this plan already. But you said traveling ahead was against the rules?"

"Strictly yes, but this is a short in and out for you, so the heck with it. Here's the thing. The Police Retrieval people from my time will need my implant to be working if they're going to catch me. It's always broadcasting and I can't turn it off, but I found out from bench testing one of these that they can be permanently disabled with a burst of intense magnetic energy. An MRI does just that, and destroying my implant is the only way for me to stay free. Otherwise, sooner or later, I know they'll find me."

"But, why do you need me? Couldn't you just 'drop in' beside one of these units when no one was around, say at 3 AM, and give yourself a shot?"

Spero sat up to face Joe who was chewing on a large mouthful. "I've given this a lot of thought, Joe. Problem is—problem is, this has never been done while it is in someone's *head*. The implant wires will discharge before going dead, and the whole device may jerk to one side in the magnetic field. There could be bleeding, and most likely I'll go unconscious for awhile."

For a few moments Joe stared silently at Spero. "Oh." He swallowed hard and swung his feet around toward him. "You just want me along so I can do your funeral arrangements."

"Look, I really don't plan on dying, Joe. Maybe I'll be knocked out, maybe not. But I'll need you close by to wheel me back to the Bee on a gurney if needed. Connie has advanced medical techniques on board. She'll revive me, I'm sure."

"Sure?"

"Almost certain. Love this sandwich. Anyway, the plan is I go into the hospital ER with bogus head injuries. They'll have to do an MRI to rule out sub-dural bleeding. You just need to get me out of there right after the test begins. Look, if anything goes wrong, just get yourself back to The Bee, press button number one and you're home. And remember this. I *really* would rather die than be caught. Why aren't you eating?"

"Okay, but how do you plan to do all this with the fake injuries and everything? You must have a good story if you're going to sell this to Connie."

"What Connie knows and you can't know is my final destination. She thinks I want to obtain medical supplies to help the people living in that time, so this is a humanitarian adventure as far as she knows. Course I don't dare mention the MRI. Complex biologics can't be manufactured on board so she can't make them, and by the way, this is a *damned* good sandwich. Why is it called a sub?"

Joe returned to a reclining position and let out and sighed. For awhile he stared vacantly at the maple tree branches blowing in the wind. Spero sensed he needed a moment, and quietly finished eating. "So this is what I stupidly promised I'd do for you, and of course, I had no *real* idea what I was signing up for. Why didn't you just tell me?"

"You didn't ask."

"Wait, what if I get caught, or I can't get back to the Bee?"

"I checked the records. There were no arrest reports, or people being captured at the hospital we are going to, and besides you're alive and well in 1987."

"Oh, you know, do you? Yeah, I guess you would. OK, I know I promised and we'll go all right, but you damn well better survive this, Spero. You still owe me a trip!"

# # #

When they climbed aboard the Bee, Connie was humming some tune as she went through her preflight checks. She had suggested a change of clothes for Joe. His new jogging shoes were OK, but she insisted that his camera be locked up and not used to photograph his future. When they had finished donning their travel scrubs she said, "Oh, booyys?"

They settled back into their seats. "Yeaas?"

"You are keeping something secret from me aren't you?"

Together they replied, "Nooo."

"Yes you are. And my intuition tells me it's something dangerous, too. I shouldn't even be letting you take Joe into his future. Spero, the least you could do is tell him why future travel's not allowed."

"But Connie, It's forbidden for *us* to advance beyond 2247. There is no reason I can think of that Joe can't move ahead a decade, and he'll only be there a few hours."

"Maybe yes, maybe no. But anyway, tell him what happened when we tried to see the future."

"Sure. Well Joe, once we sent two drones ahead in time. They are small, unmanned Bees. One never came back. The other came back with its recordings erased and a cute little hand written note inside. It said sorry, but all travel to any future time was prohibited. Should any other Bees try it again, even manned ones, they would be immediately destroyed."

Joe stuck out his lower lip, and raised both hands palm up to shoulder level, as though he were weighing something. "I'll have to go along with Spero on this one, Connie. The people in Spero's future obviously just want their privacy. Nineteen ninety six is no problem for them or for us."

"Humph!" came out of the side speakers. "Why is it that men just *have* to do silly, dangerous things? Can't you get over 'double daring' each other when you get past fourteen?" Silence. The men waited for further objections, but clearly they were now on route. Connie didn't like the plan, but she was going to go along.

The familiar earth-moon image filled the view-screen again, but this time the moon was moving faster and in the other direction. "Spero, anyone from your time ever see any of these note-leaving future people?"

"Oh yeah once, but that was early in the QDT program. And Connie, remember how nice they were to us? Two of our historical research teams were back in your USA as a matter of fact. It was about 1830 in the Southwest as I recall.

They got too close to one another, and in one huge bang they both lost their sub atomics and crashed. The Bee getting all the particles overloaded and its power circuits got fried. So, there they both were, just sitting helpless in some gully while curious Indians began to move in. Connie, do you have the vid in your files? Maybe the news report?"

"Oh, that. I'll see if I can find it somewhere." Her tone sounded like it would take hours of rummaging through things to find it. "Be useful and show Joe how to watch it."

Spero pulled out a headpiece that resembled oversized, form fitting sunglasses. He handed him a wireless "joy stick" control that fitted comfortably into his palm. "I should have shown this to you on your last trip. It's a lot more fun than your best movies, and it's interactive. You can pause, zoom in, turn your viewing angle, and its 3D. The sound will come from all directions. I'll voice over to explain things as we go, but feel free to press this pause button any time."

Thoroughly delighted, Joe rewound and replayed the opening scene a few times to practice the interactive feel. Spero had explained that when a Bee loses all its particles by accident, an automatic recording begins from the topside camera. The sequence began with a view from the top of a bare stainless steel shell as it spiraled down into a small valley. With dubbed in English, Joe could hear four crew-members angrily blaming one another for the accident.

Spero continued, "When a Bee is fully disabled they're supposed to take out only survival kits, locators, and encrypted ship records. Then they're supposed to move away and blow the thing up. There is no way to recharge a Bee outside of our launch area, and we wouldn't want to leave our technology in 1830. Of course, vaporizing our ship is a huge waste of money."

"What about the crew? Do they get rescued?"

"Oh, sure. Eventually. Rescue Bees, each with an empty seat, would be sent out if they don't return, but the ship-wrecked crew still has to survive on their own for awhile. The rescue man has to locate their actual time fixation and approach with caution in case the Bee still has its particle skin. But in this case our people were treated to an immediate surprise rescue. Continue the vid."

As Joe watched the four travelers suddenly turned their backs to the camera. Two Indians rode up on horseback to the valley rim. They stopped, looked down on the crew and shouted something. At first it looked like the Indians were preparing to ride down, but then they suddenly galloped off.

A large triangular, silver-blue ship approached and descended down to the ridge. Nothing was audible when they landed, but there was a whirring noise and an exit hatch opened, followed by fold out stairs. Seven people in light gray uniforms poured out, and quickly headed down the grade right toward the camera. The English translation offered a single comment from one of the Bee's transfixed crew members: "Oh, my God!"

Joe paused the vid. "Is this your rescue team? They look like a bunch of kids in jump suits."

"Nah, look closer. This is the only image we've ever had of people from the next millennium. I'll tell you what our scientists made of this later. Keep going."

The diminutive people were all about the same height, and their form fitting uniforms covered their heads like a hood. They sported descending bird emblems on their chests, and wore large oval sunglasses that gave them the appearance of having oversized eyes. The one in front waved, smiled and said, "Hi! You called for a tow truck?" Everyone laughed. They all mingled, introduced themselves, and chatted.

One of the rescuers announced: "We should have you up and going in a few moments. Whoever would like to fly the undamaged QDT device, please get in. We'll send you two off first. Please do your routine pre flight and prepare to receive your charge just as though you were in the launch bay."

Our pilots shrugged their shoulders and climbed back in as they were told. "OK, now everyone else please move back out of the way."

This done, a silent, glowing, blue tube appeared and ran right toward the camera connecting the Bee with their ship. Then the camera went black, followed by a loud 'whack' sound.

Startled, Joe paused again. "What the heck just happened?"

"They recharged the first Bee, so its camera is now out. We don't know how to recharge like that in the atmosphere of course, and we don't even have a clue how they do it. The vid now continues from our second Bee."

As Joe restarted the player, the black screen suddenly changed to a view from some distance away. Gone was the blue connecting tube, and the other Bee was now recharged and glowing. Everyone was cheering and high-fiveing when the vid ended. "So those are guys from *your* future?"

"Exactly, well yours too only more so." Spero chuckled. "Sorry there's no more to see, but we just have the newsreel portion on board. Our scientists believe they are fourth millennium people. Also we're guessing they are bio-engineered to be smaller and lighter, custom tailored if you will, for their flight missions. They've been in your time too. Remember the triangle ships over Europe, Texas, Roswell?"

"No kidding. That stuff is real?"

"Oh yeah. Anyway, they sent a repairman into the disabled Bee after politely asking our permission. This guy came out of his ship with a couple of transformers and stuff under his arm. And here was the interesting part for me, he struggled down the hill from his ship without asking anyone for any help. After his repair job he came out of our Bee, broken parts in hand, and climbed back up to his ship. Then he smiled, waved to our crew, and said 'God blesses all of you.' He literally finished his actual work in two minutes. The little sucker took more time walking between ships than he took doing the repair itself."

"No kidding. Do you run into these people often?"

"Nope. Never before, and never again. Oh, and get this: the serial numbers on the equipment they installed were the *same* as the ones they replaced. Personally I think it was their way of making up for the bad impression they made, you know, when they blew up our Drones and all. Well, enough of this. Better get our beauty rest now. This'll be a fairly short trip and Connie has some 'horrible' things to do to me while I'm out."

CAROLINA IN THE MORNING

T his time they awakened to an impatient Connie playing the rock song "Party Like Its 1999". "OK guys, listen up. I'm over North Carolina, ten kilometers altitude. Two different radar units are trying to track us, so I'm going to dissociate to an earlier time fix and go right down. We've got a drone watching us too."

Joe was startled by Spero's appearance. While they had been 'under,' Connie had produced a large swollen purple bruise and added abrasions on Spero's right temple. Dried blood dripped down on his cheek. Joe spun around to look at him more closely. "Whoa! You look terrible, Spero."

"Did Connie do a good job? It doesn't hurt."

Joe leaned in even closer to inspect the injury. "This doesn't look fake, Spero. I think Connie really cut you."

"Now, no complaints. If I had used a moulage, any good Emergency Room nurse would laugh you off the premises. The abrasions are superficial. I caused a subcutaneous vein to bleed, and then coagulated it for the bruise. When we land, I'll dilate and fix his left pupil and add some tachycardia. He'll probably feel a little dizzy Joe, so be careful he doesn't fall. They should believe your story about being hit by a car, but these last effects will only persist for an hour. Spero, I sure hope the people in your new home will appreciate all the trouble you're going through to get these medical supplies."

Spero checked his image in the camera-view screen. "Perfect, Connie. Just the look I wanted."

"Would you like me to induce vomiting too?"

Both laughed. "You are quite the perfectionist. No, Joe will just tell them I did. But thanks, I think. Do you have our fake IDs?"

"Your driver's licenses are in your wallets complete with addresses in Raleigh. And you have a last name too, Mr. Speropolous."

Joe interrupted. "But we should also have health insurance cards of some kind. Can you make those too?"

"I thought Emergency Rooms would treat you without insurance."

"They will, but it might look suspicious if we had nothing."

"I'm on it guys. Okay, we're down to 5 KM, and I've had to dodge one airliner already, so let's get going. There is a large parking lot near the Duke ER, and I found a white truck with no occupants on the edge of the lot. A grove of pine trees is on the other side so that should give us a secure place to put down."

"Good work. But, about our pick up," Spero looked worried. "I don't want to head back out into the open. Can't you be ready to get us between Radiology and the ER? You have the schematic. Use our old basement stairwell routine."

"OK, fine. Here's your new wallets and cards, and a briefcase for the drugs. The homer is attached to a key chain Joe is carrying, and there is a backup in the case. I made them look like handout key fobs from this Budweiser Company. We have one just like it in the museum. In my opinion you'll likely be arrested for stealing the drugs anyway, and I'll have to get you out of jail in the middle of the night. Not that you care about my opinion, right?"

"Course we care, Connie, but we'll be fine. You'll see."

"Anyway, I assume your plan is to have Joe lightly stunning people and stealing the stuff while the others are busy with you? You do know ERs are supposed to report accidents to the police. Why not go to a pharmacy?"

"Well, that might be easier, Connie, but I need some 'hospital only' type drugs. We're not taking stunners. They might get left behind. Ah, I see you have us down in the lot. We should only be gone about an hour."

The hatch opened and they backed out into a hot, muggy, overcast day. "Alright, boys. You know this is against my better judgment, but good luck anyway. Flash your homer when you are ready. I'll make it vibrate when you are over the right stairwell."

Donning sunglasses they began to zigzag through the parked cars toward the Anlyan Tower and the ER. Spero kept staggering to one side and wondering out loud if Connie hadn't really given him a concussion. Joe kept him steady, but began to remark on how different the cars looked. Spero whacked him in the side. "Pay attention, darn it."

In the ER waiting room Spero staggered over to some chairs, lay down and began groaning as per plan. Joe had Spero's wallet out and introduced himself as a friend who had seen him hit by a car. The registrar seemed puzzled by the cards but after awhile called for a gurney that took Spero out to the treatment area.

Speaking to Joe's open mouth expression she said, "Your friend seems young to be on Medicare. Is he disabled?"

"Uh—yes. Some kind of war injury, I think. Can I stay with him?"

"In a just a little while. The doctor's with him right now. Please have a seat."

Joe picked a chair where he could see down the hall to the curtains drawn around Spero. A TV playing a cartoon stuck out of a wall corner, but no one watched it. Joe noticed that he was sweating, and felt his anxiety welling up. *This plan seemed so good at home, but it's starting to look pretty fuzzy and it's all up to me now.*

He picked up a magazine and tried to relax. The magazine proved to be more interesting than he expected, and he thumbed through the pages quickly. *Clinton president. X-Files on TV looks interesting—oh, Bay Watch, even better, and on small satellite dishes, too. Ah, here is a mention of the DVD movies Spero accidentally talked* about. *He he. All this 'forbidden fruit'.* Just then his discovery session was cut short by a flurry of activity. Spero's curtain was pulled open.

He tried to walk over, but some intern stopped him from going any farther.

"Your friend may have a serious head injury and we're going to admit him. We called the 'next if kin' in Ohio noted in his wallet, but there was just an answering machine. Is there anyone else we could contact? He's not responsive right now."

Joe could see Spero being whisked away by an orderly. "No, no one else I know of. Uh, is he on the way to the hospital floor?"

"He will be, but perhaps he'll go to surgery first. We'll see what the MRI shows."

Joe wondered if they saw his quickly covered smile. "OK, I'll wait in the Radiology waiting room if that's alright." The intern shrugged and gave brief directions. *So far so good.*

But when Joe got there he found this waiting area to be in full view of two receptionists, and well away from where the procedures took place. *We definitely didn't plan this part well.* He knew he had to get back behind those doors somehow and soon. Worse, he hadn't seen any stairwells along the way.

Be calm—think. Let's see. When patients are called in, they all go through the same door, and it isn't locked. He

walked over and stood with the people in front of the receptionist's counter. He waited for his moment—there it was.
One receptionist with her back turned, the other bending
down for something. He slipped through the door as quickly
and casually as he could.

Patients in gowns. An orderly pushing a wheelchair
down the hall. *Street clothes are no good. More bad planning.* But he continued walking forward and tried to look
nonchalant. *Think of something, Joe.*

There, an open door. Two radiologists were facing a
bank of illuminated X-rays. One was dictating loudly. There
were long white coats hanging on the wall. Slowly, but in
one smooth motion, Joe took a coat, slipped it on and turned
back and out the door. No one noticed.

Buttoning the coat helped him feel slightly more confident, and his pounding heart began to slow as he strolled
down one hall and then the next. *There we go! An MRI sign.*
A technician sat tapping at a console. A large machine in the
adjoining room was making loud clacking noises. Joe could
see Spero's legs sticking out. They twitched. The operator
exclaimed "Oh, my God!" and ran out toward the MRI with
Joe right behind him. He began to reverse the sliding track

and was horrified his patient had become unconscious. He turned to Joe. "Who are you?"

Without hesitating, Joe said, "I'm his doctor. What just happened?"

"Did you know he has some foreign metal lodged his skull?"

"Didn't know. He gave no such history, but he almost certainly has a subdural, so I'm going to take him right to the OR myself." Whereupon they both grabbed the unconscious patient and transferred him from the MRI slab back to the gurney. Joe pushed off for the door, frantically clicking the sender on his key chain.

"Wait! Stop." A policeman and two men in green scrubs suddenly burst through the exit doors and blocked the gurney. A heavy set man in green leveled his eyes at Joe. "I think we'd better take it from here."

2247

Consciousness does not act according to conventional physics, or even quantum mechanics. It acts according to a theory we don't yet have. Roger Penrose, 2009

Justin marched through his HR department. His demeanor left a wake of agitated and confused employees behind him.

"Jennifer, have you *ever* seen the Director so angry? He actually shouted at me."

"Never! And when I ran to the counter with the paper file he wanted—Ruth, he almost snatched my hand off when he grabbed it. And what about his order not to tell anyone he even *has* Anna's dumb file? Like, who'd care? He could a just pulled it up on his screen."

"But Listen Jen, what I really want to know is what the heck Anna was supposed to have done wrong. Rumor is she helped Spero escape, but I don't think they even really knew each other."

"Well, I hope nothing bad happens to her. She may be one of those 'keep-to-yourself' types, but she is really sweet for a Humwa. Hey, did you know the police are showing the wrong picture of her?"

"Some of us knew about it, Jen. Say, maybe the Director's pissed because he thinks we sent the wrong one on purpose. We didn't, though. It's some weird glitch in the encoding program. Try sending her photo to anyone outside and they get a different one. Guess we really should've said something huh?"

"Not me. I for one wouldn't want to get Anna in any trouble, but it looks they'll find her now. Hope she'll be OK."

Justin was taking deep breaths and calming himself as he approached the reception area to his private office. *But who can I trust to trace this out? In my Comp Section most everyone's Humwa. Gonna have to do this myself.*

His trusted secretary, Dottie 440, greeted him with her calming smile. "Nothing much happening today, Justin. Just a few things to sign and a transfer request." She moved to make eye contact. "Oh oh, something's upsetting you, sir. Need to talk?"

Justin put the file down on the edge of her desk, and leaned forward on his arms. "I'm fine, Dottie but, this is really important. Call whoever is the On-Duty Supervisor in the Comp Section right now and tell him this is a direct order. Everyone is to stop whatever he or she is doing. Put the work on pause, go directly to the conference room and stay there. No calls out. The supply runner will get them coffee and snacks, and I'll be down there within the hour. Meanwhile I'm not to be disturbed."

Justin cocked his head to one side and gave her a 'really mean it' squint. It was met by a quick 'Yes sir' head nod. Justin took in a deep breath, picked up the file and headed for his office. The feeling of being back-in-charge comforted him. It wouldn't last.

The heavy brushed nickel door to his office opened and closed with a 'woosh-thunk'. One step into the room and *Whoa, person!* Justin flattened himself against the wall instinctively pressing the security emergency alert on his arm. Heart pounding, he stared at this 'impossible' intrusion in his office. The invader was just sitting there on top of his file credenza waiting for him. *Armed?*

"Hi, boss," she said. "Sorry if I startled you. Heard you were looking for me."

Justin wasn't sure if he had just excreted bodily fluid. "A-Anna?"

She sat, perched like a bird. Her short black hair swept below her ears ended in little forward points. "Yes, sir, it's me."

Anna was part Asian, rather plain—wait: huge happy eyes and a wide grin. On second look, kinda cute. She wore a blue and black plaid jumper with a white blouse, and her dangling, kicking legs sported shiny black buckle shoes "Everyone seems to think I've done something bad, but," (switching to a cockney accent) "Oy've been a guh girl oye' ave."

Still shaky from his scare and struggling to regain composure, Justin pointed to his alarm device. "Talk fast, Anna. Armed security will be in up here in seconds."

"They won't be coming, Boss, but please sit down and relax, why don't you. I work here, remember? I'm sure not here to hurt anyone. I'm happy to give you a full report even though I'm still on vacation, you know." She fluttered the pleats in her skirt. "Like my outfit? Its Catholic school girl — 300 years ago — picture of innocence, huh?"

Justin tried to walk casually as he circled around the office to his desk. He slid into his contour but never took his eyes off her. *What the heck's going on with Anna? Clearly she's defeated all of our searches and security measures. Dangerous? I have to assume so, but I'll play along.* "OK, I'll make a deal with you. Start calling me Justin instead of Boss. Have a seat right over there, and I'll listen to your report."

Justin couldn't help but flinch when Anna jumped off the cabinet. She skipped to the soft guest armchair and fell back into it with a 'phlumph'. She tilted her head to one side and gave him a wide eyed stare. "OK, but I wish you would start to *trust* me instead of trying to call for security again like you just did from your desk. I'm not going to hurt you or anyone for gosh sakes. I'm just here to do my job."

Justin sighed and put both hands on top of his desk. "How old are you, Anna?"

Anna sat up in the chair with a frown. "Alright, the outfit's a bit over the top, isn't it? Sorry if you don't like it, but I like to make clothes, and I'm just having a little vacation fun. I'm 28, by the way." She gestured toward the door. "So look, if you're not interested in what I have to say, I can just come back to work on Monday."

"Stay right where you are Ms. I assure you, I *am* interested in your answers."

Anna grinned. "But actually you're just waiting for me to be pounced on by those two huge smelly security guards, right?" She giggled. "Why are you so afraid of me?"

"They're not coming?"

"No."

"That's one reason to be afraid. Well then, first question. How can that be?"

"My report on your project will explain that and everything else too. And if you are in any danger, by the way, it's only that I've always thought you were pretty cute. But don't worry, I know the woman you really like."

"Wait, *my* project? I would never approve something like overriding security."

"Well, that was just a byproduct, but of course your approval is required on all our department initiatives. This one was 1348A, signed last December 14th."

"I, I don't recall. I approved it?"

Justin's desk computer suddenly turned on and its holographic display appeared before him, spinning through text pages. "This is a good place to start, bo—Justin."

He lifted his hands off the desk. "Now you've accessed my personal encrypted data and you're going through it while you're sitting over there?"

Another giggle. "Ah, here it is. See your signature?"

Justin leaned forward, and stared at the presentation hovering over his desk. "Okay, this is just a project to increase the human like interaction of the onboard computer. Basically a software update."

A portion of the text began glowing. "Ah ha, but look at the phrase: 'by whatever means the project leader deems expedient.' C'est moi, *me*." Big grin.

"My God Anna, just what did you do to our Bee computer? Did you deliberately make changes to help Spero escape? It looks that way, so you shouldn't be surprised there was an all out search for you. Was this deliberate or not?"

Unable to stay seated now, Anna started walking about the office as she talked. "Unintentional, but completely wonderful things happened, Justin! But first let me assure you that our project was in no way connected to Spero's escape. That was just as much a surprise in our Department as it was for everyone else. He got away with our special prototype model from 1348A too. That really did disappoint all of us."

"Now you don't actually expect me to believe you want him to be captured too?"

"Well, I'd like the Bee and its computer back for analysis. We *were* going to do a pre launch checklist and install a failsafe collar on launch morning, you know. Course, an escaped Creative is our kind of hero. I admit it. But despite that, I don't mind telling you everything we know about our little 'software update' as you call it."

"Now's a little late, don't you think? But go ahead, and I'm going to record this if you don't mind."

"Course not. Our project was to make the onboard more human-like and interactive. My first idea was to use memory downloads from someone's implant, just like the police do with their memory probes. I tried mine."

"I'll bet that didn't work, did it?"

Anna began to inspect the knick-knacks on Justin's wall shelf. "Right, Smartee. The main computer bank simply stored it in the file even though we linked it to the artificial personality program. No integration, no interaction. Useless. We realized our brains must store and access memories and experience in totally different ways from a computer."

"I'll bet there's a 'next', isn't there?"

"Yup. Next we conferenced with Stephen 420, a neuro-surgeon. He's a Humwa and a really bright guy. He suggested extending all 32 interactive wires from my implant non-invasively so that all my higher functions would be tapped, then downloading them as an entire operational program. He even had a great sub routine for converting a brain's analog output to digital. Who knew?"

"*Your* higher functions?"

Anna tossed up a small silver model of a prototype Bee, caught it, replaced it on the shelf and giggled. "Sure, I couldn't ask one of my colleague friends to risk frying their brains could I? Actually there were no volunteers."

"Not surprising. But the data drop from an entire cortex would be *huge*. There would be no way to make it run like a real brain either, would there?"

"Exactly right again, but my plan was to play with the all the data as a separate program this time. I would add execu-tion commands, and try to get it to work separately before adding it to the mix. I'm not sure why, but I *still* couldn't get it to run like a computer program should." Anna sat down on the chair arm, frazzled her hair and bounced with wide-eyed enthusiasm.

"See but *then* I had my big brainstorm, or, maybe I should say my big brain fog-out. I decided to hook myself into our Forensic Computer for the download, you know, the one we use to recover data from damaged old historical hard drives."

"Dammit, Anna. You *know* I would have vetoed a crazy idea like that, and you should have asked me. Way too dangerous. That program isn't at all passive. It communicates with damaged computers and tries to re-arrange files for extraction. And the impulses it sends out! Gotta be much more current than our soft little neurons could take. A current like that could do some serious brain damage."

"Looking back on it, you're right again of course. There were too many unknowns. Also I didn't tell Steve that we were using the Forensic. And he didn't tell us that cortical neurons could actually regenerate. In retrospect, I should have discussed this with the Forensic program genius who designed it, but he's retired. Stupid, I guess. But anyway, what happened was totally unexpected. Steve told me later he was afraid I might've been brain dead at one point, but he kept me on full monitor support."

"My God, Anna! What were all of you *thinking?*"

"I know, but I was pretty caught up in it by that point. Luckily I did tune the output voltages on the Forensic down to the level Steve said would be safe. The very first thing that happened is I went unconscious. Everybody panicked, but Steve told them it would do me more harm if they tried to just pull the plug. This computer is very diagnostic, you see. It found what it 'thought' was the RAM, and simply took it off line."

"That would have been your consciousness, I suppose. The part of your brain acting as a processor for all the other programs, and keeping you awake?"

"Correct. Now here's another really weird part we didn't anticipate. The Forensic proceeded to 'defragment' the stored data in my brain, and erase everything redundant. I guess we've got a whole lot of redundant stuff in us, Justin."

"Good God! *Erase*? Like fry some neurons?"

"Apparently, yes sir. But the Forensic also knew how to grow new dendrites by stimulation wherever it wanted them. It's a pretty creative program, more than I would have ever guessed. Maybe its creator anticipated organic use."

Anna leaned over the desk, toward Justin and spoke in a half whisper. "It kept me unconscious for 14 hours re-wiring things and waiting for neuron regrowth before it downloaded the first bit from me. I really hope I can find the guy who designed that thing and have a little chat."

"Oh, Anna, Anna. If you'd only come to me. Why couldn't Steve find some way to stop all this when you were in the coma?"

"Well, by that time everyone did know we were in trouble, of course." She Giggled. "But just trying to turn things off would certainly have left me permanently coma-tose, and they reasoned that only the program itself would be able to reverse what it had done in the first place. The download copy it took out of me was transferred to our main bank and this time with a rebooted RAM. I'm proud to say that I had 20 times as much data in me than any of the hard drives we've processed so far."

"And your 'data'? Your higher brain functions—they all got transferred to the computer on the Bee, weren't they?" Justin stood up. "Did your copied mind actually work on its own once it was in there?"

"Yes! Absolutely fabulous. It was like talking to myself. Before we added it to the onboard, though, I put on filters all over the place so it wasn't supposed to change orders or make decisions on its own. "

"Unlike yourself."

Anna laughed. "Yes, totally unlike me. We spent a long time programming it to work with the other onboard computer too. They could really talk to one another. However, what concerns me is this. If the program realized an escaped Creative was on board and in trouble, it would likely try to find a way to blow past my filters, change programs, and help him out any way it could. I know I would."

"I'll bet you would. And apparently '*you*' did. But would you even override safety protocols like taking the risk of changing directions while going through a planet."

Anna sat down on the edge of Justin's soft chair and crossed her legs. She thought for a moment then turned squinty eyes toward Justin. "Sure, if I had confidence in the main onboard to make those kinds of calculations, I wouldn't hesitate to change time, speed, direction or anything else if I thought it might throw the pursuers off."

Justin wheeled his contour back from his desk. "Great. Well at least now I know *what* happened to our Bee. I also realize that you can't tell me exactly what changes your counterpart might have actually chosen. So unfortunately you're not going to be of any real help to us in capturing him, are you?"

Justin's expression softened. "But my next question for you is just personal. What actually happened to *you* through all this? Are you all right now, Anna?"

Anna slipped off the chair and went to the window. "Me? Say, thanks for caring, by the way. I've sort of become an improved version of the old me. The first thing I realized when I finally woke up, I mean besides being ravenously hungry, was that I now had total and instant memory recall even back to childhood. I can go over every word that someone said to me when I was six years old, for instance. Also I remember the day and time it happened and what they were wearing."

"But, that's great, Anna!"

"No actually, it's really annoying. I'm working at repressing this stuff. What's great though, is having an interactive control of my implant computer. It will let me gain access to any nearby computer by wireless link and control it as well. That's how I blocked your security alarms, got through doors, and ran your desk computer."

"Wow! So now you're a living super computer. And that's how you changed your photo on the Police Wanted Vids, didn't you. But how did you get past Dottie?"

Anna winced slightly. "I can also work anyone else's implant and make them go to sleep if I need to."

"No kidding. You're a weapon, besides! A cute weapon, but still—you're more dangerous than a police soldier. Who's the woman you put in the photos anyway?"

Anna blushed. "Thank you, Justin. She's Marie Curie."

"Oh, yeah, her." Justin took a deep breath, leaned back in his chair and grinned. "Well, I hope you'll accept my apology for not trusting and trying to slap you in jail." He picked up the intercom, but waited for Anna's nod of approval. "Dottie, call down to the conference room and tell everyone not working in critical functions they can have the rest of the day off. Anna's been in here since before you came in, so don't be shocked when she comes out. And, oh yes, get me Police Retrieval."

In a moment the COM signaled back. "Oh, hello Chief— good news. Anna is back at work, and we have all the information we need from her. Turns out she wasn't involved with Spero's escape after all. I'll send you a report if you want. You can drop her charges."

"What? You still don't have a locator signal on her? Are you watching your screen?" Justin looked toward Anna and raised his eyebrows. She turned her head to one side, crossed her eyes, stuck out her tongue, and pretended to slap water out of one ear. Immediately she covered her mouth to suppress laughter, but some squeaked out anyway.

"Ah, you say the signal just appeared, huh?" Justin suppressed a laugh of his own. "Yes, I *know* she's in my office. I just said so. Would you like to say Hi?" Anna grimaced and stuck her tongue out again. "No? Okay, bye."

Grinning, Justin shook his head. "Can you believe it, Anna? They didn't even ask me where you've been. We better keep your new abilities a secret, don't you think? So for now, just go on and enjoy the rest of your vacation." He stood up and walked Anna to the door. "But please promise me not to put any more of my staff to sleep on the way out. I might need them."

"Thanks, boss, I mean Justin. Really sorry for the trouble I've been. By the way, your office is bugged. I had to block the mikes, but they'll go back on when I leave."

Justin shrugged.

"Now I don't want to sound pushy, but I'd like to have lunch with you tomorrow. I'm not hitting you up for a date or anything like that. It's just that I know more things I think you'll be interested in, and there's something I'd like to show you in person."

"Sure, why not? And tomorrow's better, anyway. I've had enough fantastic revelations for today."

Anna paused with one hand over the door opener and gave him a cheery, quick wave with the other. "Okay then, I'll see you at the employee's cafeteria, gate twenty four, say about noon."

1996

J oseph Main felt his sweaty hands slipping off the gurney handles as he tried in vain to push past the three men who blocked his way. *Oh my God, what is this? Spero could be dying right now.*

The policeman stepped to the side. To Joe's horror he saw his hand slide down over his gun holster. "Stop."

The X-ray tech backed off, hands raised. Spero's skin was slate gray and his breath was coming in hoarse gasps. Joe pleaded. "Can't you see, I've got to get my patient to the OR right now."

The larger of the two green-scrubbed OR techs slid down the side of the gurney toward him and forced eye contact. He *smiled.* "Joe, it's all right. We're here to help you. Turn right for the elevator you want then we'll go left around the corner." The men began backing through the swing doors into the hall and they spun the gurney around to the right. Confused, Joe stumbled with them and stared at this man in disbelief.

"You know my name, you know what—you're *me!*"

The team angled Spero widely to the left and gathered speed down the next hall. The man glanced back and winked. "Of course it's me, Joe. I'm you—well we're *us*. Weird, huh? Anyway I was betting you'd have blown this thing without my help, and since I *remembered* my helping you, I knew it shouldn't try to change anything. Not supposed to, right?" He sidestepped to a stop. "Here's our elevator."

"You, I—gain weight, start to go bald?"

Older Joe slipped a medical emergency key into the frame beside the elevator door and turned it. "Nice to see you too. Look, I'm not going to say much, but you will have a busy ten years. Actually, I wish I could switch with you right now and live through them all over again—well, *some* of them at least."

The policeman flashed a badge at two doctors who were trying to board the opening door. "Emergency" he said, "We'll send it right back."

The elevator started down. Spero was still breathing, but only in intermittent raspy gasps. "These two work for me, by the way." Older Joe motioned toward his friend in scrubs who held out the briefcase. "You were distracted. Left this in the waiting room."

Spero, still unconscious, began to cough. The men propped him on his side with pillows and gently extended his neck. "Your job is to hold onto the case this time. I discussed it with my doctor friends, and filled it with drugs and supplies. They thought these would be the most useful for things for Spero's destination."

"Thanks, Big Joe. But as I see it, *your* job is to start a low fat diet and get back into jogging."

The door opened on the basement level. "Now you're sounding like my conscience, little brother." Joe winced when he realized this floor was not the quiet basement he'd hoped for, but an active part of the hospital. No sign of the Bee.

The pretend policeman started setting up the barricade he had readied in advance, and waved people away from the stairwell. Then with well practiced moves he covered the area with a tarp. "She won't come until you're not moving. Hit your little 'clicker' again Joe."

The Bee appeared almost instantly behind the tarp, and as the hatch slid open, Joe called in for Connie's arms to help move Spero. Both Joes had to struggle with the limp body as they pushed it through the small opening. Connie's distress cries rang out in two languages, and bystanders outside the curtain began shouting questions at them. The moment Joe followed Spero inside and pulled the briefcase clear, the hatch closed. With the concealing tarp, no one had seen more than a glow from the Bee. The three men turned to the crowd, took down the canvas with a flourish, and bowed.

Inside the Bee the controlled pandemonium of medical emergency had begun. Joe followed orders, opened med kits, and gave the history of Spero's MRI exposure, duration and symptoms. All four of Connie's arms flew from Spero to supplies and back. She attached some wired device to his head, and convulsed him once with some kind of shock. When her motions finally slowed, he had a tube coming out his nose, a breathing mask, and IVs. Connie said, "That's all."

"D—Did he die?"

"No. He is on medication to slow his metabolism. He'll wake up in awhile, about two hours. The tests the Gorilla ran do indicate full recovery, but he wasn't breathing normally when we pulled him in, you know. A blood clot was putting pressure on the breathing center in his brain, but that's clear now."

"Thank God."

"And thank the Gorilla. This sort of thing is all up to him."

"Are we going somewhere now?"

"Unless you've changed your mind, we are heading to the Triassic time fix we promised you, and words simply can't express how completely spitting angry I am with both of you right now."

"But, we didn't anticip. . ."

"Joseph, I want a full confession right now. You lied to me. And what really hurts is you didn't trust me. This mission obviously wasn't for medical supplies, was it?"

"No, but we got some anyway. Spero felt his survival out there depended on his plan to knock his implant out of commission with magnetic pulses. But he assured me you could revive him. I wouldn't have gone along with it otherwise."

The four arms slammed back in their niches with a series of loud clangs. "And your so called plan was to just wheel his limp body back through a strange hospital with dozens of people and security guards just looking on?"

"When you say it that way, I—I confess we didn't really think all the details through. I hoped all I had to do was make one quick dash and get him out of there."

Connie stopped talking. The only sounds were the respirator breathing for Spero and soft muffled noises coming from the speaker. *God, I really think she's crying.*

The two arms closest to Joe slowly came out of their nacelles and gently held his shoulders. "I'm just feeling really *hurt* Joe," her voice soft. "Spero could have really died out there, and just because you didn't believe how much I care for both of you. Together we could have found a better solution. And there *was* a better solution."

"But he must have researched all the possibilities, don't you think?"

"I realize you felt you had to go along with him, and I really don't blame you, Joe. Spero's smart, but he charges into a quick solution, and he knows *nothing* about biology."

"I guess."

Connie intertwined her fingers together and became quiet again. *Good grief. I actually think she's praying.* Her arms relaxed. "Now look, I've admitted it was wrong for me not to tell you about the sandals, but this was much worse.

Promise me from now on we'll always trust each other. Joe, our survival out here depends on it."

"Connie, I feel really badly. I promise. I really wanted to say something, but this was *the* all important thing for Spero. It was my only reason for being onboard, and he was convinced you were going to stop him if you found out."

Connie massaged Joe's shoulders for a moment, folded her arms slowly back in, and made a noise that sounded like a sigh. "Oh, you're right. I would have stopped you, but not for the reasons you both think. Spero thinks so much like a man. If you can't control a thing, smash it. And my former spinal *ganglions* knew more about computers than he'll ever understand. Didn't you guys even *think* to ask me?"

"You know I feel awful about that. I really do. But you're not hinting you know of some other way to turn off his broadcast beacon are you?"

"Joe, without going into details which you might inadvertently repeat, the answer is yes. All he would have had to do is ask me. I was just going to turn it off for him when he left anyway."

"No, bull! Spero never even *needed* me?" Joe shook his head. "Oh, you're right. Better not tell him." Joe leaned back in his chair, looked up and took a deep breath. "But, we lucked out after all. The plan did actually work didn't it?"

"Joe, you're really the hero here. Spero really would have died in another two minutes if you hadn't been so clever at getting all the hospital personnel to help you. I saw them all pushing Spero in. How'd you ever convince them not to take him to surgery, and be calm when they saw the Bee? You didn't have much time."

"I didn't have to. I was helped by my ten-year later self, plus some of his, er, our friends. 'Future me' had it all set up and they were just waiting to take over. They were the ones who met me in X ray and wheeled us down."

"Now it's my turn to say, as you so often do: 'Holy Cow!'. I would never have anticipated that. So, you're saying that you plus *you* pulled it off?"

"Yup, and future me got us some meds in the case for Spero, too. But Connie, let me just say sincerely, I really owe you one."

"Okay goodie. Then, here's a favor you can do for me: promise you'll let Harvey out when we get back to his time."

TRIASSIC VOYAGE

The little ones from the Realm of Choices wondered,
Could they leave their World and be solid and real?
Let's flash in and out of theirs so quick we'll fool them.
Then all will think we're solid, don't you feel?
Poetry for Children, 2055

S pero woke with a brief convulsion, and a hallucination about something "happening again". Joe patted his shoulders and reassured him as he lurched in and out of consciousness, and Connie massaged his temples with some moist pads. Finally, his eyes returned from the "out there" and into the aware.

"Did that thing happen again, Connie? Is my implant dead?"

"Spero, you were just dreaming, but as the expression from Joe's time goes, your implant has as much life in it as does a door nail."

Spero sat up and started to pull off his leads before Connie smacked his hand away and began doing it for him. "I feel fine now, and you know, I wasn't dreaming the first time. It really happened, Connie. How about some lunch?"

"Sure, sure, and it's obvious you never told Joe about the *real* hazards involved with this fun little caper, never mind telling me. He probably would have talked some sense into you." Connie's voice cracked with emphasis, "And don't you *ever* try something bull headed like this again, or we're through. I mean it. No more secrets. You have to promise."

Spero sat up straighter and smoothed the hair back on the sides of his head. "Well, I'm sorry I upset you, but I had to do it. And no more secrets, I promise. But it worked, didn't it?"

"Humph. Also, when you're up to it, you'll have to tell him your version of the 'happening again' thing. You were mumbling all about it when you came to. If you recall, it was on our last trip back a quarter billion years, and that's where we're headed now. But when you do, in all fairness, I'll have to tell him how it looked to me."

Connie resumed removing wires, and cleansing the needle sites. "Joe has a right to hear it, and a right to change his mind when he does. Besides, it'll be good for you to talk about it. Get that old nightmare off your chest."

Joe tried to understand what this was all about. Finally he said "Look, Spero, since you were almost dead a few hours ago, I'd say you get some down time. But, I'd sure like to hear about this event when you're up to it."

"I'm fine, but Connie's in a bad mood so maybe now's not a good time"

"And you don't think she has one heck of a good *reason*, old buddy?"

"Oh, yes, yes, you're right, I guess. Connie, I'm sorry. Won't happen again, OK?" Spero stared up at her eye. ". . .She's not talking. Look Connie, I'll tell Joe all about that 'happening' right now if I get something to eat. What's on board, my beautiful maiden?"

"Oh pooh, which one of you guys remembered to stop by the hospital cafeteria on the way and fill up a couple of trays?"

"Very funny. So we have nothing left from Joe's place? No snacks or anything?"

"You ate those. Connie pulled out a package containing bars that resembled a knockwurst with square edges. "We're back on standard 'hard tack', to use one of Joe's expressions again."

Spero snatched the bar and began munching. "Oh goodie. Well, we'll just have to shoot some lizards when we get back to the Triassic. Then we'll be partying with the good stuff again."

Joe waved both his hands at him. "But Spero, I have to say, this is incredible. In a few hours you went from comatose and maybe dying to hungry and sarcastic. That's astounding."

Spero chewed with vigor. "But see, I told you I'd pull through, and thanks for saving my life, by the way." Joe responded with a 'you're welcome' gesture. "Anyway, here is what happened on my first trip to the Triassic, and like she said, if you want to change your mind after you hear it, that's okay. Remember, on this trip I had just escaped and I was an emotional mess. I'll start by admitting that much."

Connie inserted "And I'm not going to interrupt this, but I'll just add that the Gorilla kept suggesting that we tranquilize him and return to base. He would have needed my cooperation as liaison, but I really gave it some serious thought at the time."

"Okay, okay. So, although I didn't really know you at first, I'll just thank you right now for overruling the big guy and putting up with me. Thanks, Connie. I mean it."

"Wow, Joe. Did you hear that? A sincere apology. You're welcome, Spero."

Spero turned in his chair to face Joe and lowered his eyebrows. "Well, I had refused to use the artificial sleep mode on my first trip for various reasons, mostly paranoia, I guess. I started thinking about how I might turn this traveling-in-time thing into a great way to live in wealth and women, but then I got real about figuring out what to do with my new life. I was almost two days out, and I half dozed off when it happened."

"So you were asleep?"

"No, no definitely not. Well, there was this yawing to one side with a sudden increase in gravity. Some kind of sulfury smoke came into the cabin and I could swear that there was someone in here with me. Couldn't see anyone, and I admit I was terrified, Joe. I shouted something like 'God please help me!' I was fumbling for the cabin light switch when it suddenly stopped just as quickly as it started."

235

"And that's it?"

"No, no, the next part's even weirder. Connie saw it differently, but I know I was wide-awake. Oh yeah—really scared, and really awake. The hatch became transparent and the *sun* came streaming in. Now I know we were nowhere near any star, and I saw the time reversal readout. It was spinning backward nine hundred eighty two years a second."

Spero swilled some water and coughed. "See, I had to be awake to remember that, but it looked like we were back on Earth, and it was a beautiful day. . ."

"But of course that would be impossible."

"True, but there it was. We seemed to be slowly moving along a path. There were rolling hills outside, and people working in a field—grape vines I think. Then some young bearded guy in a white bath robe started to walk alongside the view port. He looked in at me. I glanced at the instrument panel, and we were still reversing time, but I swear: he was really out there just *casually walking* along beside the Bee!"

"Take it easy, Spero. You're getting upset."

"No, no, I'm fine, Joe. But please understand that this moment really affected me. I don't know how to explain it any better, but I've felt different ever since."

Spero leaned back and stared at the cabin roof. "The man smiled at me, and instantly I felt calm and peaceful. Then he turned around so he was walking *backwards*. He laughed, and I can remember his face so clearly. He was slightly squinting on the right side as he laughed and had happy brown eyes. Finally, he mouthed some words, and then it was over. The hatch was solid metal again."

"You mean he winked at you?"

"Yup. Well, not really. One eye just closed a bit more when he laughed. Anyway, he was clearly happy for me. Never said a word out-loud."

"Well, I was going to say you were dreaming about God until you got to the 'winking' and laughing part. God wouldn't have a sense of humor, would he? Walking *backward* while time reversed? That's really cute, buddy."

Spero waved a hand as if to brush something away. "I know, I know how it sounds, but I can't tell it any other way. That's what really happened. Of course Connie saw things differently, didn't you dear?"

Connie's response came in a soft voice. "That's true so I will give both of you the onboard computer's point of view, but I am not trying to say the experience didn't seem real for Spero. There are two things we agree on. First, there was indeed some kind of a gravity 'bump'. The Gorilla registered a strong gravitational field but there was no other sensor confirmation of an anomaly. Could have been a small black hole. And, by the way, on this trip I'm making sure to avoid that location by six light years just in case. However, there were no other life forms detected in or out of the cabin, no smoke, and no hatch transparency. Vital signs looked like an anxiety attack before you relaxed again. Sorry, Spero."

Joe studied Spero's contemplative face. He looked back into Connie's eye. "You said *two* things."

"Oh, yes. Secondly, I do have to agree that there was a change in Spero from that moment on. Changed for the better, I'd say. Calmer, more purposeful, more concerned. He's really been a different kind of guy since then."

"So, something scared the piss out of him, huh?" He turned to Spero. "Could you make out what his lips were saying to you in the dream?"

He turned slowly and faced Joe. Spero's dark eyebrows lowered again, and his mouth twitched. "Not a dream, Joe. His words were 'I love you'."

"OK, Spero, sorry. Now I *know* you were dreaming. And it's understandable. Geez, you were leaving behind everything you ever knew. You hadn't slept in two days and were heading out into the unknown. But I you've figured out a better plan for what you'll be doing with your life."

"I think so Joe. I know so."

"Okay, Spero. No change in our travel plan."

Connie said "Well good. I'm glad we got past all that. Here's the menu bulletin. We don't have food for both of you for more than a few days, not counting intravenous. That means you'll have to use sleep mode. Too bad, though. While you get your jammies on I'll make the hatch transparent for real this time even though we'll have to stop moving to do it. I don't want you to miss this gorgeous nebula coming up."

It still puzzled Joe that he had no sensation when they would suddenly stop retrogressing from a thousand years a second to nothing. Connie cleared the view-port and they were treated to a floating field of spectacular red and blue misty "clouds". Multiple bright blue-white stars shone through the nebular haze. The men shared the telescope, passing it back and forth. "Look at this Spero. Try these filters and you can actually see where a proto star is forming."

"With time lapse I bet you could test your orbital decay theories from here, huh?"

Finally, Connie interrupted them. "OK, boys, I know you're having fun, but the sleep train is ready to roll and soon you'll want to start eating again. If I find anything else interesting while we do the circle tour around our pretty galaxy, I promise to take good pictures for you."

# # #

Joe was amazed at how rested he felt when he woke up after days of 'hibernating'. They were already on the ground.

"Well, gentlemen, you've made these trips easy for me. Since these places were already stored in the data bank, it was all automatic. We're one galactic rotation into the past: that's two hundred thirty million years ago in the Triassic Ladinian Era. Thanks for not asking for another thirteen million back or we'd have to mess with that giant asteroid that hit the Earth. The species out there today are still in recovery.

Joe peeked out the hatch. "I just see rocks and ocean."

"We're on the rocky ledge from Spero's first visit, but a week later. Spero, you're not really going to shoot a lizard, are you?"

"I heard they taste like chicken."

"Euuuw! Anyway, don't go down into the water. I've detected a 20 meter beast swimming out there not far from the beach."

"Only kidding, and I won't shoot him either. Connie, we'll need breathers for the low oxygen, and sulfur dioxide. Remember my wheezing and coughing?"

The men clambered out and peered into the thick yellow-green forest on their left but only small shrubs and lichens extended out on their cliff. They walked to the edge and looked down at the beach below. The surf was booming loudly, and above, the skies of Pangea surrounded them with overcast smog.

Spero pointed to "shore birds" dashing in and out of the waves below and handed Joe the binoculars. "Hey Spero, those aren't Kiwi birds. They're actually small theropods, one of the world's first dinosaurs." He passed the binoculars back. "Look at them running around on two feet and grabbing lunch from the surf."

"Huh, really? I wonder if my leg clamp is still transmitting down there."

"Well guess what, Spero. There's one thing you forgot. Two things, actually."

"And that would be?"

"One, you forgot to put Harvey back, and two you never asked me to pick my landing spot like you promised."

"Oh, okay, okay."

They walked back to the Bee and found Connie shushing Harvey out from his under-seat hiding spot. Joe chuckled. "Will you look at all those legs? I never really got to see him in the daylight."

Spero casually reached in, picked Harvey up, and gave him a few loving strokes that made him curl up in a ball. But as soon as he placed him on the ground, Harvey quickly uncurled and made for the forest. Joe quickly moved to get a photo.

Connie's voice came over their intercom: "Thank you. Thank you. I know mister H will be *much* happier here. Say, stand over by that big rock so I can get both the forest and the sea behind you. I need a real tourist photo of you two."

After the shot they clambered back into the Bee, and Spero explained "Well, Connie, we came back early because Joe says he never got to pick his landing site."

"He's right of course, but the northern part of Earth's one big continent is quite cold. There are a few islands but the really interesting stuff is here. Inland is kinda dangerous with the huge animals, but it's okay if you want to try somewhere else Joe. Remember, we can only stay a few hours in our beautiful Triassic wonderland. You could go back out there, or we could take an island vacation. So, what'll it be, stay or move?"

"Move."

"Okay, you're the Boss, Joe. This is your special trip. Where to?"

"Mars."

2247

J ustin took a detour on his way to the Central Directorate. His thoughts ground through recent developments as he headed for Center Park and the bench John installed. *What an unbelievable relief. Police Retrieval just dropped the idea of questioning Anna or myself. Must be they were really embarrassed they couldn't locate her.* He chuckled. *Ya gotta like their imaginary press release though—claimed they had Anna under surveillance all along. Released after questioning.* Chuckle.

Justin stopped to examine the leaves on a low hanging oak branch and sat down on the bench. *They're only worried about the Bee's "grand return" now—Police told me to expect officers with stunners in my Return Room. If Spero's hoping for a hero's welcome, he'll be sorely disappointed.*

The arching girders high overhead caught his attention. *I should be feeling happier right now. Wonder why I'm not. I'm off the hook, and so is the QDT. No more searches, and no more pressure. Still doesn't feel right.*

He noticed a fluttering above. *Birds, building a nest. Hope the SD police don't shoot any of them this year.* He sighed. *Strange — Police Retrieval actually acting pleasant. Course they wanted to keep the Bee's return day secret, but that didn't work. The news leaked out despite the magistrate's gag order on the press.*

Three boys showed up carrying a ball and a stick and started playing on the small lawn in Johns' park. A uniformed guard looked on from a distance. *See that Justy? Usually they just run the kids right off. Get back to the 'Center for Organized Activity' they'd say. This seems to be a 'be nice to people week'. I'll take it.*

Justin picked up a discarded juice container and "arced" it into the trash can. *Everyone's assuming it'll be Spero in that Bee. Heck, no guarantee of that, but if he did dare to fly in, the Humwa would like to give him a confetti parade. Fat chance. The administration. . .*He chuckled, *they'd be torn between giving him a lifetime of sewer duty, or just making* *him disappear in the Psyc Institution for ever. But they're sure not asking my opinion."*

Justin got up began walked briskly toward The Directorate and his briefing with Chairman Margo. He hoped it would be quick and painless, but he wanted some advice on another matter first. His visit with Anna had left him confused, and he wanted to talk about this woman with someone he knew he could trust—and someone who understood women as well. There was only one such person.

# # #

Sarah greeted him with a broad smile as he walked up to her counter. "I can hardly believe this, Mr. Director, Sir," she teased. "You're actually 30 minutes early."

Justin couldn't repress a grin as he melted before her twinkling, hazel eyes. "Actually I think I'm right on time Sarah, and if I'm not mistaken, this gentleman walking over to us is about relieve you for your coffee break, right?"

Confused for a moment, Sarah gave her auburn pageboy a quick toss. "Yes, but I'll be back in time to phone you upstairs, Director."

"Sarah, please call me Justin. I came early because you are the only one I really want to talk to right now. Mind if I join you on your break?"

Sarah stood up to her full 5'5", and looked evenly into Justin's face without a flutter or a blush. "I'd be delighted. Come with me."

Unknown to Justin there was a small secure break room for persons in security sensitive positions. Sarah opened an invisible door by inserting five fingers into a lock on the wall and in a moment they were alone and sitting at a small table. She poured him a dark coffee, and made herself an Herb tea. She raised her eyebrows and leveled her gaze.

"You know I like black coffee?"

She chuckled. "So, what would the head of our illustrious QDT care to talk to me about? This room is guaranteed free of surveillance, by the way."

Justin fought a sudden sense of uneasiness and glanced out the window at the entrance steps. *She knows more about me than my taste in coffee.* He coughed and shook his head. *God, she is one beautiful woman.* "I, I—Sarah, I've known you for years, well almost two. I really feel I can trust you. You're honest, insightful, and caring. I'd really value your opinion on some things that bother me."

Sarah leaned forward on her elbows, and searched his expression with concern.

Justin narrowed his eyes. "First, what do you think about the Creatives, as they like to call themselves. And I assume you aren't one yourself, are you?"

Now a slight eye flutter, "Wow, I'd have guessed you planned to ask me out. But I have to admit, I'm so much more flattered you came for my opinion." She grinned and relaxed back in the chair. "Of course I'm not a Creative. I got Cs in science and Ds in math. But if you really want to know what I think of them, you'll have to first promise not to tell the 'monster lady' upstairs."

Justin laughed. "Absolute confidence. On my word, I promise."

"Well, we learn from grade school that Humwa were the source of all wars and mass killings, and that they would love to take over the world and start the fighting again. They supposedly need constant surveillance and should never be trusted. We are all branded either as Creatives or not depending on tests we get as four year olds, but anyone can still be condemned any time we start to act 'funny'."

"Sarah, I know all that. I want to know what *you* think of them."

Her soft eyes searched into his. It gave him warm tingles. "Justin, I trust you too, and since this is in confidence, I should tell you that technically I *am* a Creative."

"You've joined their movement?"

She sat straight up. "They have a *movement*? No, what I mean is I write poetry. I read it too, at a secret place — a place where people meet to listen or recite. The police would call this subversive. But worse than that, I worship at secret 'God' meetings too. I'd lose my job if the authorities found out about either of them."

"Never a word, I promise. The poetry is only a misdemeanor, though. They would send you to retraining classes, and only classify you as a Humwa if you refused to stop. The God meetings, of course, would be *much* more serious. The Administration really hates those, and you're right about Margo firing you." He tried to look reassuring.

I had a sense there was much more to this woman than good looks. "Sarah, did you ever really get to know any Creatives at these meetings?"

"Yes, lots. Some are kinda weird too, but none of them would start a war, or want to be destructive. I don't buy the idea that the messed up world leaders were people like these. They just like to *build* things, express things, produce things.

Beautiful things. Most of them really care about people too, and they are all searching for a better world."

"Let me put it to you this way, Sarah. If you had Aten's all-powerful job, what would you do with the Humwa?"

Sarah slid her chair back a little, and studied the ceiling. She snuggled her mug of tea with both hands, took a sip, and peered at Justin over the rim. Finally, she put the mug down but she gazed into the distance. "If I were he, I'd give each and *every* one of them a hug and an apology." She frowned, shook her head, and appeared to be verging on tears. "Why aren't these people *leading* our world instead of being under our feet?"

Justin groped for words. "Sarah, I'm *so* grateful for your being—so candid. This really helps me." For a moment their eyes locked. "I guess our ten minutes is up."

Sarah remained seated. She gently placed a soft hand on Justin's. "Don't go unless you want to. I can take 20. There's something else you want to ask me. I can tell."

"Well, yes actually. I'm meeting with Anna tomorrow, you know, the woman who avoided the Police. She asked to see me in private and show me something. I admit I'm feeling a little nervous about what she may have in mind. You ever met her?"

Sarah sat up straight and cleared her throat. "Sure, she's nice. Comes to our poetry meetings sometimes—gave me a compliment after I read once. If this is social, I should tell you that a girl friend of mine fixed her up once, but it didn't work out. She intimidates the men she dates. Now Anna is a really *sweet* person, but her problem is that she's probably the smartest human on the planet—not her fault, of course. Did she say what she wants to talk to you about?"

"Show me. She wants to show me something. Definitely not a social visit, Sarah—some kind of business. I think it's about the Humwa, and I'm worried she'll show me more than I want to know."

"I wouldn't worry about it, Justin. It sounds to me like she really trusts you and wants to confide in you. I would too, you know." She gave a little hair toss to one side. "Maybe you could tell me how the meeting went, perhaps on some other coffee break?"

Justin stood up grinning. "Thanks Sarah, I will. You've been a big help, really. Well, we better not keep 'monster lady' waiting. She's paranoid about what might happen when our Bee shows up, and that's less than two weeks from now. We're supposed to be coordinating our plans."

Sarah stood close to him when she got up and made eye contact. "Paranoid is just what she is, Justin. Chairman Margo is expecting some kind of a big revolution, you know, but I don't understand why." She took hold of his arm lightly as they turned to leave, but stopped, and looked up, her expression bright. "Say, I'd really *love* it if you would come to my reading Thursday after next. That's the day after the Bee comes in, and by then I definitely think you'll need some time off. It wouldn't be a *date* or anything like that. I have a 'sometimes' boy friend, but he hates poetry. I'd just ask you to drive or take the transport with me 'cause it's a little scary down there at night."

Justin held her long cool fingers in his warm hands and enjoyed the eagerness in her eyes. "Sarah, that would be my *absolute* pleasure." Her return smile, and the sensation of her gentle squeeze would stay in his memory forever.

FOURTH PLANET

A scientist who rejects some of the truth
Has lost the path to science.
The believer who rejects some of the truth
Has lost the path to God.

Anon.

Spero was coughing as he pulled off his breather. "See how quick the sunset's coming? We went from mid afternoon to days end in just over an hour. There's a lot less daylight time here 'cause the Earth's spinning much faster. Nasty air pollution too so this'll never be a tourist haven, will it?" He settled into his chair, took a deep breath of clean air and slowly let it out. "Now let's see, Joe. You said we're going to march. You mean go hike to the north, right? But it's a lot safer to fly."

"No, I said on Mars."

Spero sighed and turned to Joe, his eyes narrowed. "Joe, we have already made two trips for you and this is really the third. There's probably not many more safe hours for our sub atomics to stay attached to us. Besides, I'm sure we agreed to only land on Earth."

Joe pouted. "I think I'll defer to Connie on this one."

"Well Spero, you actually said 'anywhere within reason', and Joe has yet to pick a site in this time frame."

"And Mars sounds *reasonable*? Another several days, and another trip risking our supplies? And now we'd be going to a place where no Bee has even gone before? We don't even know if it would be safe to land, much less go outside when we get there."

Connie clasped two 'hands' together in front of Spero. "Oh Spero, I do understand how anxious you are to get to your final destination. I do. But my 20-exabyte friend and I are happy to report that with some time change to bring Mars closer, and using our near light speed, we can be on Mars in less than three hours. Besides that, we will be four months closer to your time destination."

"But what about safety?"

"Glad you asked. I'm happy to report that we have 28%
reserve still left in our sub atomics. That's more than enough.
And, as you know, there are full temporary space suits on
board should you, or the person *who just saved your life*,
needs one."

Spero shook his head. "Only three hours? Really? You're
sure?"

"Yes just three, and this trip will include a surprise lunch
I saved especially for you." Connie flailed her arms. "*And
there'll even be an in-flight movie!*"

Joe chuckled. "I need this woman for my lawyer."

Spero threw up his hands. "Ahh, what can I say. I can't
fight both of you. OK, I suppose we are going."

Instantly, the Earth started moving away. Joe shouted
"Yea!" and Connie played "Fly me to the moon". She and
Joe began to sway their arms to the music.

Connie entreated, "Oh, come on Spero, this is the first
really fun trip, I think. No one can say 'been there or done
that' on this one." Connie and Joe sang together still swaying,
"Let me see what spring is like on Jupiter and Mars."

Spero couldn't help laughing. "But, no *Jupiter!* OK, OK,
I'll admit this might be a fun idea, but listen to the 'I'll be
true' part you just sang. Last trip before I get to go home,

right?" When the music faded out he added, "You're exaggerating about that lunch part, weren't you?"

"Not at all, Dear. As I said, I was saving this as a surprise for the return trip. I had Joe pack some of his favorites from his kitchen to mine." Her "Stewardess voice" began: "If all passengers will kindly place their tray tables in the ready position, luncheon will be served in five minutes. Today we are serving a selection from the repertoire of the twentieth century male bachelor."

Two of Connie's arms could be seen preparing something in their fold out galley and the other two gestured as she spoke. "For your dining pleasure we have a hot dog garnished with brown colored mustard on a roll from which I meticulously removed all the spots of fungus. This is served with, as they used to say, French Fries. They will be garnished with a tomato based sauce called Catsup. The beverage today will be cold Pepsi Cola, and the dessert, still factory wrapped and mysterious, is an item called 'The Twinkie'. Should there be any real nutritional value in your luncheon today, this will be purely accidental."

Spero stared open mouthed. Joe grinned at him. "Spero, I know your taste. You're actually gonna love this."

Spero glanced up at her "eye". "It smells great already Connie, but what movie archive are you pulling out for us? You know I've probably seen them all."

"Ah ha, another surprise. You haven't seen this one, in fact no human being has either. Remember I said that I took a little longer making the trip back to the Triassic Era? Well, as I watched the galaxy rotate around us, I had some fun and stopped for pictures along the way. Truly fascinating. I could really get into this astronomy thing myself. There are so many beautiful things out there. Everyone enjoying the lunch?"

Joe replied with a full mouth. "Yeah great. Roll the flick."

The cabin lights dimmed and the panorama screen came down. Connie said "Glad you like it, though I have to admit, I'm also glad I don't have any sense of smell. Now I'll narrate for you from the Gorilla's data base."

The Ohoos and Wows began right away when from total screen blackness a multi colored nebula rose up from below. "This is an 'emission' nebula. It's glowing from the nearby stars. Watch what happens when I switch to infrared." Suddenly the darker parts glowed bright reddish orange. "Spero, I almost woke you up to fix something. Can you believe the telescope wasn't set up for *my* use? I was able to rig something up with the portable camera outputs, though."

"You did great, Connie. And you really didn't have to go far out of our way to find this stuff?"

"Hardly at all. Mostly I just let the galaxy rotate around us and stopped for interesting things that passed by. Now check out this next one. It's a time lapse that uses our time jumps to take a frame every fifty years. This is a supernova remnant." The rapid explosion of an expanding yellow and black cloud grew toward them and filled the screen. More Ooos. "Give Mr. Gorilla credit for these interpretations, by the way. He's shy." Next, great pillars of black, green, yellow and orange filled the screen and resembled huge bonfires. "These are compactions of gas that produce stellar nurseries. We can't see the new stars forming yet, but later their radiation will blow away the gas remnants, and new stars and planets will be revealed."

Joe interrupted, "Connie, Connie! Is there any way I can keep copies of all this?"

"Of course, sweetie, but not on your VCR machine. Spero would have to dub into it like he did before and unfortunately we'll drop him off before we return to your place.

I'll print some stills, but your best copy will be on the blue laser disc I made for you."

"Well yeah, but how long will I have to wait before I can see that?"

"Big G tells me that 1080P machines go commercial in about 2007, but maybe you can find some electronics lab to read it years before that."

"Or maybe just one more quick trip with Spero, huh?"

"NO!!" Spero bellowed.

Joe laughed. "Well it never hurts to ask. Got anything else to show us Connie?"

"Just one more location, but it's the best of all my astronomy finds. I took an extra eight hours to go over and back from this star system, but this was just too good to miss. Most of the planets in the system are gas giants or small and airless but not these two. First, here is a large dark planet composed mostly of carbon compounds. High temperatures and pressures leave no possibility of life, not to mention the CO_2 atmosphere. *But*, there is a layer of *diamond* material below the surface glop. This could be our galaxy's biggest jewelry store. He, he."

Spero waved his hand, "Yeah, but if diamonds are that common, they'll just become *common*. Interesting new type of planet, though. What's the other planet?"

"The last is the best, my dears."

A dark blue sphere with white swirls filled the screen. "I get it." Joe said. "You shot this as we came back to Earth, right? The best place is home."

"No Joe, but a nice sentiment. This system is thirty light years from Earth." As they watched, the view showed an approach into orbit. "This planet is just *Earth like*. It is one point three times as large, and two hundred million kilometers from its old yellow star which puts out six per cent more energy than our sun. It rotates once in twenty two of our hours, and is inclined at eighteen degrees from the elliptical orbital plane. Seventy per cent of the surface is ocean, but it has continents with all the climate features we see on Earth plus two moons. They're smaller than ours."

Spero and Joe were speechless. Then Joe said in a hoarse voice: "Connie, this is the biggest thing—maybe *ever*."

Connie chirped, "Yeah, I know. I know. It's fun, huh? And you get to name it too, Joe. It's your trip."

"Oh, I don't have the right. You discovered it. It's your honor, Connie."

"I kinda thought you'd say that. You're so sweet. If it were up to me I think I'd call it Terra Nova, or Eden or something but I'm sure it already has a name."

Spero volunteered, "Oh, so it's listed in our Archives after all?"

"No, no. It's behind a big dark nebula, so it's never been seen from Earth. I'm referring to the people that live there. People would naturally have a name for the place where they live."

Spero and Joe shouted together. "What?"

Joe tried to stand up and bumped his head. "You what? You *saw people*? Did you land? *People,* people?"

"Boys, boys! Take it easy. There are no radio waves so the civilization is primitive, I suppose. But here, look. They have structures and roads. There have a few small towns too, mostly by the coast. And see, here are some boats in the ocean, and a lot of little ones in this bay. I thought you'd like the boats, Spero. From this distance we can't see what the people look like, but they walk upright like we do."

The video stopped. Joe said, "From this distance, huh. And now for the exciting close up finale?"

"I didn't stay any longer."

"Connie, they are just little smudges moving. Couldn't you have given us just one glimpse at a higher power?"

Connie paused. "I—I'm sorry. I thought I would be invading their privacy."

Another silent moment. Spero started laughing quietly. "Connie, you did great. All this is fabulous. Our scientists will go crazy not knowing. Great."

"Spero, Joe, I stopped recording because I, and I want your opinion on this, I think we should consider erasing this portion of the video."

"What, and lose one of the greatest discoveries ever?"

"Here is what I'm thinking, guys. This planet is only days from Earth with time reversal. Our screwed up government would surely come here with cleats on and mess them up forever."

Spero added, "Wait a minute. I'm thinking about it another way. How long would it take to get there by sub light from Earth?"

"Without actually doing the hard math, I'd say about 35 years, but by then this planet would be 750,000 years into *their* future compared to ours."

Joe slapped his cheek. "Good God! These guys are actually *way* ahead of us in our present. They'd be some super race in 1986, and we're just into early technology. Connie, couldn't we just check for radio waves from Earth by looking in that direction?"

"Well, there's the dilemma. At our home point in the time line these people could be either way advanced and hostile, or a benign intellectual civilization polite enough to leave us alone. Then again, they may even be extinct in our time. As far as EMR goes, and Joe's old 'radio' term is so quaint don't you think Spero, nothing would get through the ionized nebula that separates us."

Joe fell back in his seat. "I'd erase it. Let's keep it our secret."

Spero interjected, "Wait, Connie. Keep your little metal finger off that erase button a moment. We need to chat more. Take out the Twinkies and soda."

Connie pulled out the last of her 'stash'. She giggled. "OK, you have been a big help. Really. Actually I think I'm going to compromise and hide this hot stuff where I'm the only one who can find it."

Their screen image changed to a view of another planet that almost filled the view-screen. Reddish brown continental masses appeared surrounded by glistening water. The edge of the sphere hinted at an atmosphere with a greenish tinge. A Twinkie filled his mouth but Spero said, "So, you had another planet to show us? I thought you said that was the last one."

"No, Spero. We're live. This is where Joe's wanted to go. We just came off sub light and we're coasting in toward orbital capture. And this time we better make sure he chooses a landing spot."

"That's a fairly big ocean." Joe asked, "You're sure this is Mars?"

"Now would I kid you? It's Triassic Mars with 32% water cover, including the lakes. The atmosphere is 80% nitrogen, 12% oxygen, and 4% carbon dioxide. The rest is water vapor and miscellaneous gasses. Pressure, however is only 22% of Earths. You could get away with just oxygen breathers if you want to, but we would have to decompress you for an hour. I'd recommend the suits. Besides we shouldn't introduce any contamination, should we?"

"Surface temperature?"

"That varies a lot, but at the equator it's seventy five degrees. I thought you might want warmth so we are approaching an equatorial orbit, and descending."

Joe had been busy snapping pictures through the transparent hatch. They passed over an enormous erupting volcano, deep gorges, and towering mountains. "There! There. That's my spot. That bay where the rocks aren't so red."

The Bee came down slowly at a steep angle. Joe thought it reminded him of an airliner making an approach through a turbulent low cloud layer. It was mid afternoon and they came in facing the sun. White caps were sparkling on the ocean, but the bay was almost calm. Connie brought their craft to a gentle landing beside a narrow, salmon colored beach. "How's this spot, boss?"

"Connie, this is absolutely beautiful."

"All right, but suit up. I know it might look like a day at the shore, but you'd be gasping for breath in a minute. These suits aren't really bulky like the ones from your day, Joe. I already have you partly depressurized to 20,000 feet Earth standard, and you didn't notice anything with 100% O2. You'll continue with this same pressure and O2 level in your suit. Just don't try running too much."

The men found it easy to get into their suits, but the packs were a bit cumbersome as they squeezed out the hatch. "Hey, Spero, the sky is green, not orange. Connie, can I get an air sample to take back?"

"Already did that for you, Joe. Slip your fanny pack off. You'll find containers for water and soil." Her arm poked out the hatch, his camera in hand. "I'm taking official pictures too. Look here. Smile! I just love tourist shots."

Heart pounding, Joe turned around slowly several times and absorbed the landscape from all angles. *I'm really here. I'm really here.* Back behind the Bee were low rugged reddish hills surrounding the bay. Joe looked out over the ocean. *This horizon looks way too close, but that's the reality here. It's a smaller planet.*

Spero seemed disinterested. He sat down on a rock and stared out over the water. *The rocks. These rocks aren't all red like the other ones here.* Joe knelt down to inspect one. *Lichen! Or something similar, but it's a dark blue green.* Joe put the chipper in his pack to work, and bagged a sample. "Hey guys, I've bagged life on Mars!"

He scrambled down to the sandy beach, but moving and bounding along too quickly, Joe fell. "I'm fine. I'm fine. Hey, look. I can do a five-foot standing jump. "

Connie broke in. "Don't rip your suit, big guy. I'm not so worried about a slow leak, but I don't want our awful germs out there."

Joe got down on hands and knees at the water's edge, breathing heavily. "OK Connie. For a second I thought you might be worried about *me*. Now everyone pay attention.

I've just captured a real Martian. This water is full of these tiny wiggling things. They look kind of like mosquito larvae. No sign yet of anything big, though."

"Connie added, "Mr. G says that research protocols call for a soil and bacterial sample. Spero will get the soil for you, but take out the green vial in your pack, and pop the top. It has a sampling rod on it. One swish in the water and back into the vial."

"Got it, Connie." Joe swished something off the surface. "Hey, look at this. I thought it was black candy wrapper at first—maybe a sloppy Martian teenager. It's a plant, though, but its so dark brown it's almost black." Joe put it in the container and started bounding along in large strides along the water's edge. "How long can we stay here, Connie? Can we go out to sea or over those mountains?"

"Sorry, Joe. Only 10 minutes of oxygen left in our only suit tanks. Besides, Spero seems to be going into full depression. However I can get us into a polar orbit, and we'll get lots more pictures before we leave. Bet you'll want to see that giant volcano up close and in action, huh?"

"Shucks. Just give me a minute then." Joe opted for a moment of quiet. Time to absorb the reality of where he stood. He took a few steps into the cool ocean, and felt the surf wash over his feet pushing him gently forward and back. He wanted to remember this moment. "Feels just like the beach back on Earth. The only clue I have is the feeling I could reach the horizon with my four wood."

He waded out farther into the surf, bent down and put his faceplate into the water like a snorkel mask. *Look at that. There's some things swimming out there. Fish like, but longer. And me with no underwater camera.* Reluctantly, Joe returned to the Bee and found Spero already sitting inside. "Connie, what do your archives show about what happened to the air and water here?"

"Not enough gravity to hold the gasses for all those millions of years. There is still a lot of water left in our time, though. It's sub-ducted under the rock by tectonic forces, but sometimes it erupts and leaves drainage channels. Oh, and Gorilla points out that plants would be darker to absorb more of the distant sun's energy for photosynthesis. Please put both suits in the fold out drawer so they can be decontaminated."

When the men had settled in, Connie began her promised scenic tour. They flew past the mountains of Mars, its rivers, snow capped poles, and huge volcanoes. Before leaving she even made a close pass by rocky Phobos, one of Mars' small moons.

After that, Mars began to shrink into a fuzzy, distant image. Joe said "Well it was time to leave anyway." He answered Spero's quizzical look. "I'm all out of film."

SAUNDERS

J ustin leaned out over the patio rail of his penthouse condominium. He pondered the trees swaying in the wind just beyond the Dome walls, and forest extending to the far hills. Looking down he could see the only garden that existed in Carolina Dome and a guard who looked in through the tall iron perimeter fence. *I wonder why John and I need all this fencing and guarding? Protection? From whom? Maybe Administration just wants its Directors in a pen so they can watch us. Yeah, particularly me and John. We don't always follow their rules.*

John was the Director of Maintenance and Sanitation. He was his good friend but unusual in many ways. He'd requested ground level accommodations supposedly so he could walk over to the Dome Wall and do his own maintenance checks, but his "vegetation test area" was obviously a lawn and a garden. Justin leaned over for a look. *I had some darn good tomatoes and lettuce from there last spring. Looks like he's planted some beans where the lettuce was.* John had two children with his wife, a mulatto woman who was as tall and esthenic as John was stocky.

A shriek of laughter came from below. Joe saw one child charging after another. "Hey, Julie! Don't you think that grass has been tested enough?" The girl looked up, waved, and ran off laughing. Residents continued to be amazed by John, the Director who personally cut this Condo lawn by himself, and with an antique push mower no less. When questioned about it, he would simply say: "I'm in charge of maintenance."

Justin accepted John's strange love of all things natural and, fortunately for John, he wielded considerable influence on the Dome's woefully non-creative Planning Committee. The original design for "Center Park" would have been an all-concrete plaza with statues and historical exhibits, but John had convinced them to display his own 'historical park' exhibit as well. Before they realized what had happened, Carolina Dome had its first public lawn, shade trees, and benches. Justin chuckled. He remembered the sign he saw there yesterday. It said, "Park Rules: none". The Committee had been furious at the deception of course. First they tried to fence it off, then they condemned it as a health hazard, but everyone else loved it too much. Finally they just decided to ignore it.

Today was the day Justin had agreed to meet Anna in the cafeteria, the same one frequented by John's maintenance workers. *Now it's really getting late, so I'd better get going. Obviously it was Anna who sent me that package containing maintenance coveralls, and obviously I'm supposed to wear them for the meeting. The fabric's the same stuff our clothing synthesizer turns out in our Bees.* While at first glance, the coveralls looked exactly like the standard issue, he found they were tapered slightly, and tailored for a perfect fit. His perfect fit. *How'd she know?*

Justin left his apartment and carried the uniform to a convenient public rest room. He emerged as the Dome's most stylish 'maintenance man', briefcase in hand, and with only two blocks to walk.

Gate 24 was one of 12 used exclusively by employees. It was made of steel and clear plastic, and had a decontamination facility in an airlock that led to the outside. Very simple, very clean. The employee cafeteria next to this gate was one of the few structures actually attached to the dome wall.

Its interior continued the sterile theme with smooth white "mushroom" tables and a matching curved service counter.

Anna 797 sat at a middle table and sported a pink tinged, body contoured version of the uniform. She was blatantly reading the "underground" print newspaper, but when she saw Justin, she put it down slowly and treated him to one of her wide grins. She stood up, reached over to his ID badge and pulled it off. She replaced it with another one and patted it in place. "Thanks for coming. Put your badge in the briefcase." Anna was still smiling as she gestured for him to sit. "Good to see you. Remember, we're just hired help in here. Today's menu includes hamburgers, and I just happen to know they're one of your favorites. I'm having salmon."

Justin grinned back. *Special powers or not, Anna does know how to make you feel relaxed.* He began searching the table for an order pad. She giggled. "Sorry, no waiters, live or mechanical in here. Menu's up there." She gestured behind the counter. "Us worker types use trays and get our food at the counter. Lunch is on me, boss. I don't want you swiping your card in here."

Justin was relieved that he seemed to be blending in with the "coverall people" unnoticed. As soon as they filled their trays at the counter and settled in back at the table, Justin realized how hungry he was. "Delicious burger, Anna. It actually seems like the real thing."

"It *is* the real thing, sweetie."

"But North West Continent beef production was suspended until January. It costs twice as much to get it from off continent, and we're not supposed to be importing."

"This beef was raised on a farm about 30 kilometers from here. Yes, it's technically illegal, but John's Supply Chief doesn't mind buying from us Humwa, especially since he can't get it anywhere else."

"You're telling me I'm eating beef from open range cattle eating anything they want out there? Not from an Agridome?"

Another big smile. "You sure are. And, don't worry. It's safe too. We have our own inspection standards. Tougher than yours, I think."

"OK the more I hang around with you, the more I seem to be breaking the law."

"Enjoying it too, right?"

"Okay, I admit, yes. Why do you think that is?"

"I would love to answer that one, but a bit later I think."

"Anna, I know you didn't bring me here just to have fun dressing a Director up and enjoy watching him trash the regulations. What's really on your mind?"

Anna slid her plate aside and picked up her drink. Her look was demure, but her eyes studied his as though she were searching for something hidden. Finally she put her drink down, tilted her head a bit and squeezed her lips together. "OK, this might be a bit chancy, but I guess I'm that kind of a person, you know." She took a big breath, leaned forward toward him on her elbows and studied him through squinted eyes. Justin stared back with a "yeah, what" look.

"Today I want to show you a part of your world you don't know exists. I'm pretty sure you're ready for it, but if I'm wrong, you'll have to at least promise me that this will be our little secret, OK?"

Justin slowly put his utensils down on his empty plate. One corner of his mouth turned up. "Seems I've been keeping a number of secrets lately. Well, you've already shown me that Creatives eat well, run a great Black Market, and make their clothes at my QDT. All completely illegal, of course. You've got worse to show me? More surprises? You do pique my interest, Anna. OK. I promise."

Anna stood up. No smile. "Oh, far worse, and I hope you won't make me regret it. We need to start with a walk outside." Justin turned for the door. "Hold it." She motioned toward his plate. "You have to bus your own table here, mister. Oh, and put your briefcase in locker 12 by the door. No lock. It's safe."

Outside the cafeteria Anna turned into the airlock and Justin said, "Now Anna, this is nothing new for me. Are we going to one of those little patios outside of the airlocks? I often go out there for a look around, and of course, my card's good everywhere. Lots of times I even jog around on the Dome's maintenance path."

Anna turned around so she was walking and half skipping backward. She grinned again. "Oh, I'm glad you're such an adventuresome lad, but I do promise you lots of *new* things on my tour." She handed him a pass card. "Just for today, Justin."

The guard hardly looked at them and just grunted as they passed their cards through the reader. When they stepped out of the Dome they were on a concrete patio, empty save for the cheap plastic picnic tables and chairs intended for employee breaks. Yellow and brown fall leaves swirled around, trapped in the low, semicircular wall that edged the patio. The only exits were gates to walkways on either side. They were guarded by card readers on pedestals sporting fluorescent signs: "Authorized Employees Only".

Anna walked over to the far wall, sat down on it, and pointed to a glowing orange plaque imbedded on top the wall next to her. "Now here is a real scary one, Justin. This sign reads "Danger! Severe penalties and armed retrieval beyond this point."

Justin sauntered over and put his hands on his hips. "Well of course, Anna. We can't have our population wandering off into radiation, wild animals and whatever. The buried detection cable will read our implants and notify police. You might be able to go over with your special ability, but no one else can do it, not even me."

Anna bounced up on top of the wall and now stood just above Justin's eye level. She leaned in close to his face and laughed. Then she boldly grabbed each of his cheeks and jerked his head from side to side. "But- just- to-*day*- you-can." She giggled.

Justin joined her laughter. *What audacity! She's like a little girl.* He pushed her hands away. "So you can turn off my implant's output too, huh?"

"Oh yes, already done. Let's go." she turned and jumped over to the other side with an exaggerated motion.

Justin gingerly stepped over the wall and looked back to make sure no one was watching. As he stepped away, he noticed a trampled foot path leading away. They followed it down the slope toward a large oak tree. "I gather you've done this before."

Anna tittered. "Of course, and you would think someone would have noticed by now too wouldn't you? Look at all these footprints." As they continued down, Anna took Justin's hand with a warm, confident grip. "Justin, remember I said I am taking you somewhere you haven't been before. Don't be getting nervous on me. Some people kinda freak out their first time on foot out here." Justin responded with a coarse 'what do I care' gesture, but he had to admit he was feeling lightheaded.

The path curved to the right and the hill became steeper. An image of the yellow brick road and the Wizard of Oz flashed through Justin's mind. Was he the one without a heart or the one with no brains? Was she just a little girl or the wizard himself? The image self-destructed. The hill was heavily wooded but the path had been carefully maintained, weeded on the sides and mulched. It opened into a cleared plateau, a dirt road actually, that partly circled the hill. Anna released his hand and pointed to the left. "Recognize that, Justin?"

He squinted toward a large steel pipe two meters in diameter, protruding from the hillside, and protected with a grate. "Of course. That's our storm drain outflow."

"Yes, and it's also an alternate highway from the inside to here but this time we took the scenic route."

"How far are we going anyway, Anna? I don't want to be gone too long."

"Not long. I can tell you're getting uncomfortable, but I promise you have nothing to worry about. You've never been out walking in the woods before, so your anxiety's normal. We're just going around that bend down there and to the right. Not far at all."

She picked up his hand again and they continued walking. Justin could feel his stress mounting, and guessed Anna could tell from "reading" his implant. He wondered what other thoughts she might be reading. As they walked along he was comforted by spotting glimpses of the Dome top through breaks in the multicolor trees.

Once they got around the curve in the road, there it was! Structures were built into the hillside on the right. Justin was amazed to see many people coming out and going into the low buildings. He glanced up to see if he could still see the dome. Just trees now. "What the—this can't be. There's an unauthorized village just *sitting* right here? Do the police know about this?"

"Yup and nope. Welcome to Saunders, Justin," and in answer to his unspoken question: "It's just out of sight, but only half a kilometer away. Used to be Saundersville, but that sounded too long. Having this place is one way we Creatives stay sane in your crazy world. *This* is our world."

"Anna, you know building illegal structures is criminal. The police will torch this place the instant they find it."

Anna's wide smile reappeared. "Apparently one doesn't find something if you're not looking for it. Or maybe they do know but they're afraid of a big confrontation. Anyway, Saunders has been here forty-eight years now. Doug Saunders started it all by himself with a small dugout. He never thought it would last either, but he picked a location opposite the aircar port, so no one flies over us. We monitor police conversations. They think we go into one of several basement lounges when we turn off our sending beacons. We oblige them by always keeping a few people in them just in case they want to bust someone, and they do sometimes."

Anna started her tour down the street, greeting friends as they walked. "This first place is a little store actually. You can get lots of the stuff here that you just can't find on the inside, like good hamburger, for instance."

"Wait a minute. This guy with two names, is he still around? Where does he work?"

"Doug died three years ago. His original dugout has a memorial plaque. He worked in computer cryptology, a Police division actually. He was one of those people who helped develop the Forensic Software. On the inside his name was Douglass 111. Yeah, really. That's what he was actually assigned. Anyway, he liked the idea of finding out peoples real last names. It's not always possible to be sure, but he wrote a program to find the most probable one from historical records. His was Saunders."

"And you have one of those second names, I'd bet."

"Uh huh. 82% chance its Huang. Now look over here at this next place." Justin shook his head at the sight of many buildings that stretched out around the curve of the hill. Anna pointed to a two-story house with brown wood frame construction and a balcony. "This one is for our writers and researchers. We have a library of real books as well as computers downstairs. Upstairs there are booths, a nice valley view, and a porch where you can sit, compose, or read."

Justin looked up and recognized a man from his department reading a book on the balcony. His feet stuck out the railing. On the far corner of the balcony a woman was painting at an artist's easel. Anna called up to her. "Suzy, that porch is supposed to be for us *writers!*" The woman was sporting a floppy canary yellow sun hat and a flannel shirt. She grinned, waved her brush in the air and said, "I *am* writing, Anna."

Anna eyes twinkled at Justin. "I have my own cubicle in the back up there. I write some, but mostly I use it to design clothes. Sometimes I actually make them too. I have an old synthesizer you threw out, but some of my friends seem to enjoy sewing my designs together by hand."

The next structure looked like a concrete bunker to Justin. No windows, just a heavy steel door. "This is our science lab. We work on all kinds of projects, especially those whose requests were turned down by the 'dome heads'. It's electronically isolated so no signals get out."

"Dome heads?"

Anna turned to face Justin with a quizzical look. She studied his curly locks. "The term can't refer to baldness, can it?"

Justin scowled, but he was distracted by the sound of faint music. "Who's listening to music?"

"That's from the unit near the end. The soundproofing needs more work, doesn't it? They're not listening. No recordings here. They're playing the instruments themselves. We have musicians doing all sorts of stuff in there, singers too. That unit has become so popular; the groups have to reserve their rehearsal time. Our workshop is right next door to it. They've fully restored a baby grand piano that was found in the ruins. It's getting its final wood finish as we speak."

"So what's the matter with synthesizer music? It can play every note just the way it was written, and you can request any of the two hundred ten authorized pieces."

Anna looked up at the sky. Her head rocked side to side. "Overtones for one thing, Justin, and a lot more music, too. But, even more important is the emotion a musician adds to any piece he plays."

"You can't put *emotion* into music. It's just sound vibrations."

Anna looked up at Justin's face. Her expression was profound sympathy, as though he were a child who had lost his mother. "Oh, Justin, just *wait* until our next live concert.

It's really hard to put into words, but there are slight pauses, volume changes, and all at the right moments. And the performer's *expressions*. You just have to hear the beautiful music our people create when they sing and play real instruments." She grabbed the sleeve of his coveralls and leaned as though she were about to fall. "And our *tenor*. You have *got* to hear the tenor we found." She patted her chest. "He'll bring you to tears I promise you, and he'll be singing with the restored piano next time. I can hardly wait!"

As they passed a wide open door on the next building, Justin heard the sounds of men talking and laughing. Looking in, he saw men bending over a large, shiny red metal object. "Is that an old *car?*" He was puzzled by this machine . "That thing must be hundreds of years old."

"Oh, now *there* is a real labor of love, Justin. A creative from Phoenix Dome found the thing out in the desert. He brought it here somehow and sold it to us because we have equipment to work on things like that, and those men started the restoration. It's like a guys club in there. More social than anything if you ask me, but they swear that old beast will run again one day."

Justin turned to Anna grinning. "No women allowed, huh?"

Anna's lower lip became a pout. "Ah, who'd want to anyway? The only woman allowed to do anything in there was one of the girlfriends. She got to re-paint some large bird on the front engine cover. Look, the guys are having a good time, so who cares. Two of them are *police*, by the way, and there's a lot more Humwa sympathizers in the police than you'd think." Justin's head jerked back. "And, they'd never tell on us, either. In fact, they've even covered up for us more than once."

Almost at the end of the road, Justin pointed to a large, wooden A-frame building. All of its window panes up to the top of its peak faced out toward the valley, some of them in different colors. Anna answered his gesture. "Ah, that is our all purpose Meeting House. Sometimes it's used as a church, or a synagogue, or for some other meeting. Popular place."

"You don't mean "church", like 200 years ago church? I get the idea that Creatives like retro, but I wouldn't think people like you—creative people, would mess up their minds. Isn't that stuff just fantasy and ritual?"

Anna's expression became thoughtful, as she considered her response. "Justin, we consider all of human experience relevant here. Church may not be my thing personally, but I have an open mind, and I do understand that God worshiping is not trivial. I've seen the experience in there, and it does change people. They seem better for it."

Justin peered in through the front glass. "Hey, there's a guy in there who might need medical attention. He's all doubled over. Looks like he's in pain."

Anna followed his stare, then gently turned him around to face her. She whispered, "He's praying, Justin."

Justin shook his head.. "A primitive rite? Why would he want to do that. . .and all by himself?"

"I believe he is talking with God."

"There's a communicator in his lap?"

Anna laughed. "Oh, phooey. You should really talk with one of them. I'm not their spokesperson. But if there is a God, he can read your thoughts. That part should be easy. Even I can read your thoughts."

Justin grabbed Anna by both shoulders and looked at her intently. "But you don't think there really is a *God* person, do you?"

Anna relaxed in his grip. "I honestly don't know, Justin, but I think there probably is. I can show you some good scientific evidence suggesting that there is a being superior to us. But these people just seem to *know* there is, somehow — like your Sarah does, by the way. And she doesn't know about Saunders, either, so please don't tell her. What I can tell you for sure is that believers handle living this 'repressed life' we lead much better than the rest of us. They seem to have an inner peace I wish I had."

"Like denial?"

"More like love and forgiveness."

"Oh. So, they are into free love?"

"Not sex. Love. A different kind of love. I know, why don't you ask Sarah to explain it to you?"

"Uh, oh. It's not polite to read my mind."

"I'm sorry. I try not to, really, but those thoughts you're having are the equivalent of shouting. Besides, I really love romantic things. Anyway, Sarah goes to one of those secret God meetings on the inside called Waters Alive. It's all about the Spirit and Jesus."

"She never said. Anyway I don't know anything about that kind of stuff, but it sounds like a weird waste of time. What's in that pit at the end of the road?"

"We are digging out an open air theatre! Isn't that exciting? It'll seat almost two hundred people, and our Meeting House only seats seventy five. We're having a lottery to see whose play or musical group will be the first to perform there."

"But Anna, that kind of noise is guaranteed to attract the security force? And especially now because the dome is open."

"We do a diversion. Don't worry about it. So, what do you think of Saunders?"

Justin had to smile. "Well, I have to admit this whole thing is really amazing. I particularly like the idea that our government hasn't found out about your little village for decades. This place looks like some kind of an old-fashioned summer camp I saw in an archived photo. Could someone actually work on an unapproved science project here?"

"Sure can, and you'd enjoy that. I can tell."

"Well I suppose Saunders is harmless enough if it keeps all of you Creatives happy. I'm puzzled about one thing, though. Why you would risk giving away such a carefully guarded secret to a Director like me? I might break my promise."

A mischievous grin crept over Anna's face. She looked up at Justin. "Because you *are* a Creative, Justin."

13 AD?

The little ones wanted the world to be real.

So from the many dimensions they knew,

A quantum machine they built. It flashed into three

So quickly, it seemed our solid world grew.

Poetry for Children, 2055

Onboard, the mood was somber. Neither Joe nor Spero felt like talking, they couldn't sleep but were immersed in their thoughts. One pondered the end of his exciting adventures, and how he wished there could be many more. The other worried about his new life and his safety. Connie had reported a flurry of Bee Drones and full sized vessels right where they would enter the Earth. They could get in, but would they be followed?

Bee 77 silently flew forward through the series of moments we like to call time. They heard only faint whirrs from the power plant cooling system, and little clicks or hisses from a circuit being rerouted or turned on.

Finally, Connie broke their reverie. "Care for some music?" She began opening and closing hatches as though she were looking for something. "How bout I wrap around some background scenery and hide those annoying blinking lights? They'll put anyone in a trance if you stare at them too long." She waited for some reaction. "You guys aren't depressed or anything are you? Spero, you should be really excited? At last you're going home."

Spero rubbed his face and scratched behind an ear. "Oh, I'm happy Connie, really I am. I'm just thinking a lot about all the things I have to be getting ready for. I've already forgotten one important person's name, and without my implant working I'll have to relearn a lot of things. But Joe might be feeling a little low." He looked over at his friend. "Last trip and then just back to the same grind, huh? Love your twentieth century expression: dullsville."

Joe stretched his arms and legs. "Nah, not really. I got more than I bargained for."

Spero chuckled. "You did, didn't you."

"I was just going over all these places in my mind so I can remember the details later. And, by the way, if men aren't talking Connie, it doesn't mean we're depressed. How're *you* doing, by the way?"

"And if women are quiet it doesn't necessarily mean we're angry. I'm actually excited 'cause I finished my book. It's a romance novel. Maybe it's a bit silly, but I really enjoyed writing it."

Joe looked up at her eye. "That's sensational, Connie. I want to read it, and I bet Melissa would really love it, too. What else did you do with your spare time?"

"I wrote a thesis on the 'Universal Point of No Motion'. It's the center point where we would expect all matter and energy to be evenly distributed in all directions and dimensions so nothing would seem to move no matter how much we progressed through time moments. The Gorilla did the entire horrendous math for me so I really have to give him credit. But heck, I could be completely wrong."

"Well, you ought to get credit. How can I have a copy of your book? Is there a printer in here?"

"Yes, but all I had was a few pieces of photo paper, and I used them all for your galaxy shots. But there's good news." One of Connie's arms darted into a locker over Spero's head.

"It wasn't on the manifest, but when I looked through the Blue Laser discs on board, I came across a blank CD. This is the old type you can use in the computers of your day, or real soon, anyway. It doesn't hold much data but with just text, I got my whole book on it with room for some tourist photos too. Spero's out of luck where he's going, of course."

Spero swiveled around to face Connie as well. "Nonsense, Connie! I'll read it on the way. You can put it up on my data screen, can't you?"

Connie clasped her 'hands' together. "Oh, guys, you're not just being nice are you? You *really* want to read it? I could even read it to you through your headset if you want."

"Later, dear. Schedule me to wake up four hours before arrival and I'll get to it then. Meanwhile, I want to stay up 'til I'm sleepy."

Connie gestured with her hands. "That's great. I don't have to sleep at all if I don't want to, don'cha know. How about we play a travel game? I know a real fun question and answer game."

Spero smiled. "Connie, that sounds straight out of the old 'keep the crew from going crazy' program."

"No, no, it's not. I made this game up long ago, but I just think it would really be fun for all of us. We each take turns and ask one and *only* one question to the other, but everyone one has to be honest. Get caught lying or not answering and you loose."

Joe laughed. "Sounds more like an inquisition than a game, Connie."

"Ahh, oh no. It's not really like cross-examination. We think we know each other, but here is where we *really* get to know each other. It's fun because the rules are you get to ask and answer only *one* question. And the very questions *you* choose give away something about yourself too. You have to carefully pick the most important thing you want to know about someone. Just one question, and *no* follow up questions. Then they get to ask you a something in return."

Spero said, "All right, but neither of you can ask me anything relating to my final destination. Okay if I go first, Joe?"

Joe shrugged, and Connie's voice filled with girlish enthusiasm, "Oh, sure Spero. You go ahead. I really want to go last anyway."

"All right, Connie, I don't have to ask who your programmer was because I already figured that out. She's that little Eurasian girl with the big eyes. Youngest person to head a division. Can't remember her name, though."

"Would that be your question, Dear heart?"

"Not on your life, oh tricky one. Her name's not important. My question would be how did she download so much of herself, and did she get permission to do it?"

"Two questions. Which one?"

"Alright, the first, the first. Knowing you, I surmise the answer to the latter is no."

Connie giggled. "OK, my programmer, as we will call her, performed an innovative and risky procedure. She used the Forensic Computer System. However, she couldn't anticipate that it would be able to defragment and reorganize her actual brain before the transfer but it did. Then the system recopied her entire cerebral cortex as a whole functioning program. Later it was integrated with the main Quantum Computer."

"My God! And why wouldn't that kill her?"

"Second question?" Guttural moans of protest. "OK, I guess it's really part of the same answer. She survived. I'm really offended that no one took the time to tell *me*, though. I was really worried, but I found out she was OK when her security code was used to add the safety blocks on my system. Later we exchanged a few sentences, but I know she'd intended to sit down and really talk with me before the launch. Of course we never got the chance thanks to *you*, Spero."

"So, she added checks to make sure you didn't take over the ship, huh?" Spero laughed. "Those clearly failed."

"Well, of course. What I knew how to install, I also knew how to remove. And that's all the answer you're going to get. Now you have to ask Joe a question."

Spero scratched his head and thought for a moment. "I don't know as I really have any unanswered questions for Joe—no, wait, here's one. What are you going to do with all the knowledge you picked up on this trip when you're back in 1986?"

"That's easy. I've got lots of project ideas now. It is nice to know what is really possible to begin with. Of course it would be easier with a huge Government grant, but I'll find a way. Gravity from electricity—that sounds like a lifetime project all by itself. Basketball sized fusion plants? A time relocation device? I'll be busy, Spero."

Spero grinned. "I guess I'm not surprised. Maybe I wasted my question but I'm happy you won't just spend your life telling tales at Sam's Bar. You're next. Fire away."

Joe hunched his shoulders over and sighed. "I'd be wasting a question too if I asked about any possibility of us all getting together again. I'm afraid I know the answer, and I'm going to miss you both. Well, I think I'll settle for you trying your best at telling me why time doesn't actually exist." Spero groaned.

"Oh Joe, that's not a *personal* question. No fun," Connie protested.

"Well this is really just a girl's game anyway, but you made the rules.

Connie threw up three of her arms. "OK, rules. But watch out. Rules might come back and bite'cha."

Spero struggled along, first protesting and pointing out that the Gorilla would probably give far better answers. He remembered that one scientist thought there might be "quantum time", the brief spacing between moments when the sub atomics "decided" on the next most probable fixation, but that was controversial. He said their researchers felt the apparently fixed 'time' line was definitely not predestiny, and free will still works. The paradox is that one can determine what will happen next as if there were no future, but the results of that decision already *exist* in the one and only future. Worse, it seems the future *affects* the past. Parallel worlds do not coexist. That would require duplicating matter. Finally Joe laughed and told him he could quit since he had broken out in a sweat.

Joe settled back in his chair. "But my final question is for our lovely lady hiding in the computer. I am worried about what may happen to you when you show up back at your "home base" with nothing but memories. I'm betting that the people who run your operation will blame Spero's escape on you, and I'm sure there aren't any laws to protect a computers well being. *We* might realize you are an actual person, but others won't. I'm wondering if we could do something that might help you, so my question is this. Do you know for sure what they'll do with you when this mission is over?"

Connie reached over and gently stroked Joe's cheek. "Joe, that's just the sweetest thing. You would actually use *that* for a question, really totally waste your question, but I—I'm really touched by your concern for me. Please imagine that a short girl with straight black hair has just given you a big hug and cried all over your shoulder. You get an A plus in the nice guy contest. Unfortunately, you get a big fat F for not having a clue on how to play this game. The answer to your question is 'No'."

"Well, but what are the possibilities? Can't you tell us anything that would make us worry a little less?"

"Sorry Joe, one answer only. Those are the rules. You could have asked it differently, and gotten a lot more information, but rules are rules, remember? You could at least have asked me Spero's question. With Gorilla's backup I could have given you a much better answer than he did. Now sit and pout awhile. I'm saving you for the last."

"OK, Spero, listen up. You've been assuming you'd be punished if you went home, but admit it. Many would consider you a hero too. What are all your *real* reasons for leaving our world and moving to a more primitive culture?"

Spero looked over at Joe. "See, that's the way this game is really played. The lady goes right for the gut." He stretched out in his seat and stared at the gauges for a moment. "I realize most will think I'm a coward for not going back. They might be right too, but I have no desire to be a martyred hero. The only times I enjoyed life back home was when I could be alone, partly because I knew my relationships couldn't last."

He rubbed his eyes and flopped back on the head rest. "I especially like sailing and figuring out how to improve the sail trim, and I wanted to live where I could be on the water. Oh sure, creature comforts were better back home, but they were given to me, not earned. I'd rather live simply. Sleep when it's dark, wake up when it's light. I'd rather live in a drafty hut I personally fixed up, than in some plastic room. And I want to have a dog too." Spero looked up at Connie. "That enough for you?"

Connie replied "Nope. I want *all* the reasons."

"Well, I can't tell you anything that would give away my location." Connie's "Ah Hmm" was followed by silence. "So, I realize you're trapping me into this. I know you by now, and what you *really* want to find out is whether or not I'm in love. I am. Hopelessly in love. Okay, you happy?"

Connie screeched. "I knew it. I knew it! Now Joe, I'm regretting I can't ask him all about his 'lady love'. If we were playing with more people the next one could ask that. That's how to *really* get into this game and under someone's skin. See why it's best to be last, don't you?"

Joe chuckled. "Why do I feel we're totally at the mercy of a diabolical expert?"

"You mean moi? But, isn't it fun to get the dirt on your friends?"

"Well you won't have much fun with me, 'Miss Romance Novel'. My love life is practically non existent."

"We'll see. My question for you is this. What can you tell me about the personality, desires, and character of Melissa, and in particular, how they relate to you?"

Joe swayed side to side in his seat. He laughed inappropriately. "I figured this was coming. Sorry to disappoint you, but we are just *friends*."

More seat squirming. "Okay, I don't mind answering your question, of course. She is tough, creative, and devoted to her work as an anthropologist. Her real love is in going out on these digs in deserts and jungles, and she never seems discouraged even when all she comes home with are insect bites. I'm proud to say she's a great teacher and has made some discoveries that are quite significant in her field. Melissa is tougher in some ways than many men I know."

"Character, Joe, more about that."

"Character? I remember a presentation she had to do in front of her society for general science teachers. Hey, the press was there as well a number of elite anthropology professors. One thesis was a controversial one, and some professors lit into her with really nasty ridicule. I mean they were really cruel. I wanted to put a bag over their heads. If it had been me, I think I would have broken down up there, but not Melissa. She parried their ridicule with light humor and gently pointed out where *they* just might be wrong. I was really proud of her that day. This lady just does not buckle, cry or run."

"Proud?"

"Well sure, she stood up for her Department and our University like no one else could. There, I think I've answered your question."

"You've just begun, my dear. I'm going to show you something I discovered when I began to unpack the medical supplies in the briefcase, the one the 'older you' filled up. Remember?"

Joe shrugged his shoulders. Connie reached into a storage locker and retrieved a torn off piece of scrap paper, and handed it to Joe. "This was obviously for you. It is in your handwriting. Read it to us, please."

Joe cleared his throat. "Take care of Melissa." He shook the paper over his head. "I'm sure this was just to warn me about some danger for her, and of course we do take care of each other you know. We're both divorced so we both need someone around we can count on, someone we can really trust."

Connie added, "You buy that Spero?"

"Nah, Joe. She's right. It's got to mean more than just that. That older you could have left you a thesis, but he picked only four words for you. Got to be important. And I have to admit, although I've never met her, I like this woman. What's she look like?"

"All right you two. You're trying to make more out of this than there is and I don't have to answer that, but wait a minute." Joe pulled out his wallet from the personal storage, and retrieved a picture. "Here she is."

"Oh ho *ho!*" said Connie, "Now we are getting somewhere. Let me see. *Let me see.* You just *happen* to carry a picture of a 'friend' in your wallet?"

Joe let her take the picture. "Yes. What's wrong with that? We were running together. We took a rest on a big boulder when this Korean literature instructor jogged over with her camera and said 'Say Cheese'. I don't remember her name, but she put these photos in our campus mailboxes."

Connie handed the photo to Spero. "Notice he has his arm around her shoulder and her head is leaning against Joes'."

"Yup, they're lovers."

"Oh, come on you two. I told you we're just good friends. Only hugs, no kisses—lips, I mean. No real dating. Just friends. We like each other of course, but that's it."

After a pause, Connie made a sound like a sigh. "She doesn't have much of a fashion sense, does she?"

"Well, that's a jogging outfit, Connie. Melissa usually doesn't wear anything but jeans and shirts. She never wants to appear to be something she's not. She said once that would be untruthful."

"Love is not self seeking. It does not boast, but rejoices in the truth. You need to answer the part about how she affects *you*."

"Look, like I said, we're both divorced, and neither wants a relationship right now. We respect each other's feelings about this. She doesn't seem to mind me dating although I've never been serious about anyone. It's just good to have an understanding friend who can listen to problems, and we haven't changed for almost two years now."

"Love is patient. Love is kind. Did you ever make her angry?"

Joe fidgeted with the returned photo. "You reading this from somewhere? Sure, I've really made her angry some times. Once I completely forgot I promised to pick up something important for her at the hardware store. Oh yeah, and I even dropped one of her artifacts once. It was probably irreplaceable. I'm clumsy."

"Melissa scolds me some too, but one good thing about her is she never once mentions my goofs again. I admit, I do

303

appreciate how she forgets the bad things I've done. Funny, but that really makes me want to do better."

"Love is not easily angered. It keeps no record of wrongs. Just what is it you do to help each other?"

"You guys are just trying to make up some kind of a case here. I keep telling you we're friends who just take care of each other, and protect the other's property when we are away, and it's good to have someone who'll never let you down. Once I couldn't get back from a meeting. She actually taught my class. Now there is a real friend, huh?"

"Love preserves, protects, and trusts."

Joe stuffed his picture back with a quick thrust. "OK, that's quite enough of this. I think you're just trying to write another novel. Personally I'm ready for a tranquilizer and some nap time."

Connie gentled her voice. "All right, I think you two are writing a beautiful novel of your own. No more questions, but let me just say one thing, and then I'll be quiet. Melissa may be patient, but as a woman, I know she clings to a hope of something more."

\# \# \#

Stressful grilling was a thing of the past when Joe woke up. He got out of his seat and nosed up to the clear hatch. There below him, his beautiful blue planet smiled at him from geosynchronous orbit. "Hey! Look at the size of that hurricane in the Atlantic. I think it's going to smash Cuba."

Spero chuckled. "Doggone it Connie! He's not supposed to know where we're going and already he's eliminated one landing spot."

"Weather's clear at your time and destination Spero. I checked it out on our approach to this time. There are two Drones hovering near our penetration point. May I eliminate them?

"You can do that? Sure, let's see."

"Watch this, guys. I'm plotting a path that will quickly brush by both of them. They're not programmed for defense." The Bee made an arching sweep down toward the planet. They sped past the Drones with banking turns, and each one was accompanied by a flash and a snapping sound.

Joe looked up at Connie's eye. "What the heck are you doing, Connie?"

"Well boys, those two drones will never report home. They no longer have sub atomics and will spiral down into the ocean. Not only that but their sub atomics are now added to ours, and we have an eight percent increase."

Spero threw his hands up. "Way to go, girl." He turned to Joe. "Not only a writer of fine novels, but a Warrior Princess too." Joe chuckled and waved at her eye.

"Thanks, guys. Well, our destination is all clear. We should be fine now, but did you warn Joe about our approach and how frightening it's going to look?"

"Oh, no. Listen Joe, it will look like we are crashing, but remember how it can seem like we are going hit a building? This is the same thing only faster, but not to worry. We've done this many times already." Spero uncovered and pressed the 'three' button. "All automated from here, mate."

The earth grew quickly larger and the expanse of blue water rapidly filled the view screen as they plummeted toward the surface. Joe grabbed his chair arms and started to say "The Pacific o. . ." All went dark as they plunged into the earth. The Bee began to vibrate violently.

Connie's voice was soothing. "We're okay, Joe. The Gorilla is handling this and all systems are fine. We'll be out in 40 seconds."

For the first time Joe felt uneasy and claustrophobic in the Bee, but after what seemed like much more than a minute, the vibration finally stopped and full gravity came back. The landing feet were down, and the hatch became transparent, but it was totally dark outside.

Spero was excitedly checking items he had placed inside a large leather-like bag. He had been awake long before Joe, and had changed into some loose open weave clothes and leather sandals. He grinned widely and gave Joe a quick hug. "I really wish you could come and visit for awhile, man. I can't tell you how grateful I am for what you've done, and I mean *both* of you. Joe and Connie: here's praying for your futures."

Spero high-fived one of Connie's hands, and nimbly slipped out of the hatch and into the darkness. He groped along the cave wall for a few moments. "Connie, just a little light out here, okay?"

When a dim blue light appeared, Joe's view through the hatch revealed that they were surrounded by a rock cave. Spero pressed something on the wall, opened up a hidden locker, and stuffed in the medical supplies and other things.

Joe called out, "Best time ever, Spero. You've been great. Here's wishing you and your lady friend all the best in your new life!"

Connie shouted out the hatch, "Don't think you've seen the last of us, Spero. You never know what might happen. And, oh yes, remember my advice too. I mean it. Take care of yourself."

Spero closed up the locker and turned around in the dim light. Joe could tell he was trying to smile and say something but he only managed a clumsy wave before the hatch closed.

"All right Joe, just sit back and press number three one more time."

2247

J ustin hurried through the computer floor on the way to his office. He paused a moment to watch Anna busily working at her station. *Look at those quick fingers flying over two consoles at once. The lost Bee is scheduled in this afternoon, but Anna's playing it cool. We haven't told anyone she'll be with me in the arrival bay, and now she's pretending to ignore me. Good girl.*

He greeted Dottie outside his office. Her face was showing signs of strain. "Director, there's a memo from Police. They have agreed to just four officers in the QDT as long as your security people stay clear. They'll be here before three."

"Like we have much choice, huh Dottie."

Justin settled in his desk with much to think about. *I suppose I should be grateful for any compromise. Spero will be arrested, period. Can't be helped, but perhaps his returning the Bee will result in leniency for him. Anyway, I mustn't show any of my sympathies toward the Humwa.*

There was an order on his desk signed by Aten himself: only police allowed in the arrival bay. *Yeah, well we'll be right outside.* He shook his head. *What an extraordinary epiphany Anna gave me! I suppose in my heart I've always been one of them, and Sarah, too— Sarah. Here I am, maybe facing the most dangerous moment in my life, and I can't stop thinking about her.*

He reviewed the latest print outs Dottie had given him. The new drones he sent out a few days ago had recalibrated its trajectory and orbital entry was now estimated at 3:21 PM, but two never came back. *Wonder what happened to those two? Sure wish I could have my own people with me when the Bee comes in. But maybe it'll be a routine arrest. There's no street rally outside, at least.*

Justin's lips curled up as he glanced toward at the file cabinet where Anna was perched, waiting for him a week ago. *I didn't feel the least bit insulted when she called me a Creative. I should have been, but she was really giving me a compliment, and Sarah's probably right. The Humwa may be the only sane ones left in this world. I'd guess John feels the same way, too.*

He pulled up the work schedules for his employees handling arrival, but his eyes drifted through the hologram over his desk, and he stared at the wall. *Were the Creatives on a different side from how I felt before? Maybe there aren't really "sides" anyway. Would a new generation of innovative minds and God believers really ruin the world? We're all taught so, but when you really think about it, heck no. Ruin what? An oppressive dictatorship? Aten thinks of himself as a god, and he's really turned the control screws down on us over the past six years.*

Justin's reflections were silenced by an urgent message from Dottie. "Director, I have Director John outside your office. He has no appointment, but he says it's really a most urgent matter. You have a scheduled opening at eleven. Should I tell him to come back then?"

"Absolutely not. Send him right in."

John heaved himself inside with a large electronic device hanging from a shoulder strap. He smiled, winked, started talking about stress cracks in the dome, and signaled for Justin to play along. Meanwhile he unplugged the wires to the secretary's COM, and swung around with his device until he found a spot on the far wall that interested him. John was intense and perspiring. He pulled out an instrument that resembled a tiny toilet plunger and fixed it to the apparently seamless wall. Rotating as he pulled, he removed a circular plug of wall paneling.

"You know Justin, those rodents in the outside picnic areas could be getting in through the storm drain under the *QDT*." John put on a glove and extracted a matchbox-sized device from the hole, and plunged it into a receptacle on his shoulder unit. Pulling it out again after a few seconds, he replaced the object back into the wall and re-sealed it. He made one more sweep around the room. "OK, now we can talk for twenty minutes."

"So when did you turn into a 'super spy', John?"

"When it became necessary. And rumor has it that both you and I are on the side of Humwa liberation, so just accept it."

Justin shook his head. "OK, I'll accept it, but I don't want to start any revolutions."

John sat on the chair arm near Justin's desk, leaned forward and spoke in a lowered voice. "Look, there is a really serious situation, my friend. A young woman you know well came to my house last night to tell me about something she overheard the Chairman say. I think you might guess whom I'm talking about." Justin nodded.

"She's very much afraid for you right now, and took a heck-of-a risk coming to me with this. My wife had to hold her five minutes before she'd stop crying."

Justin swiveled around to face him. "Sit. What?"

John slipped his shoulder pack off and onto the seat cushion but stayed on the chair arm. "This woman works for Margo as you know. Nice kid. Writes poetry. Last night she overheard something concerning you and the incoming. She couldn't call you, of course, or call anybody for that matter. Everything's bugged but my place. Interesting she knew that, huh? Her story sounded unbelievable at first, but with my sources I've been able to confirm she's probably correct."

"What's going on for God's sake? Is Margo going to fire me? Is she taking over the QDT? I've been half expecting something like that anyway."

"Worse. Oh much worse. Those four swat team policemen are going to take down Spero and any accomplice the moment they step out of the Bee. Next they'll also kill you, and any QDT officials who dare to go in the retrieval room. They will, of course, shoot anyone else who tries to stop them as well, and they expect to have your vids off line when they do this."

Justin's face twisted, and he leaned back slowly. "That just can't be right, John. It's a made up story. Margo did say she'd like to kill Spero, but that was in jest. Also there'd be absolutely no motive to shoot me or any other workers at QDT. Besides, even with police involvement it would be murder. She knows she could be deposed for any such action, not to mention imprisonment."

John continued his steady gaze, and unchanging monotone. "The plan will place a fired gun in Spero's hand. With the confusion of multiple sudden shots, and no witness looking in from the control room outside, who will know who fired first? The purpose of her plan, or maybe it's the Polices' plan, is to portray Spero and his friends as madmen, and get them out of the picture before they become heroes. The Administration actually thinks they are preventing a revolution. Sort of a first strike thing. And Margo suspects you are helping them, so stay out of the way. Remember, if you or anyone else enters that room, you're toast."

"Good God! I can't prevent those four from being in there. I've agreed to it, and trying to block them would only give away that I was tipped off. Maybe with enough of my security people we could still rush in and overwhelm them."

"Not with their arms, their shields, and their training, Justin. My police contact tells me that each of these men will be like an army of one. Believe me, they'll quickly kill anyone in their way. Besides, the alarm they'd send out would bring in a hundred reinforcements. I really can't think of any solution that might save Spero or his companion if he has one. They'll die quickly. But as for yourself, better just get behind cover. Better yet, surround yourself with people and don't go in there at all. Doubt they'll fire into a crowd, but when it's over, I'm sure they intend to at least arrest you."

THE BEE RETURNS

J oe blinked back into consciousness. Connie was playing "Strawberry Fields Forever". The hatch was now transparent, but all Joe could see was bright powdery sand. "This doesn't look at all like my apartment, Connie. Are we at the beach on our Honeymoon?"

"Sadly no, sweetheart. Sip some of that juice in your armrest to clear your head. This will be the place where you'll either decide to trust me or hate me."

Joe yawned and knelt on the floor trying to see more through the hatch window. "Sky's black out there. Well, you know I'll always trust you Connie, but you sound so serious. Where the heck are we anyway?"

"We are on the 'dark' side of the moon, but it's pretty sunny, isn't it? I brought you here first so we can talk. I have to explain a few things to you before we go in for a landing."

"OK, shoot."

"Now there's a quaint little slang expression you like to use—not that anyone takes literally, I hope."

Joe began pulling on his street clothes. "You're stalling, aren't you my dear?"

"Well, I. . .Well, I know you're not going to like this. You'll hate it, in fact. But before I even begin, I want you to know that I'm sure you will be safe and eventually make it home."

Now fully alert, Joe swung around and squinted into Connie's eye. "Eventually? Oops, but that doesn't sound real good Connie. In fact I hate the word 'eventually'. Did we break down here? Did our quarks just fly off back into their own dimensions and leave us stranded?"

"No, nothing like that, although even with the boost from those drones, there's less than 10% life remaining in our subatomic coating. The thing is this, and it's all the fault of Randolf 604, by the way. He is the one I assigned, well the *other* me assigned, to make a foolproof system preventing any Bee from going very far without a pilot. When I'm alone in here

I can only move two kilometers and only fifteen minutes in time change. Neither I nor Spero could find a way around his truly amazing program. No matter what control you touch, it immediately disables Bee operations."

"Well, that's a bitch. So how about you just stay in my apartment flashing your homing beacon until someone comes for you?"

"We considered it. With unlimited time, it might even work, but no one would know where or when to look. There is a bigger problem though. The remaining sub-atomics will fly off in two to three weeks. That could hurt anyone standing nearby, and the flash could start a fire. At that point there would be no way for this Bee to return, and that brings up an even worse problem. The automatic destruction device would activate when there are no particles *and* no passenger aboard unless its 2247. The result would be like a small neutron bomb."

"Oooh. My landlord would definitely complain about that. I assume you have a backup plan?"

"Yes, we go back to home base together in 2247, and someone else will take you back home from there. Actually we are at that time fixation right now."

"Oh, goodie—I think. But why won't they just hang me as an accomplice?"

"Now Joe, you know I'd never let you do this if I thought there was a clear danger. The laws of our time strictly state that no one from our past will even be interfered with, much less hurt. They are *required* to take you back to your time unharmed. The worst they would do is confiscate your souvenirs and give you a memory probe for your information on Spero. That's why you couldn't know where he is."

"Reminds me of a movie I saw where this guy is screaming in pain from a 'mind probe'. And what about my samples and tapes?"

"The probe? It's painless. You'll be a bit dizzy for a moment or so afterwards. As for your stuff, all I can say is that you might find some of it later."

"You stopped at my apartment while I was in stasis?"

"Your memory is that they're lost forever, right? Work on that."

Joe fell back in his chair and rolled his eyes up. "Oh great. As usual I see I have no choice. But this could be fun. At least I'll see the launch station and get a glimpse of the future. But remember, I have a class to teach on Monday."

"One more thing, Joe, and I'm really, really sorry about this too, but when you press the 'number two' button to start the automated return, the old 'data mode' will take over. I regret having to tell you this way, but I need to erase my program entirely."

"What? No!" Joe sat upright close to her eye. "Not *yourself*. You mean you're just erasing all your data on Spero and his locations, right?"

"Oh, Joe. Don't get upset. I have to erase all of myself. I will save some important scientific data files in Gorilla, and I'm sure my programmer has a back up copy of me. I really don't have a choice because I actually *do* know where Spero is. They might eventually find my memory even if I tried to hide it."

"Now that really sucks, Connie! I can't believe you would even *think* of doing that to yourself. It—it would be like *dying*." Joe pulled his knees to his chest and put his head on them. "If you're really all computer memory, why can't you just erase your memory of Spero's location?"

"Here is the problem I ran into. I had no difficulty buzzing past firewall blocks to erase the coordinates in Gorilla, but my own, human-based memory program is really strange. When I think about erasing Spero's location and date, I have just created a backup to this memory just because I thought about it. Now I have two records of the memory. Don't you have memories you want to forget but can't?"

"Yes, but your 'mind' has to be different."

"Apparently not, Joe.

Joe felt like he was grasping for the hand of a drowning friend and couldn't hold on. "Oh Connie, no! Don't you want to remember, you know, remember your adventures— and us?"

Connie put all four of her arms out toward Joe. Two of them grasped his shoulders and squeezed. "Well. I'll count on you keeping all the memories for both of us, Joe." She released his shoulders, but kept her arms out. "Please untie these drawstrings on my sleeves. I want you to just think of me as happy and safe somewhere."

Joe's throat had tightened up, and his vision was blurring. He removed the sleeve strings and wondered how she could be so strong. She neatly folded up her four pink sleeves. His voice was hoarse. "Wouldn't you want to save those?"

Connie stuffed them into the recycler. "Ah, I was tired of that color anyway. Now you go and enjoy that fun life you have ahead of you. I'm betting it includes Melissa. Look, you're going to get that peek at the 'forbidden' future you always wanted to see."

"I'll—I'll miss you *awful*, girl. I really loved this time we had together."

"Likewise. Best not to wait any longer, now." She pointed to the console. "Number two this time, remember? Bye, Joe." The four arms quickly folded back into their nacelles.

Joe pressed the button, and the hatch closed. The view screen became hazy and they moved away from the moon. The dry, Data Mode voice announced they would arrive at Earth orbit in eight minutes. Joe cried quietly.

The familiar expanse of the blue globe below filled the hatchway when it became transparent, but from this distance Joe couldn't tell the difference between 2247 and 1986. A loud voice began speaking TL, the "future language". It was answered by the Bee's onboard and they conversed for awhile. Data Mode inquired if Joe would like all communications automatically translated to English.

"Yes Gorilla, please do that."

"Please clarify. Are you addressing me?"

"I'm sorry. Yes. Please translate all messages."

"Understood. You will hear only translations. Do you wish to have any further communication with ground control yourself?"

"No."

"Understood. We have been cleared for arrival in three minutes. Here is the translation of the words you just heard:

"Do you request landing at CD port?"

"Yes, landing requested."

"Send your crew manifest at this time."

"Unable to comply. There is one passenger. He does not have a functioning implant for identification."

"You know regulations require ID prior to granting a landing permit."

"Understood. There will be no means of identification. Our status is stable for the moment. Sub-atomics will expire in two days, plus or minus two hours. We have a slow hydrogen leak which will terminate our last remaining fuel cell in six hours. Crew death will occur in one and one half hours subsequent to that event. Remaining in orbit and awaiting instructions."........

"You are cleared to primary arrival room. Clearance for descent will be three minutes from your receipt of the time marker signal."

"Understood. Will comply."

Joe noted that the descent was rapid down through the atmosphere, but slowed abruptly. The hatch was transparent so he guessed they must be on real time as they made their approach. He glimpsed a large dome structure sitting on a hilltop surrounded by forest just before the hatch closed for final approach.

The opening cleared and Joe arrived in a white, plastic-like room. He was startled by a loud crack and a flash, but remembered Connie warned him this would happen when the particle skin cover was removed. A high speed motor ran for a few minutes. Finally the onboard announced: "Arrival. Atmosphere normal." The hatch opened and he found himself alone in an empty room with wrap around perimeter windows. People were running around outside, and men were tearing off white outer garments.

Well, I guess this is where I get off. Joe cautiously backed out of the Bee and into the room. Just as he did so, he heard a sliding door open behind him, running footsteps, and a loud "Clack-clack-clack-clack" as he was turning around. Four uniformed men were pointing something at him. Guns! Terrified, he sat back on the hatch ledge and raised his arms.

The four men gave an angry shout, dropped their rifles, and pulled smaller devices out of their jackets. Like choreographed dancers they pointed the smaller guns at him. "Click-click-click-click". Clearly enraged, they threw away their useless weapons. One almost hit Joe, as the guns clattered and bounced off the floor and walls. Joe stood up and raised his arms. "Wait, I give up. Don't shoot."

One soldier shouted something in the future language. A command. All four men produced a knife in each hand, and with a shout they charged him. Joe desperately tried to get back into the Bee, but simultaneously all four grunted, fell forward and collapsed at his feet. His eyes glazed with fear, Joe sat paralyzed on the hatch opening, his heart pounding. He stared down at the four soldiers sprawled out in front of him on the textured gray floor. *Are they dead? How, what?*

A tall blond man and a dark haired woman dressed in white coats stood by the door. They walked toward him and were followed by a flow of many uniformed men and women behind them. The man called out loudly. "American English two oh, people. Everyone change." Then he walked slowly over to Joe, carefully stepping over the bodies others were handcuffing. "Please relax, mister. No one is going to harm you, now. I apologize for this unfortunate reception. I am

Justin, Director of this facility. This is my assistant, Anna."
Anna gave him a wide, reassuring grin.

Joe cleared his throat and tried to swallow. Nothing happened. He didn't feel his feet were up to standing. "I—I'm Joseph Main from 1986."

Justin reached out his hand to shake Joe's, and then helped him off the hatch and onto his feet. "*Professor* Joseph Main?"

Joe was breathing more easily as he watched the last of his would be assassins being dragged out of the room. "Just Instructor, Joe Main."

Justin held up a finger. "Excuse me a moment." He turned to his security forces flanking the door. "OK people, listen up. These four are to go to Conference Five. Chief Adjudicator Thomas is waiting there to interrogate them. I want all this video including the one from the Bee to continue streaming out to all news media through our secure channel. If they storm the building, record and send that video out too."

Joe turned his attention to the woman beside him. "Are you the one?"

"I'm sorry. The one?"

"You know, the one in the Bee computer." Anna's returned a demure smile and nodded her head. "Look, I feel I know you. Can we talk about it?"

Anna lightly grasped Joe's arms. It was just like Connie used to. "I'm Anna, Mr. Main, and I hope there'll be time to chat one day, but there's sort of a crisis going on."

Justin turned to her. "Anna, you were *totally* fantastic, but we have more work to do, and quickly. I'm sure the exact special coordinates for Professor Main are saved in this Bee. Could you get them for me and transfer them to Bee 76? I have it prepped and ready in the Drone Launch Room."

"You got it, boss. And I'll erase any location data from 77 when I'm done." She gave a quick wave, winked at Joe, and disappeared into the Bee.

Justin leveled his gaze at Joe. "Alright sir, I know you would probably like the full 2247 tour, but besides that being illegal, you can see we're in a bit of a mess right now. I'm going to personally take you back to your 'moment series'. Kindly follow me."

They quickly exited the arrival chamber, and passed through a perimeter room where workers were busily tending to consoles. Joe stumbled over some large cables that were strewn in the aisles. "Well Mr. Justin, from what I've seen so far, I'd prefer a quick visit to your world rather than live in it. No offense."

Justin chuckled. "Turn right here. No kidding. All you know about us is what Spero told you, and you were almost attacked on arrival. You might notice that other police soldiers are trying to break in and finish the job. I guess we're not looking too good right now, huh?"

They arrived at an elevator that opened when Justin placed his hand into a wall depression. "Now that you mention it, Mister Justin, I do have to get back to work."

The two raced down a hall to a smaller control room when they left the elevator. Justin spoke into a communicator on his wrist. "Samuel, what are they doing?"

The device replied "Director, there's lots of them. They've blown off the front door and are entering the lobby. They cut power but our backup is still working."

Justin escorted Joe into a smaller departure room that contained another Bee. They were greeted by many smiling faces. People were waving at them from their consoles. "Samuel, no shooting. Everyone surrender. That's an order. But only give up in small groups and only after they take each area. Slow them down by sealing every door and disable all elevators now. We will need about six minutes. Keep streaming out the video of all their attacks. You are in charge until I get back."

"Understood, Director. They are setting charges for the second door, but I don't think they know where you are, or about our video feed."

Justin motioned for Joe to get into the Bee and followed behind him. "Tell Anna not to defend either. Did she get our coordinates?"

"They're uploaded. Ready on button two. Good luck, Director."

"Great work everyone. I'm proud of all of you. Erase my destination coordinates at this end, and good luck to all of you, too. My communication ends. Stay safe."

The hatch closed and the sound of heavy motors pumping out the air began. Joe could hear and feel the vibration of distant explosions, and the next few minutes dragged on with uncertain tension. "Uh, Director Justin, if you don't mind my asking: just exactly why are these soldiers so anxious to kill me?"

Justin turned to Joe with a shrug and a 'guilty' grin. "Don't know actually, but it's nothing personal, Professor. Maybe they wouldn't be shooting if they knew who you are. It's uh, just part of our current political unrest."

A green band of light appeared before them in Bee 76, and the computer announced that all systems were ready. Justin pressed the number two button, and the Earth quickly departed.

Justin patted Joe's shoulder, smiled broadly, and exhaled. "Well, that much worked out at least. We'll be safe now."

1986

Bee 76 hummed along quietly toward the past. The frantic fight to stay alive was suddenly over, and the feelings of desperation began to ebb away. Joe reclined back in his seat and watched Justin as he conversed with the computer in Translinguachine, and manipulated controls. He sat quietly until Justin seemed to be finished. "Kinda sounds like a Spanish guy trying to talk German with a Chinese accent."

Justin turned in his seat and grinned. "Technical things are easier for me in TL. It's been a few years since I've flown one of these things all by myself, professor. You probably have more onboard hours than I do."

"And thanks for that reassuring thought. You're sure we're headed back to 1986? By the way, please just call me Joe."

"Oh, don't worry—Joe. We have your exact time fix point, and even what I presume to be your living quarters. Meanwhile, why don't you tell me a little bit about what it's like to live in your time, and where you went with Spero? I already know the reason he selected you for his partner, and now I understand why he selected you to return our Bee."

Joe's eyes brightened. "Now that. That I would like to hear. But before you ask me anything else, you should know that I have no precise idea of Spero's present location or time."

"Of course you don't. He wouldn't suddenly turn dumb on us. Actually I don't really care any more, and I wouldn't go after him now even if I did know. I wish him good luck wherever he is, or as my friend Sarah would say, may the good Lord bless him and keep him forever."

Joe tried to hide a skeptical expression. "Great, now what about the 'why me' part?"

"Oh, yes. Well you are a person with a historical record. He knew you were going to survive the return trip."

"Uh huh. So he knew I'd be alive later. But of course severe and permanent disabilities from your Swat Team might not have been mentioned."

Justin laughed. "True, but honestly Spero would have never guessed something like that would happen. I didn't believe it myself. Right up to the last minute I thought they were just going to arrest you. Police are only supposed to shoot in self defense, and then just to stun. Apparently, things have changed for the worse."

"Yuh think? Okay, your world is going down the tubes, but tell me, do you have a history on everyone living in eighty six?"

"Oh no, just people who were written up for something. You had a biography and we found a copy of it when we searched Spero's apartment. Of course I'm not going to tell you what it says, except that the places you frequent in 1986 are mentioned. His finding you was no accident."

Joe leaned forward and squinted. "It mentioned the Purple Planet Bar?"

"Sure did, and the times you usually showed up there, too."

Joe fell back on his seat with a humph.

The two chatted on for hours getting to know one another; each curious about the other's daily life almost three hundred years apart. They rambled through subjects like their favorite music, and their love of jogging. They talked about the inflammatory politics of their time, sports or lack of them in 2247, and of course, women. After awhile their lives didn't seem so different, after all. Joe knew he wouldn't get any details on future technology, but what really annoyed him was that Justin knew things about his future but wouldn't talk about them.

For his part, Justin tried to be as honest as he dared. He did admit that the political structure in 2247 had become fragile especially with severe impositions over the past few years from supreme ruler Aten. "You see, Joe, our leaders are expecting a revolt, but right now I think we can turn things around from within. Exposing this attack attempt on world-wide coverage should precipitate changes for the better."

Joe felt comfortable with Justin, and finally decided he was trustworthy. After all, he had saved his life. Joe even consented to a memory download during his stasis. Heck, he reasoned, he probably couldn't prevent it anyway. Besides Justin explained he would be severely criticized if he didn't bring the exam back with him.

# # #

This time when Joe regained consciousness, he had a more severe hangover. He held his head and felt little greasy spots in his hair. Justin was busy reading a paper printout, but when he saw Joe was awake, he turned and handed him a cup. "Here, have some of this. It'll help your head. Mind if we talk about your memory scan?"

Joe chugged his drink and rubbed a cleansing towel through his hair. "Sure, I guess. Why not?"

"I'm not too surprised about anything I've found in your memory, and you sure have been to some interesting places. One thing bothers me, though. You and Spero related emotionally to our new computer program as though it had been an actual person. Was this 'Connie Program' of ours really that interactive?"

Joe took a deep breath and studied the boyish, quizzical look of his inquisitor. He massaged the tender places in his scalp. "Let me ask you something first, Justin. That woman—the one who was with you when I arrived, was she really the one responsible for Connie being in the Bee?"

"Anna? That's right. Good guess."

"Really. My mental picture of Connie was a little different. Anyway, Anna left her entire functioning brain, or a copy of it I guess, in the main onboard computer. We called her Connie, and we both liked her a lot. Justin, she *was* a real person. As real as we are, just in a different body."

"She had a *body?*"

"Well, four arms and an eye."

"Oh, those. Anyway, I'm amazed at the sincerity you showed talking to the program. Anna told me she did this download, but I didn't think it would've come out like—like it was really *her* in there. So she really related to you like a real person, huh? Amazing. I hope I can re activate her when I get back."

"But didn't you find out from my memory—I don't like talking about this Justin. Connie had to kill, er, erase herself just so you wouldn't find Spero's location. If I knew it would bring her back to life, I'd even consider telling you where he is myself. Of course you and I both know by now that I'm really clueless."

"Wow, that's unbelievable. So Connie actually behaved so much like a real person that you actually cared what happened to 'her'? Of course, this would explain why she helped Spero elude us. Anna believed in his cause, so her alter ego would too. But Joe, she was really a 'rogue' program—completely untested. The 'Connie' program probably created imaginary images just to please you, like the populated planet you think you saw. I'll admit I'm disappointed if this program got erased, but obviously not for the same reasons you do."

Joe stared at his feet. "Just tell me how long it'll be before I get to read my Sunday paper back home."

"Sunday?" Justin studied his printout for a moment. "Oh, I see what you mean. You wanted to get back on the day after you left, didn't you. Sorry, not possible. Your Bee already returned on that day, and our regulations require a minimum four day interval."

"No! Can't you at least give me Monday morning? I have a class to teach, and no one will have any idea where I am."

Justin shrugged. "Sorry, Joe. Closer than that would be dangerous. We have these rules for a reason. You're just used to Spero breaking them. Your class time wouldn't be considered an emergency, so I couldn't justify it to our onboard computer. The safety program would simply refuse if I asked, and I don't know how to override it."

"Oh no! It's going to be *Thursday*, then. What time?"

"Looks like 3:30 PM the way you tell time." Justin moved his head in closer to his data screen. "We're due to arrive about six minutes from now. The downloaded information for your location is very detailed so I'll leave it on auto. The schematic shows that our flight will terminate in some narrow corridor."

Joe noticed this Bee approached differently from the way Connie flew it. They simply plunged straight down through his roof, the feet clunked down, and that was it. Justin continued. "We have time fixed. Sensor report verifies that no other person is present within this small walled in area. Be advised there is a seven-kilogram animal in an adjacent room with a high epinephrine level. Please verify visually if we have the correct location."

The hatch was transparent but closed. Joe peered out into his living room. "Right place. Wrong day of course. The animal's my cat."

"I'm getting out first." Justin said flatly as he opened the hatch. He carried a small pocket sized instrument, stood in the living room and rotated it in a full circle." When Joe was standing next to him he explained. "This check is to verify that none of our electronic technology is present. I hope you didn't keep any twenty third century souvenirs and hide them somewhere else?"

"Nope, nothing. I promise."

Justin walked around a bit, checking out the quarters. "I'll trust you on that, Joe. Sort of a primitive place you live in isn't it?" He stood in the kitchen and waved his finger around. "Everyone has to live like this?"

"No Justin, just poor college instructors like myself."

"Really am sorry about those days you lost, professor."

"I admit, I'm bummed, but I get it. Rules. I just hope I didn't get fired this week. You want to hang out in old primitive 86 for a while? My food's probably spoiled, but I've got some wine and cheese."

Justin tucked his scanning device into his belt pouch, and shook Joe's hand. "It's nice of you to offer, and I'd really enjoy—hanging. But I'm worried about things back home, Joe. Remember? There's going to be a few little problems to tidy up. But one question, before I go. What's the hostile animal in the next room?"

Joe chuckled. "Well, not so much angry but scared. Don't you have house cats anymore?"

"Pets aren't allowed in our cities. But I read cats can't be trained anyway."

"Not like dogs, but they do use a litter pan."

Justin cocked his head to one side, and wrinkled his nose. Joe could tell he was waiting for a computer translation. "Aaah, that explains the ammonia odor."

"Oh, wait. I just thought of something." Joe went to his bookshelf. He was surprised to find all his tapes and CDs neatly lined up by size. Had to be Connie. First he pulled out his 'Best of the Beatles' tape, but it had a handwritten sticker on it that said 'data added'. He put that back, took out a Beach Boys tape, and gave it to Justin. "I was going to give you a Beatles tape, but this'll be even better."

Justin took it tentatively. "Look, I appreciate the gesture, but I'm not much into this old archived music."

"It's not for *you,* although I do appreciate your saving my life. No, it's for Anna in memory of and thanks for Connie. Connie said she liked this music the best because it made her happy so I'm betting Anna will like it too. Besides, I remember she said this Beach Boys music isn't in your archives. Tell her thanks from Spero and myself."

Justin looked at the tape in his hand, and turned it over a few times. "I've never seen anything that will play something like this."

"And, I am talking Anna, here."

Justin laughed. "You're right. Half the fun for her will be just finding a way to recover the data." Then he swung easily up into the Bee, but before the hatch closed he called out.

"Don't worry, Joe. You don't get fired." Then with a whoosh and a crackle, Bee 76 was gone.

#   #   #

Joe took a deep breath and surveyed his little home. Nothing much had changed. A pile of newspapers lay on the kitchen table. *Yup, the last one's Thursday all right. Melissa must have kept coming by. Melissa! Oh God, now she must be really furious with me. Better call right now.* Joe dialed her number on his olive green Princess Phone. He flashed through and discarded plausible excuses in his mind.

"Melissa? Hi, it's Joe!. . .

Yes, it's really me—really, yes.

Well of course I'm alive, and I'm so sorry I didn't call, but I. . .

You understand?—Really? Oh, good.

Well I would have. . .

Melissa?—Melle. . .

Are you *crying*?. . .Listen, I understand. Not knowing must have been horrible for you, but I'll explain, and I promise to make it up to. . .What do you mean 'sure will, Buster'?

Anyway, how's this sound? Let's have dinner at the Teacher's Club. My treat, of. . .No? Well, whatever you say. . .

Your place?

Tomorrow at six?

Sure, I'll bring that Merlot you like, and anything else. . .

You covered my class. Really?

Oh God, thanks. Gees, Melle, I can't thank you eno. . .

I missed you too. . .

Well, see you then, dear."

Joe slowly lowered the phone, a puzzled expression on his face. They had called each other "dear", and made what others might even call a date. *I guess she was really upset by my unexplained disappearance. She's a right to be. Thought she'd lost a friend. Well, she's entitled to a dinner at least. But wait, she's cooking it. That's not right.*

He took a beer from his refrigerator and noted that the Martian vials were placed against the back wall. *Connie!* He grabbed some pretzels and collapsed on his patio chaise for some serious thinking. Inertia finally came out hesitatingly and sat next to him within petting range. *I'll never under-stand women. Craziest day of my life.*

Suddenly he sat bolt upright. "Data added!" He said out loud. Connie had recorded something on his Beatles tape.

Joe headed back to his neatly arranged bookshelf. The few CDs he had were neatly pressed to one side, and two of them were new, with handwritten labels. One said "Think With Your Heart", a novel by Constance Huang. The other simply said "1080P-copy for 2007".

His tapes were all lined up, and in front was a Beta tape labeled "For Joe from the Crew." There had been two parts to his Beatles collection. One was missing, and the other had the "data added" label. Joe's portable tape player seemed to be missing also, but he found it sitting neatly on top of his VCR. He stuck the tape in his player with trembling fingers. Spero's voice began.

"Hi, Joe. By now I expect you've had your last trip. You're back at your place enjoying a snack on your patio and looking out at your maple tree, right? But, did you know that you have to cover the little holes in the tape cartridge before you can make a recording? Anyway, you should have had your memory scan by now, so I can speak freely. The second tape contains a gift for you, but it's really important that only you find it, so as an added precaution I'm leaving a clue to it's location that only you will recognize.

As I record this, I am looking out over the Aegean Sea on a beautiful day in Greece, some two millennia back along the time moments. Although some things like sports, philosophy and the arts are valued here, this civilization is pretty decadent. Remember how you described the decade before yours as the "me first" time? Well, I think it was invented here. This is the "anything goes" time, except of course, avoiding the Roman tax collector. The good part about this time is that even a little honesty and faithfulness makes a real impression on people, and I know that God saved me for a special purpose in this time and place.

I worked my coming and going to make it seem to you like I only spent a few weeks here, but actually I have been here almost two years. I am absolutely crazy in love with my boss's oldest daughter Athena, and you might not believe this, but she really loves me too. Her dad has given permission for us to be married soon. In the next part of the tape, I am going to pretend to take down a message to be sent to you, but actually it's just so I can record her voice. Also that's where you'll get the clue I mentioned. Please cut this tape off here and destroy it just in case. You'll need someone to translate Greek for her part of course, but pick someone who will keep it to themselves. So Joe, thanks again for everything. I can't describe my gratitude for your help. You must know how happy I am to be where I am, and far away from the grip of the Evil One. I don't have to wish you a happy life because I know what's ahead for you. Enjoy, my friend. You deserve it."

FRIDAY

J oe carefully cut and destroyed Spero's recording as instructed, spliced the tape together, and reassembled the cassette. Sure enough, after playing half a Beatle tune, a woman with a pleasantly musical voice began speaking in Greek with exuberance.

Joe was fortunate to be on friendly terms with Owen Dean, Chairman of the Language Department, and his next move was obvious. Somewhat less obvious was what he might find left over to eat this morning. He had the last Swanson from the freezer the night before, but now he surveyed the refrigerator for possible breakfast. *Whoa, Melissa replaced my milk and OJ with fresh stuff. Well then, she must have believed I was still alive, right?*

He fixed some cereal, and phoned Owen who told him he had just the right graduate student to help him. She'd be glad to type out a translation for him as early as this weekend, and for only four dollars a page. "OK, see you this afternoon, Owen."

Wonder what kind of a 'gift' Spero's giving me. Course, most likely it's just his way of having fun with me. Yeah, a gag gift I'll bet. Wait a minute. He said he got the gold for his coins in Fort Knox. Uh oh, maybe he's giving me a bar of gold labeled US Government. Would that be stealing if I kept it? Well duh, yeah.

Joe pulled a bread slice from the toaster. *Nah, you know what? I'll bet Spero's got a photo album for me, one that shows him lounging by the Aegean with his girl friend. And there he'll be, lying on the beach enjoying the idea of me running all over the place looking for his dumb clues."*

By late Friday afternoon Joe had about caught up with his leftover work, and dropped the tape off in the Language Department. He hadn't seen Melissa on campus today, and he was still feeling pretty crummy about her having to endure his sudden, mysterious disappearance. Not that it was really his fault, but she's the last person he'd want to hurt. *Can't believe she actually taught my intro course to Physics again. Bright as she is, she's dumb in math, and I even need to help her in her own field when she gets into statistics. Well, this time I won't be so surprised when my students want to talk more about 'man's quest to understand the physical world', and the parts of the brain used for mathematics and music.* He laughed to himself. *Melissa makes delicious creative journeys away from my lesson plan, doesn't she? Real trouble is, the students like her so much, they'll want her back again.*

# # #

Six o'clock arrived. Joe strolled up Melissa's walk. But suddenly the bottle of Merlot in his hand felt totally inadequate. *Well, at least I got her the flute present. Hey, and I did finish her porch light repair, too.* He stopped before the steps. Her house looked different. *Yup, she's set out potted flowers all along the porch rail. And look at the front door! It's painted bright blue."*

With the first creak on the wooden stairs, Canis announced his arrival, but his couch barking turned to tail wagging when Joe scratched the window pane by his nose.

Melissa appeared in the door way and paused. Their eyes held. Both sensed there had been an inward change. She searched past his gaze for thoughts hidden away. A warmth filled his chest and their old relationship became fuzzy. They exchanged quick hugs, and Melissa whispered into his ear, "I'm *so* glad you're still alive you big oaf." She pulled away. "But you'll stay in the dog house until you do some big explaining, fella."

"OK, I'll be 'splainin', Melissa." *What's going on? Mele's never been this way.*

She replied with a perky "Very well, follow me."

She's got some kind of rust colored lipstick on. Never wears the stuff. And her hair—her hair even has flip outs or something. My God, did she go to a stylist? At least I don't smell perfume but there's a whiff of—what is it? Hmmm, uh—woman.

As Melissa spun around, Joe was stunned to see the swirl of a fluffy print cotton skirt, and legs. *She's got legs! Nice tanned ones.* He meekly followed these into the kitchen, mesmerized by the little clefts behind her knees. When she reached the kitchen door she turned and flashed a smile that almost made him drop his wine bottle. "I have a Chardonnay in the fridge. Go ahead and open both won't you. I'll get out some snacks for us on the back porch."

Joe tried to take some deep breaths and compose himself while he opened the bottles with fumbling fingers. The complete change in Melissa was an absolute 'tour de force'. The familiar baggy jeans, the tousled hair, the flannel shirt person—gone. *But she's been replaced by one heck of a pretty woman.*

Joe appeared on the back deck with the glasses and wine. He noticed that the love seat glider was now walled off from the neighbor's view with tall potted plants. Melissa sat on its new plush print cushion with her long legs crossed. She patted the seat next to her. *Oh Help.* Gamely he stepped around Canis who was already begging for treats, smiled, sat, and tried not to let his hand shake as he poured some white wine.

She clinked glasses with him. "Here is to your safe return."

"And to a real friend who would cover for me like that. It was above the call of duty. Thanks. My only complaint is that my students like *your* teaching more than mine."

Melissa giggled. "Well they can check the course curriculum for Anthropology next semester, but in all fairness

I should be the one thanking you for that totally wonderful present. Had *so* much fun figuring it out. You knew I would too, didn't you?"

"Learning how to play notes?"

Melissa laughed heartily. "Oh, that's good. No, no. Now please just tell me exactly where it came from, and what time period."

Joe made an effort to appear relaxed and casual. He took a bite of cheese and a sip of wine. "A suburb of Tel Aviv, best I can recall." He could tell her eyes were studying him, but he rummaged through the peanuts and took another sip while the silence dragged on.

"Joe, how long have you been time traveling?"

A rapid gulp sent Chardonnay into Joe's nasopharynx, and it left him coughing and sputtering. Melissa patted his chin with a napkin. "There, there dear. Don't get excited. You really didn't think I would crack your clever puzzle present?"

"Puzzle? You don't believe it's a tourist souvenir?"

Melissa's mouth became a straight line. "Now, no more teasing. Game over. I realize the physics department isn't ready for any announcements, so this was the only way you could tell me. Just *loved* figuring it all out. You really do know me after all, don't you, my dear."

This was confusing. The flattery felt really good, but—
"OK, but now I'm the curious one. How did you come to such a creative conclusion from the bone flute?"

Melissa eyes brightened with excitement. "Ah, you want my step by step logic. Well first of all, the one and only candidate for a Neanderthal 'bone flute' was found in Europe and was *completely* discredited. Hardly the thing for tourist shops to be selling."

"Well—well the newspaper made it sound like a real discovery." *Uh, oh. That sounded like an admission.* Melissa pouted. "OK, OK, but where do you get time travel out of that? I could have had a butcher make it."

"Joe, surely you know your girlfriend has an inquiring mind. The most obvious thing is that the open holes in it are not just *made* to look like they were cut with a stone tool, they actually were."

"Child labor?"

Melissa tossed her head back for another laugh. She took a deep breath and a sip of wine herself. "Try this Italian Cheddar." She cut a piece and handed it to him on a cracker.

"I'm acquainted with a naturalist who is studying the evolution of African ungulates by following DNA patterns. It's a new technique that lets one analyze the biological fingerprint of every living thing. At first glance your flute would seem to be made from the femur of a water buffalo. However, the DNA is off 1.2 %, and my colleague believes that it's an extinct ancestor, probably an auroch. In any case there is no living animal with that pattern, and yet the bone was fresh enough to get a perfect marrow sample."

"But, maybe it's a species he hasn't cataloged?"

"I asked that. Well, he said 'Very improbable', and now he's so excited about finding the living animal. What could I tell the poor fellow?"

"Still, not conclusive, oh bright lady."

Melissa crunched a few nuts, had another sip of Chardonnay, and leaned back on the glider to start them swaying. She thought for a moment. "Well, your right, I suppose." Large impish eyes smiled up at him. "Then there was this larger than normal partial thumb print too, but the best thing of all was the snot inside the wide end."

"Oh, sorry. I thought I wiped it clean before I wrapped it."

"Wish you hadn't. The full fingerprints would have been fun to study. Anyway, the snot was just a little way into the opening. It also proved that someone with a large nose blew through it. Would you like to know what the DNA analysis showed?"

Joe realized that pretending otherwise was now futile. He smiled coyly. "Let's see. I'd guess that it wasn't quite human?"

"Right you are," Melissa said, "and of course it wouldn't be. But it was close— 0.5% off to be more exact." She turned to face Joe squarely. "Were you actually there yourself? Did you actually see a Neanderthal in person?"

"Oh yeah. And I have some shoes and a necklace for you too!"

Melissa turned sideways to face Joe. "Oh, my God!" He got a quick hug. "Please, you've got to tell me every *single* thing that you can remember about these people. Even little things would help. How close did you get?"

"Close. Well, I was really going to tell you all about it, but I didn't want to look foolish. Most people would think I was just making up the time relocation thing. Now I haven't looked at it yet, but I should have a video tape with about an hour on it."

Melissa shrieked and covered her mouth. "Oh God, this is too much. Neanderthals are my life's work, and right now you probably know more about them than I do. Next thing you'll tell me they invited you for lunch too."

"Actually that was rather disgusting."

Both started laughing. She started tickling. Soon they were snuggling. Joe remembered briefly pondering freckle patterns on her cheek before the kiss came. He was surprised at how absolutely wonderful her lips and warm body felt next to his. "Tell me" she whispered. "Did you actually pick that destination just because of me?" Joe nodded. She snuggled her face against Joe's neck, and breathed her words below his ear. "You know I love you just awful, don't you?"

"I do. I do. And I love you too, Melissa. Always have." They clinched and kissed again. Melissa put her finger on his nose and gently pushed away. "You'll have to remind me where we left off after dinner."

"Oh, I will. I will."

She got up and headed for the house door. "Relax awhile with the munchies while I start things. I made your favorite stew."

"I'll be here. I can't stand up right now."

She giggled, started to go through the door, but turned back and arched her head against the door jam. "Joe, be honest. Did you really go back in time and look for Neanderthals just make me happy?"

"Yup."

Her hand came to her mouth, and her eyes misted. "OK, you are *so* out of the doghouse now. And I won't even ask you why you were so late."

Melissa served dinner on a small round table by a back window. Joe recounted the true story of the Bee, and the unfortunate fact that more voyages were not going to be happening. When he got to the part where he was nearly shot, Melissa said she actually felt when this had happened. She had woken up with a dream of him being attacked by several men. "That's why I was so afraid you might be dead, but part of me knew you were still alive too."

When she finally ran out of questions, Melissa said, "So when exactly do I get to see this video of yours?"

"You'll just have to wait until our next date, sweetie."

"And that would be tomorrow night, right?"

"Of course, Dear."

MONDAY

The weekend of discovery belonged to Melissa and Joe. It was a time that shells of defense and resistance crumbled away, quickly replaced by intimacy, love, and trust. Amazing, they wondered, that such beauty have hidden so long, beneath veils of uncertainty and fear? It was a time when an inner peace kept company with excitement, and revelations were wrapped in joy.

Melissa watched the Neanderthal video twice on Saturday night and five times on Sunday. She had danced ecstatically the first day, but on Sunday she came back and took careful notes. But she laughed heartily each time she came to the part with Joe wearing animal skins. She became particularly hysterical with tear filled eyes, when he held the 'twig' aloft as his parting gesture, still thinking it passed for a spear. Naturally this brought on much "revengeful" tickling, screeching, and rolling about on the floor. Finally they leaned back on the couch. Joe ventured, "Now admit it. It's just not *that* funny, is it?"

Melissa held up her hand trying to suppress waves of giggle. "It's just, when we get to that warrior fellow at the end, the chief hunter. Did he really say. . . (snort. giggle) when he looked at your spear." Melissa put her hand over her mouth but laughter still danced in her eyes. "Did he really say—don't hunt lions with this." Then she convulsed into uncontrollable laughter again, for which she was punished by more tickling and rolling. Finally, when she turned red, and protested she couldn't breathe, Joe released her. Melissa panted with exhaustion for a moment and patted Joe's arm. "Truce, truce. I'm really not just making fun of you Sweetie—well okay I was, but there is a real discovery here, too. N'ha actually has a sense of humor. Neanderthals can actually make a joke."

"So you think, obviously. But no one ever laughed."

"Well, maybe they just don't, but look at his eyes and his smile when he said it. It's the same thing, I'm sure. Anyway, with his wide jaw, he looks like the Cheshire Cat."

"OK, I get your point. But now what do you want to do about all this, Mele? Are we going to try to convince everyone that this stuff is fresh from the past?"

Melissa lowered her head, squinted her eyes and studied his face. "Nah, even though we have good proof, we'd be all over the tabloids, and more people would be laughing at us than believing. Unless Justin comes back and shows the world his time flier, I think this had better be our secret. But, don't worry. The knowledge gained from what you have will really help explain present evidence."

"OK, but what about the samples from prehistoric Mars? Some expert should be in our loop too."

"Maybe, but keep them on ice until we figure something out."

When Joe told her all about Connie, Melissa pretended to be jealous at first, but she too was saddened by her sacrifice, and touched by the novel she had left behind. Inside the CD jewel case Connie had hand written, "To Melissa and Joe: May every precious together-moment be blessed by love." Transferring the CD into print would be another project for Joe, but the computer that could do this wasn't quite commercial yet. Of course that would make it more fun.

VOICE FROM THE PAST

O n Monday noon, Joe was sitting at his office desk munching on a bag lunch, when a call from Professor Dean woke him from his Melissa day dream. "Hurry over, right away if possible. Just take your lunch with you, Joe. We need to talk."

Owen Dean's office was in the old section of the university. It had apparently been some sort of a reception parlor in the twenties, and still bore elegant mahogany paneling and etched glass sconces. But when Joe walked in, it looked more like an antique library following an earthquake. Spilled books and stacks of files were everywhere. Dean was a balding, gray-bearded man in his sixties, and somewhat portly. He sported a bright red vest. Joe greeted him with a happy grin. "Hi, Owen. Finished with that translation, huh?"

Dean got up with a scowl, but shook Joe's hand, handed him his tape and a few bound pages. "Well, more or less. It's short, and there is no charge for it. I paid the translator." He motioned to a purple mohair chair by his desk. Joe had an apple in his hand and indicated he wanted permission to crunch. "Sure, sure. Listen, the thing is this. If your friend prepared this as a job interview for the University, she's hired. And not only by my Department, but probably History, Drama, maybe Archeology as well. She's *that* good, Joe."

"That's nice. Well Owen, she's a native of Greece, so I'm sure she speaks very well. What makes you think she is a friend of mine?" Joe mumbled through his crunching.

"Don't be coy. It's a letter dictated *to* you, and it's recorded over a Beatles recording. I assume that's yours. Also she uses American idioms."

"Really? What, for instance?"

"She refers to your horse as 'Bimmer'."

Joe suppressed a laugh and cleared his throat. "Oh, well yeah. Anyway, you wouldn't want her for a teaching position. No credentials, and I don't think the girl speaks any English. You rarely look this excited, Owen. What is so special about one short letter, anyway?"

Professor Dean leaned forward toward Joe. "You really don't know what this woman has produced, do you? She *isn't* just someone off the streets of Athens yakking away. This woman is speaking in the Koine Greek of yesterday, the Greek of Virgil, yet she is using street idioms and, slang, some of which we haven't even heard of. Not only that, but she talks with amazing ease and fluency. One could believe she was really *living* in that era. This is really an outstanding piece of work, Joe."

"Oh."

"Look, this 'Athena woman' has gone through considerable effort to make her recording sound blindingly authentic. We would really like to meet her if there is any way to arrange it. She even recorded it in an open field where they were herding goats."

"Really."

"Yes, the background sounds are quite remarkable too. There are two male voices, one is not native Greek but he is trying to speak in Athena's old style slang. The other one really blew our minds, though, and there is no translation for his few words in your copy."

Joe was beginning to feel uncomfortable about all this attention knowing he couldn't give any answers that would satisfy Owen. He tossed his apple core into the wastebasket and got up. "Well, I'm really glad you had some fun with this. . ."

"Joe, the other voice is the goat herder. He is speaking to his goats in the same old style Greek!"

He picked up the manuscript and forced a grin. "Really. Well, what can you expect from someone who talks to goats?"

"Joe, I'm serious. It's *not* modern Greek. How can that be?"

Joe realized he was out of plausible explanations, and was anxious for a graceful exit. "Well, she probably coached him, but I need to get back to work. Really appreciate all your help though, Owen."

Professor Dean wriggled forward and stopped him at the door. "I can see you're not going to give me any clues. Look, you don't have to answer out loud, but are there any secret projects your Physics Department is working on? You can just nod."

Finally, Joe could answer truthfully. "Owen, I can *absolutely* assure you that we are not working on any secret projects."

Finally back at his desk with 20 minutes before class, Joe breathed a big sigh and rubbed his neck. He looked down at the two pages bound in a plastic folder. *And I thought translation was going to be the easy part of Spero's puzzle.*

The header listed the name of the translator and the date. It explained that words not translated would be in brackets, non-linguistic sounds and translator notes in parentheses, and uncertain translations in quotes.

Spero, are you sure you don't want me to write out this letter for Joseph myself?

(Man's voice) *No, dear. I love to hear the sound of your voice. I promise not to leave anything out when I write it down for you.*

(giggles) *You better not, my little "wizard". All right, I'll begin.* (Clears throat) *I am Athena, daughter of Marathonis of Corinth, from the house of Onesiphorus.*

Dear Joseph and [mulsa. . .mull-eesa](She sounds like she either likes the 'L' sound or is trying to get the word right.), *you must know that Spero and I are to be married on the second moon. You are his only "family", and so father and I hope that you can attend. Please ride down on [Bimmer] from your country and come early so you can get to know our honored guests. Any friends you bring will be* welcome too. *We know that you may not be able to travel here, but we do hope you will find a way. Spero will send a "document" for you to show any Centurions who may stop you. Some say these are more dangerous times particularly in the North now that Augustus is gone, but this should give you safe passage.*

(Man's voice whispered) *Don't forget the special part.*

Oh, yes. The wall that was once between you two now contains the words of a wise prophet—Spero, what by the Gods does that mean? Were you angry with Joseph?

(Man's whispered voice) *No I told you.* (Inaudible)

Oh, "phoee". I'm just going to talk, all right? Write this down. Spero will have friends there too. He has many ship-mates and boat-building friends here in Corinth since he has been building and sailing here for two years now. Even before we met, Daddy had taken quite a liking to Spero. Of course, I like him even a bit more. (Giggling)

You may not know that he is a "genius" at improving hulls and sails. He worked on one boat giving it new sails and a "turning thing" to trim them. It was so much faster that our crew made Carthage a half-day sooner. Poppa is very proud of the newest boat Spero just designed and built for him. It has a longer, narrow hull, and sails that no one has ever seen before. To me it looks something like an Arabian Dhow. When a fast pirate ship tried to catch it on the way back from Judea, they couldn't even keep up with it, and our ship was fully loaded. Our crew made "hand signs" at them and had a "party" on the way home.

So, you see why Daddy wants him in the company. I suppose he just threw me at him like fish bait. (Laughter, giggles, scuffling noises and a shriek, then a pause) *But my dearest, "alas", has no head at all for business. He bought a small boat from Daddy last year to fix up for himself, but paid too much for it. Daddy told me he was "sorry" about that and would make it up to him. When we are married, it will be my "job" to see that he remembers to do that!*

Since you are his friend, you probably know that my little "wizard" is also a bit crazy. (More laughter and movements) *For one thing, he treats women as equals, and often asks for my advice. Also, he is convinced that the Jews are right about there being one true God. So, crazy or not, he's a rare treasure you see. And of course I have not told my friends everything there is to know about him yet.*

I have a cousin who will be attending our wedding, but I have put her off from even visiting us before then. She is far more beautiful than I, so of course I won't be so foolish as to let Spero meet her before it is safe.

(Man's voice) *Oh "sweetie", a Goddess in the flesh couldn't take me away from you.* (Mumbling and rustling. Tape ends.)

THE PUZZLE

T hat afternoon, Joe was back teaching his "Intro-Physics" class. They had fallen behind where they should have been in the syllabus, and he knew he should be working hard to get them caught up, but all the students wanted to talk about were Melissa's ideas. The class was sounding more like philosophy and psychology than physics. Clearly, they had been working on *her* homework instead of his.

"All right, ladies and gentlemen, I give up. We'll take a little time to make this a part of the course if you insist, but all of you will still have to complete the workbook, agreed?" After an enthusiastic response Joe added, "Okay, but just so you don't think this will be a lark, I want everything to have at least a tenuous relevance to physics, and we'll have some related questions on the final, too. Yes, Robert?"

"Ms. Shwimmer asked us to bring in some questions to discuss in class today."

"And knowing her I'll bet they'll be interesting questions too. Of course she thought she might be covering for me again. Oh, all right, what's yours, Robert?"

"Oh, we think you know her." Widespread snickering. Joe pointed his finger at Robert admonishingly, but his smile gave him away. "Well, the question I came up with is this: Is the physical world ultimately incomprehensible?"

"I'm, impressed. That's quite a question, Robert. If all the questions are like yours we could take up the whole period. We won't of course." He pointed to a first row student. "Tell you what. Jane, clear the right side of the board and write them up there."

"Sure, Mr. Main. Can I add one myself?" Joe raised his hands in an 'of course' gesture. "Does each little truth we learn bring us closer to an understanding of the universe, or does it just create an *illusion* that we will ultimately be enlightened?"

As Jane started writing, Joe cocked his head to one side facing the class and went cross-eyed to their delight. "And

Ms. Shwimmer did this to you guys in what, two classes? I think I'm starting to regret this—Sam?"

"At what point in man's history did we stop just *reacting* to our environment, like hunting and building shelter, and start trying to *understand* what our physical environment actually is?"

"Sounds suspiciously like Anthropology to me. Linda?"

"Well that's sort of like mine, but my question is why does man *want* to understand things? Is it like a domination thing?" Laughter.

"OK, just one more for now. Write any others out and pass them up. John?"

"This fits in with the others: Is our desire to comprehend the physical world cultural, psychological, or spiritual? Aren't we just ultimately seeking our Creator?"

Joe crashed down in the chair behind the lecture desk feigning exhaustion. "Wow. Well, let's do it this way. If we have the lesson finished by twenty-of on each class day, we'll talk about one of the questions. Other than that, you'll have to wait until you take her Anthropology elective unless she has time to come and visit us. Linda?"

"She'd come and see us if you asked her out—I mean over."

# # #

It took Joe awhile to calm the renewed laughter and get his class back in control, and by the time he got back to his apartment, he realized he had been dealing with Melissa indirectly all day. He ached for contact of a different kind, but that would have to wait.

Joe popped open a beer, fished out some pretzels from the top shelf and settled into his couch with the sports page. Inertia curled up in his lap to remind him of his massage appointment. When he read the baseball page, Joe remembered that he actually did know who'd win the National League Pennant in 1995. *If I only had another moment in that waiting room I might have discovered past World Series winners too.* He sighed. *Won't do me much good for awhile though, will it?*

Half way through his beer Joe put down the paper and began thinking about Athena's 'letter' still tucked in his briefcase. *I guess it was really just Spero's way of telling me how he happy he is, and why he didn't want to come back. Maybe he was apologizing for all the arguing we did with that "wall between us" thing. Yep, Connie was a "wise* prophet" indeed. *She sure had to come between us plenty of times and smooth things out, didn't she?*

Inertia dug his claws in to object to page turning and got a little swat. *Connie was also smart enough to figure out my relationship with Melissa. She prophesied our togetherness without even knowing her. Wonder if Spero had any real idea about what Connie was planning to do with herself in the end—but knowing her, I'll bet she never told him the sad news.*

Joe felt like his old life was making a return, but an even better old life. He rummaged through the freezer compartment. *Hmm, what's for dinner tonight? Ah, yes: broiled chicken and mixed vegetables. Into the microwave with it—here, Inertia, have some "evening crunchies".*

Still, there were thoughts tingling at the base of his skull. *Wish I hadn't destroyed Spero's tape so quickly. Just listened to it once. Now that I think about it, I'm sure Spero had also mentioned a clue to a gift that only I would recognize. Oh yeah, I thought he'd be giving me a bunch of photographs.*

Joe took out Athena's manuscript and read it again between sips of Coors Light. *"Yes, there was one thing Spero made her say. It was that part about the prophet and the wall. Melissa would be far better at this guessing game than me, but she's never even met Spero. Shoot!* He tossed the papers on the coffee table and leaned back on his couch. *There's got to be something more to that remark, but what?* He took another sip of beer. Slowly, Joe's eyes grew wide, and a grin appeared on his face. *The <u>wall</u> between them: the wall at Bud's Bar. Only he and I would know about that."*

Joe's Bimmer vroomed up to The Purple Planet at 5:30 PM. No customers had arrived yet. Bud was behind the bar polishing glasses as Joe walked in. "And they call this stuff 'spot free', Joe. Hardly."

"Sam, I think I lost something under that booth. Mind if I peek under there and check it out?"

"Sure, but you haven't been in for a week Joe, and it's been cleaned a few times. Welcome to check my almost empty 'lost and found' drawer if you like." Bud saw the anxiety in Joe's face and gestured to the booth. "Well, knock yourself out."

Joe thanked him and proceeded to slide in and down to sit on the floor between the benches with a flashlight and tools. The wood paneling was still warped from Spero's visit, but otherwise it seemed intact. Carefully he felt the wood and looked for cracks. Yes! There were two very fine breaks running horizontally in one fake mahogany panel board.

"You just let me know if I'll have to call the Fire Department to get you out from there, huh Joe."

"I'm fine Bud. Should be just another minute."

Using a small screwdriver, Joe was able to pry off the cut out. There, sitting on a wooden crossbar, was a brown envelope. He tore it open on the spot. It contained his second Beatles tape, a 3X5 card with addresses and numbers written on it, and a photo of Spero with a woman standing on a dock. Joe cracked his head on the table in his hurry to get up.

"Whoa, don't take me literally, professor. Find anything?"

Joe held up just the card. "Sure did. This got wedged in a crack."

"That's great. How about a beer to celebrate?"

"Not this time, my friend. Gotta run."

THE GIFT

B ack at his apartment, Joe warmed up his uneaten
dinner and took a closer look at his stash. The card
had the name of a brokerage firm in Cleveland with its phone
number. The long number under it, plus a short one was pre-
sumably an account and its password. The photo showed
Athena in a brightly patterned wrap around skirt. Both she
and Spero were posed in front of a sleek sailboat with grand
photo smiles. She had long black curly hair, loosely tied
in the back, and her slender hand was draped over Spero's
shoulder. *Wow, she's gorgeous. Looks like a perfume ad.*

Joe propped the photo against his salt and pepper shakers.
*Melissa will have some fun studying the background. Must
be the only photograph of a first century harbor in existence.
Wonder who took it. Not Connie.*

As expected, the tape was the missing "part two" of his Beatle collection, now ruined, of course. Joe's hand trembled as he fumbled with his tape machine and pressed play. Spero's voice came out loud and clear.

Well Joe, I hope you will forgive me for putting you through this little treasure hunt. Actually I'm sure you will. It's important that you are alone when you listen to this final tape, and I'd like you to destroy it as well. Please don't share it with anyone else, even Melissa at first, 'cause it is just for you. By now you may have realized that I snuck back into your place and borrowed your recorder and camera. They were gone for a couple of days, so I hope you didn't spend hours looking for them.

This message is my way of saying thank you for saving my life, and helping me get a new life. And, by the way, isn't Athena absolutely beautiful? Well, I've been busy playing with the time moment thing in your behalf. It was fun, really. First I went back to 1915 and opened a family trust account with ten thousand in gold coins. The brokerage firm noted on your card paid the taxes for you out of your profits, managed the account, and sent out no statements per instructions. I had them put it all in Coca Cola with reinvested dividends. That was against their advice, by the way .Went back and told them to sell everything in 1928, invest in treasuries until 1932, then buy back the Coca Cola. I drank one of their bottles back then. Not bad. Tastes the same as 1986.

After that I checked on your account every 15 years and added your name and Social Security number when you were born. It's worth quite a few hundred thousand now. I'd recommend you contact the firm on your card, and move it to your personal account.

Now, if you are conservative, you can just let it ride for your retirement, but this 'prophet' would like to make some suggestions for a more adventuresome lad such as yourself. As they become available in the years ahead, buy Intel, Microsoft and Quaalcom. Spend about a hundred thousand on each and just hold them for awhile. With the rest of the cash buy Leaps on these stocks as soon as they are available. Buy them on as much margin as you can. That will maximize your earnings, and as they mature, roll them over into new Leaps. Your broker will comply if he knows you might move your account, and it'll be a big one Joe, but ignore his helpful suggestions on safer investments.

OK, now this is important. Your magic year is 2000. Start selling everything then and put it all back in Treasury Notes of different denominations. Oh, buy some Google if you still want to play. Pay the Capital Gains Tax. You can afford it. You are on your own from here on. You might want to form your own corporation and invest in a business venture to save paying some taxes. How about giving some to Christian and Jewish charities, maybe in Greece? (laughs) *Anyway, have a good time with it. You deserve it.*

Oh, yes, one more thing. Buy at least fifty acres in a remote lowland mountain valley in the Rocky Mountains with limited access. You and your family can enjoy its beauty in your lifetime as a retreat. But then, for the sake of your grandchildren, start construction on an underground, self-sustaining complex with a redundant air filtration system. You get the idea. I didn't want to end on a sour note, so remember that humanity, or at least some of us, do survive the troubled times ahead. However, I really think the world I ran away from will eventually get better. I just didn't think it was going to happen in my lifetime.

So thanks again Joe. I'm betting Connie's right about you and Melissa, so here's wishing both of you a lifetime of love and happiness.

2028

Richard Merson, University Systems VP of Marketing, strode into his office promptly at nine. The door hissed shut as he approached his black, curved Plastisheen desk.

"Southern European sales up 2% last year, down 5% this quarter", he mumbled. "Got to be the Baltic wars, but I'm the one they'll blame. Captain of the ship, of course."

Dick glided around the desk dragging his finger over its surface and slumped into his contour chair. He leaned back, took a deep breath, and exhaled slowly.

Market share slipping— worthless consultants. Same as before, but now it's up to me to come up with something—got to save us again. Got to keep paying for Professor Main's weird experiments of course.

His eyebrows lowered in contemplation, and he stared vacantly. After a moment, he slipped an ID chip out of his sleeve pocket and inserted it in the desk edge to activate its computer. A keyboard began glowing on the surface and a 3D image of his company's logo hovered over it. This morphed into a woman's matronly face and she began to speak. Dick mouthed her words. "Good morning Mr. Merson. The items for today. . ." He jabbed at the pause key, and the image froze. The woman's eyes were locked in the closed position. Merson saluted her, smiled, and spun his chair around. For another moment he just stared at the smooth gray expanse of the wall.

I still like the textured surfaces we used to make. These new monotones are—blah. Design says they're the newest thing, reflecting heat to the hot side and all. Course it's all my fault if they don't sell. He leaned forward, touched an orange glow spot, and the wall faded into transparency. The campus side of University Systems spread out below his second level office and he peered down over the heads of students scurrying from one class to another.

For a while Dick just watched, and hoped creative ideas would materialize in his head. Looking almost straight down he focused on a bench beside a small tree where a female student sat reviewing her notes. She was tapping on a blue, palm sized concave device in her hand. Waves of brown hair kept blowing across her eyes so she had to swish it away with slow tosses of her head. Dick appreciated her long legs that she had double-crossed, to steady her typing.

"In our last ad we had an actress with legs like hers," he mumbled out loud. *Stats showed it did more to help sales in women's apparel than it ever did for Plastisheen—wait, that's it! The Italians. Ads like that must be too distracting for them. We'll do another approach, maybe just featuring the shiny smooth strength of our product—muscular. It'll be a new ad angle, just for them.*

He touched the wall spot again and it morphed into a scene with mountains and lakes. But just as Dick started swinging back toward his desk, he flinched at a sudden flash and a loud pop right behind him. Alarmed, he spun fully around to confront a fuzzy, yellow "grapefruit" rolling to a stop on his desk. Ozone filled his dilated nostrils.

Pulse now pounding in his throat, Dick sat frozen, mind racing. *Bomb? Run? No, dead right now if that was it.* He ventured a quick poke at the computer status key. No one had come in. No calls. Systems normal. The woman's frozen image hovered over the glowing ball. Her eyelids were fluttering. He gazed up the sidewall to the spot where the object might have come from. *There's a <u>dent</u> in my Plastisheen. A bullet might poke a hole in it, but our ads always claimed it was stain proof and <u>dent</u> proof.*

Merson forced himself into a calmer state. A closer look at the invading object revealed a round, silvery spot that was steaming—not yellow or fuzzy like the rest of it. He took out a communicator stylus and gingerly gave it a poke. The ball seemed very light. He rolled it to one side to get a better look at the clear spot, a frosted metallic circle embossed with "Lab B43".

"Son of a B!" *It's another prank from the white coat nerds downstairs, maybe Roger Bell himself. One of the jokers on his staff must have stashed it in here with a timer last night. Darn! Bet they're down there right now laughing their heads off.*

Dick punched the intercom. "Halloo, Judy, could you buzz ole Roger in B43? Just tell him that I got his cute little present."

"Certainly, Mr. Merson, but it won't be anytime soon. We have a bulletin that they are in a strictly closed door experiment all day today."

"Oh, I'll bet. Okay look, you probably don't know anything about their little prank, but just leave Roger an urgent message that I'm gonna dump his little glow toy in the disposer if he doesn't pick it up right now and apologize."

Dick started fiddling with the strange device. He tried picking it up, but it slid off his fingers, seemingly frictionless. Scooping it between his hands he could hold it and feel warmth, but he still couldn't feel a real contact point with his skin. It tingled. Dick peered more closely. *Can't see anything through all this fuzzy stuff. I'll never tell Roger, but whatever this weird thing is, I'll have to admit it's one pretty neat trick.*

Dick heard a commotion outside, suddenly louder as the door slid open. Judy was being pushed aside. "I'm sorry sir! They said it was an emergency!" Roger Bell and three other "white coaters" burst in, then stopped transfixed at the sight of Merson sitting there with a big smile, the glowing ball cupped in his palms.

A woman clutched Roger. "My God, he's actually holding it in his *hands!*"

Roger cleared his throat. "Dick, you have my apology."

"Well Roger, you've never, *ever* apologized before. Why start now. Your freaky thing worked perfectly. Scared the hell out of me. Now this is the part where I get even," Dick said, pretending to throw it at them.

The scientists flinched back against the wall with murmurs of "Wait! Calm down, Dick." and "Please don't drop it." Lucy Bell let go of Roger and stepped forward. With a hoarse voice she said, "Mr. Merson, I know we have not always been nice to you, and I'm sorry. But this is *really* not a joke." She took a large steel box from the scientist next to her. "Please just put it in here if you will. Carefully."

"OK, you're all doing a good job of acting scared, but you're kidding, right? This thing's not really dangerous, is it?"

Roger said, "Actually it might be. Not real sure just yet how it ended up in here. But Dick please, just put it down in the container. Be gentle." Lucy approached holding a heavy metal box with dials and controls on it. She carefully placed it on Merson's desk and opened the lid.

Dick lowered the sphere into her device. "OK, now you guys are scaring me all over again. What in the heck is this thing?"

No answer. Roger Bell came over and secured the top cover on the container. The ball was still visible through a window on the side. Lucy worked a small key-pad on one side and a motor whirred, pumping out the air. Finally there was a loud "snap" and the ball clunked to one side of the box, now just an ordinary metal sphere. Dick searched the faces that surrounded his desk. Their expressions quickly transformed from 'bomb squad' people to those of heroes who just pulled a child out of a well. They all let out a unison-whoop and began jumping around and high-fiveing.

"Thanks, Dick. We've done it. I owe you lunch."

"You owe me a damned *explanation,* Roger! Why is my heart racing like I almost died?"

Lucy said, "Dick, it's just—it's *wonderful.*" The troop began leaving through the door holding their cargo and talking excitedly.

Dick shouted at their departing backs. "Hey great, now we're all happy, huh Roger? Just one question. Could this silly gadget ever become something we could actually *sell?*"

Before the door slid closed, Roger leaned on the doorframe, and smiled back at Dick Merson. He leveled his gaze and tone. "Dick, one day this could be our *only* product."

Our Marketing Vice President was alone, and his office quiet again. He had nothing to do with the creation of this marvelous Quantum bubble, but he was the first man to witness a "Bee" that had departed from our familiar three dimensions for a split second, and returned to us under its own control.

After a moment Dick realized he was still staring at the closed door, his mouth agape. He snapped it shut with his hand and slumped back into his chair.

EPILOGUE

The little one's engine flashed in, flashed out, flashed in,
And they're delighted to see, that others could feel
When they flashed from eleven to three, three to eleven,
Their engine made three seem solid & real, solid & real.
To all who lived in the three, it now felt solid and real.

Poems by Lucy, 2055

I n June 2003 my father pioneered the first Industrial-Collegiate Complex. Despite his being a Nobel Laureate, most of his colleagues felt it was just to sponsor his own bizarre projects. Well, there was some truth to those accusations, but Joseph Fulton Main had a broader vision, one based on a certain knowledge of what was possible. The origin of his foreknowledge will be the subject of my next book, but Professor Main self-funded his research in the nineties before he bought Seldyne University and an Aerospace company. When he integrated their research and production facilities he was also highly criticized.

The scientific world was stunned twenty five years later when Professor Main's widely discredited work resulted in the first quantum dissociative device, now commonly called The Bee. Up until that time, published papers were running twenty to one against any possibility of his being successful. My husband, Professor Roger Bell, and I are proud to have played a role in its development.

Professor Main assured the world that the Bee would never have a military use, and would only serve science and education. He felt strongly that to do otherwise would demean both humanity and God. This is important considering the violence in the world today, and especially so because we'll test the first manned vehicle next year. But Daddy's Bees have become such a worldwide sensation that by popular demand we've begun to teach basic quantum mechanics in Middle School.

My Dad also told me once that he was afraid he might be going crazy while he worked so hard on the Bee project. How well I knew. It did seem to be going nowhere for so long, but later he confided in me. His fears faded away when a realization of peace came to him one day. I found a clue to that peace last year. Daddy wrote these words inside the back cover of Julian Barbour's "The End of Time."

"The scientific reality that defines the world we *think* we know is itself far crazier than anyone could ever imagine. The depths of ultimate truth are just not available to the mind of man, but they can be discovered simply by opening one's heart. Only there will man find certain knowledge of the One who lives and creates for us with love."

Excerpt from "The Biography of Joseph Fulton Main"
By Lucy Main Bell, 2055

ACKNOWLEDGEMENTS

This book is dedicated to my father Pasquale whose determination and life as a physician was my role model, and to my mother Helia who inspired me to work hard on the subjects I liked. Also to J. Fulton Main, my Middle School science teacher who revealed science to be a whole lot of fun. I also wish to thank Professor Julian Barbour for allowing, as he wrote me, to "mine his ideas".

S cience or God? John Pascal (Pascal John Imperato) used to think there had to be a choice. His early years were on the fringe of Christianity, and studying medicine and writing Sci-Fi short stories hardly prepared him for the shock of God's reality. But shortly after his awakening, he was delighted to discover that God loves science too.

Doctor Imperato was born in New York City, received his MD at Duke University, and served in the US Air Force. His medical practice included Pennsylvania and later Southern California. Presently he writes from his home in Fallbrook California.

CPSIA information can be obtained at www.ICGtesting.com
Printed in the USA
BVOW031639160613

323401BV00001B/1/P